S.J. DAVISON

Angel of Death

1

Chloe watched her sparkling silver heel tumble to the street as she clung to the building ledge. Kicking off the other shoe she wondered if there would be a chance to pick them up later.

"These are one of my best pairs, Chloe." Her friend Jenny had followed her lead, watching her own shoes clatter to the pavement below. Somehow short skirts and heels proved not to be the ideal evening wear for escaping a raging inferno. "I better get them back."

Jenny slipped.

Chloe reached out to steady her friend with one arm while clinging on to the wall the best she could with her other. If she didn't look down, she knew it would she'd be okay. The approaching sirens suggested more help than the gawkers gathered below, who seemed more interested in filming their plight than offering any assistance.

"I told you I heard somebody in the yard," Jenny protested, having regained her balance. Shuffling along the ledge beside Chloe, her tight black dress became covered in brick dust."

"And I told you to help me stack the bloody leaflets so we could get out of there. Now just shut up. We're nearly there and maybe some burly fireman will rescue us."

"Now that's the best thing you've said all night." Jenny's voice brightened.

It had been Jenny's idea to go out for a drink with the lads after work, even though Chloe had told her she had to help sorting the leaflets for her father's election campaign. As usual, her friend had persuaded her to go along, accompanied with the promise she'd help Chloe with the sorting after the drinks. At least Jenny had made it to the campaign office before the complaining began and the help dwindled to nothing. Not that Chloe had expected any different.

There was a sudden rumble from the building and Chloe was sure she felt the wall move. Glancing to her left, at the window they had just escaped from, she could see flames visible through the billowing smoke.

"Thank God," Jenny said. The sirens echoed off the buildings in the street as the first of two fires engines came careering down before screeching to a halt below them. "Shall we wait here?"

Chloe looked past her friend to the roof they were heading towards. It was the next building and flat enough for them to jump onto, only there was a gap they were going to have to try and cross. It made sense to wait. Her arms were tired, but at least her bare feet had sufficient purchase on the ledge. "Are you okay to hold on?"

"I think so." Jenny nodded. "Shit, Chlo that was close."

"I know." Jenny had been looking out of the window convinced she could hear sound in the backyard. Chloe, frustrated at her friend's lack of help, had ignored her and got on with the job her mother had given her. After all, she had to help as it was for the good of all the family.

They'd smelt the smoke at first, opened the door from the large room to be greeted by a thick gray cloud pouring up the narrow stairs. With no other exit and having tried to block the door with anything they could, the smoke had squeezed through every crack filling the room. They'd used the window to shout for help until the flames had reached the door and climbing out of the window was their only option.

Glancing below Chloe could see the firemen were wasting no time in setting up their ladders.

"Hold tight ladies, we'll come and get you. Don't move anywhere until we say." The booming voice of one of the firemen was reassuring. Not that they had plans to do much else. The wind fluttered at Chloe' yellow summer skirt as she tried to remember if she was wearing decent underwear. Then tried to shake the ridiculous thought from her head. Though no doubt her mother would ask.

"We're still on for going shopping before we go on out on Saturday, right?"

Chloe allowed herself a giggle at Jenny's question. "Yes, I gotta feeling we might need some new shoes."

2

The dispatch calls had alerted Alex to activity that might be of interest. He'd been expecting a fire and noting the address of the call had smiled with satisfaction. Gary had done as instructed, despite Alex's doubts. Drugs were a useful tool for manipulating people until they were too far gone they didn't care anymore. Perhaps the prize on offer was the greater temptation.

Revenge often was.

More intriguing was the report of two women in need of rescue. It couldn't be, could it? That would be just too delicious.

Alex leant forward in his computer chair and selected an image from one of the smaller screens in the array of displays, bringing it onto the large high definition monitor that dominated the long dining room table.

Several other screens, of differing sizes, perched on the same highly polished table each displaying reams of numbers or images from whatever data source Alex wanted. With most of the small town's systems compromised, he could virtually go where he pleased and watch anything he wanted. Even inside people's own homes, if they were foolish enough to have webcams.

The current focus was a single camera trained on a building

spewing ever thickening grey smoke and flames. Of interest, the two figures precariously balanced on a thin ledge on the first floor of the building.

He didn't have to zoom in to recognise them.

"Chloe Evans and Jennifer Mabbut," he murmured. "What are you two doing there at this time of night?" It wasn't a great surprise Chloe was there, as it was the campaign headquarters for her father, but Jenny was no player of politics, and neither of them looked dressed for an evening of campaigning. Unless Jenny was up to her old tricks and trying to sleep with as many constituents who promised to vote for her friend's father.

The fire dispatch calls boomed out of the speakers on the table indicating the fire engines were getting closer. Flames were coming out of the window the two women had escaped through. There were people in the street watching the drama unfold and though he adjusted the camera to try to identify them, he couldn't focus well enough. He wanted to see if Gary was there, Alex knew the homeless drug addict liked to watch his handiwork in progress.

While it was the building he'd told Gary to target, Alex had not anticipated the two women would be inside. He had other plans for them. Much better plans than being caught in a burning building. Still, it was exciting to watch them clinging to the outside wall dressed in their finery.

Zooming out brought the fire engines into view as they halted in the street, their occupants spilling out before going about their tasks with impressive efficiency. Alex watched them, appreciating the well-drilled manner they adopted as one team unwound the hoses to tackle the fire and another began constructing the ladders to reach the two stricken women. Sometimes, he had watched rescues not bothered about the outcome, but today he was banking on their success, urging the crews on as the first fireman shimmied up the ladder towards Chloe.

A second ladder was thrown against the wall just as an ambulance pulled into the street and, after a few minutes, Alex watched the girls descending the ladders under the careful guidance of two firemen. He smiled as Jenny threw her arms around her hero when they reached the pavement. There was a fireman who would get lucky tonight if he played his cards right. Chloe was more restrained with her thanks.

"Always having to play the politician's daughter now, my dear." Alex glanced at the empty glass on the table and considered what flavour smoothie to have next. The glass had left a stain on the expensive dark wood of the table which, up until Alex had taken over the house ten days ago, had been treated with the utmost respect.

Not that the owners were able to care anymore.

After watching the fire for a while longer, Alex flicked the screen onto the financial markets which were open around the world. Alex didn't need to do much more than briefly check the numbers, as there was another screen running the software which farmed all the data he needed from the markets and managed his financial affairs. His own software used in his own company.

He plumped for a banana smoothie, punching up the subtitles on the news, so he didn't have to hear the droning voices and asinine opinions of so called experts. Music by Oasis acted as background noise; nice and loud, as there were no neighbours to complain.

Prominent politicians had descended on the small town of Oakwell today, each articulating why their candidate should get the nod from the townsfolk. For a moment, there was a shot of the expected victor, the grinning face of Thomas Evans, Chloe's father, as he narrated all his wonderful achievements. Breaking news rolled in red across the screen about the Prime Minister due in the town tomorrow, in support of Thomas Evans.

The Prime Minister would have made an excellent target, but Alex wasn't ready for such a challenge. The security that would surround a person of such importance was too much for his current skills. As disappointing as it was to let the opportunity of a much bigger fish go, Alex was smart enough to know his limitations.

It was satisfying that his current scheme was proceeding after flying under the radar for so long, invisible to all the authorities as he integrated himself with the town, its systems and its people.

He leant back in his chair and took a long slurp of his smoothie.

3

"Hi Dad, I've made you breakfast."

After being called out in the middle of the night to a crime scene with no crime, there was no greater sight for Detective Inspector Zack Carter than his daughter's wonderful smile. The smell of cooking bacon mingled with freshly brewed coffee certainly helped elevate his mood.

"And this is why you're my favourite daughter." Zack shrugged off his bright yellow jacket, about to throw it over a chair until he remembered how Mary would have nagged at him. Turning, he hung it on the back of the kitchen door. Zack could feel the dampness under his arm where he'd been sweating despite the early hour, already needing a shower. It was going to be difficult to get any sleep during the day as the heatwave continued.

"Gee thanks." His daughter gave him a playful scowl at the lame joke. Fifteen-year-old Miley was the only child of his all too brief, but wonderful marriage.

"You're welcome." Zack jumped onto a stool in the breakfast area while Miley placed a plate of bacon sandwiches, dripping with butter, and a large mug of black coffee in front of him. They might not be good for his heart, but after a night call out, they were always good for his soul. "What gets the modern-day teenager out of bed so early on a Saturday?"

"Shopping."

"Figures." Zack bit a chunk out of the sandwich. It was fresh bread and tasted good.

"And what hideous crime took you out in the middle of the night?" Miley was always interested in what he was investigating.

"No crime, just a car wreck."

"Why did they call you then?" Miley slid onto the stool opposite.

"Some rookie cop in a town where nothing happens thinks when something does happen it might be the crime of the century. He's more interested in trying to get on to one of the TV cop shows than actually being a cop."

"The youth of today." Miley flicked back her brown hair.

Zack laughed.

"Who was it? In the wreck, I mean. Were they okay?"

"Dead at the scene." The coffee was good. Seemed crazy after watching a young man pulled from a car smash that he could get enjoyment out of a simple breakfast. "Some local hotshot who'd made his money from houses and gambling." The car had been a total write-off, having left the road before crashing into a tree. A once blue Porsche was now mangled wreck encasing a shattered body of a twenty-nine-year-old man over whom two loving parents grieved.

"That's bad." Miley broke through his thoughts.

"You meeting Alice and Emily again?" Until recently Miley had failed to connect with many people in her new school. She'd been in a tight crew when they were in London. A group of like-minded young teens intent on breaking the glass ceiling with their intellects and, in Miley's case, computer skills.

In small town Oakwell, there weren't the same sort of people, and those she did hang with were the typical nerd crowd that she at least had something in common with. Then she'd become friends with two of what was apparently Oakwell School's cool clique, and now her persona had changed beyond recognition. Still, it was good to have the confident Miley back.

"Ye and maybe a couple of others."

"What are you buying?"

"Well, now you come to mention it." Miley slid her laptop from near the wall so Zack could see the screen. "What do you think?"

"Jeez Miles, you serious?" Her normal clothes were all manner of jeans and jumpers, big enough that she could hide away in. Zack had worried she'd start wearing glasses just to blend in with computer crowd as a stereotypical nerd.

"What's wrong with it?" Miley screwed up her face at him in a way which should have made her look ugly, only somehow it made her more endearing. Usually her face was hidden by a curtain of brown hair, but lately, she had been pushing it back behind her ears to reveal her soft oval features. Looking at the dress, Zack thought she was taking the confidence thing to a whole new level.

"There isn't a lot of it." Low cut, strapless and coming halfway down to the model's knees it was far too revealing in all the wrong places, and not what he envisioned his baby girl wearing.

"Don't get old on me, Dad." Miley swung the laptop back round. "You've wanted me to make more friends, be more outgoing, and now I am."

"You'll have bloody disciples if you go around wearing that." Zack put his hand out, stopping the laptop so he could see the price. "Poor ones too. That's over a hundred quid, Miles."

"I've got the money. You know I can afford it."

Zack knew that was true. After his brother Jake had dropped off an old computer, when she was seven, for her to play games on she'd become obsessed, not with the games but how they were created. Soon she was writing her own small games she had shared online for her friends to play. Miley had even moved into the world of paid work carrying out small programming jobs advertised on freelance sites. Zack had been impressed at the money she was able to make.

Now it seemed she wanted to cast off her nerd image for a whole new one.

"I thought we were saving for the holiday? And what about your tuition fees?"

"I'm doing good with my freelance work, and I gotta chance to get in with some cooler people. You know Emily's mum is an agent for some bands. I might get to go to some gigs. I can't go in my nerd clothes."

Zack laughed. While she'd always been a part of the computer world, Miley had still been conscious of being perceived as a geek. "You don't need to dress like this to be cool. It's not happening."

"What do you know?" Miley snapped down the lid of the laptop, almost trapping Zack's fingers. "You've nagged me about how I've been hiding away in my clothes, so don't be such a hypocrite." She hopped off the stool before stomping across the kitchen towards the hall. "Oh, and Dad." She stopped, turning towards Zack her sweet smile returned. "You couldn't give us all a lift to the shops, could you?"

4

Alex didn't need to see Gary collapse beside him on the park bench to know it was the homeless man. People like Gary gave themselves away. Their body movements, the twitching of an addict desperate for his next hit. The whiff of a man for whom social niceties had become optional.

"I saw your work on the news." Alex looked straight ahead, across the large expanse of grass that formed the central park leading to the imposing building opposite. The front of the town hall was still in shadow, waiting for the morning sun to climb across the blue sky before it too was bathed in the heat of the Indian summer. In the shadows, Alex could make out the people perched on the stone steps of the main entrance sipping takeaway coffees. Perhaps some would be complaining about how warm it was already. They would be the hottest steps in the country soon enough.

Alex allowed himself a chuckle.

"You wanted it done," Gary said.

"It wasn't empty." Alex tilted his head towards Gary.

"Didn't know anyone was there." Gary shrugged.

"You'll need to do one of the other candidates tonight. Elliot's father works out of his yard."

"That's not part of our deal." The homeless man brought

both hands out of his coat pocket. While second-hand jeans and a loose T-Shirt under the sports jacket gave him a look of any other guy in the town; it was his unkempt hair streaked with grey, and dishevelled beard that demonstrated to the world he'd given up.

"Our deal is whatever I say it is." To emphasise his point, Alex slid the small gold packets sporting the image of an eye from his pocket. Gary steadied for a minute, but Alex could see he was almost drooling. "Our deal put Chloe Evans out of bounds, remember?"

"I said I didn't know she was there." Gary's eyes remained fixed on the gold packets Alex was tapping against. "It won't happen again."

"I don't imagine it will." Alex turned his palm over. Gary snatched the packets from it and Alex knew the homeless man would want to get away as soon as he could to take the hit. "So, you'll do it tonight?"

"Sure." Gary pocketed the packets before rubbing his hands up and down his thighs.

"And remember what I said, Gary. Chloe's off limits," Alex repeated as Gary rose to his feet.

"She's got it coming to her. Her and her precious daddy."

"She'll feel your pain," Alex said. "Chloe and her father are part of my plans. Justice will be done."

"Chloe doesn't know what pain is. Everything she got was because of me, the life she led, the places she went. I lost fucking everything."

As Alex watched Gary scurry off through the park, he knew it was getting harder to keep the homeless man under control. Still, he'd been useful, and there were a few more tasks before he was no longer needed. Alex respected his love of fire even though Gary's creations were crude and without imagination. For a former art teacher, Alex thought Gary would have appreciated turning the fires into a performance. Then again, his real interest in art had been photography; especially his subjects.

Looking at the town hall, Alex breathed in the fresh morning air. The doors were still closed because bureaucracy didn't like to work on Saturdays; that would be too useful for those needing help. The wealthy didn't think the poor needed or deserved help on the weekends. Not that Alex had much time for that layer of society. No one had to be poor in this world if they didn't want to. It was idleness which kept people in poverty. A simple lack of the guts to drag themselves off the streets towards the riches that were on offer to any who were willing to work for them.

No, Alex had no time for the poor.

He just hated those who wielded false power even more.

5

Seeing Jenny's beaming face as she sat on the edge of shopping centre fountain was the antidote Chloe needed to a foul morning.

"Your mom let you out of her sight then?" Jenny patted the space next to her that she'd saved with her handbag. The place was buzzing with Saturday afternoon shoppers who needed to see and feel what they were buying, not just click on a button.

"Eventually." Chloe let out a sigh as she sat down. "She can't decide whether I should be wrapped in cotton wool or paraded to the media as some sort of stunt woman."

Jenny let out a laugh. "Maybe we could be TV action girls. Our careers may not yet be over."

"Well, mine definitely is," Chloe said.

"A career as a politician's daughter beckons."

"Not if I can help it." Chloe shook her head, letting her blonde hair fall loose so she could tie it back more comfortably. The moment Chloe returned with her tail between her legs from the London fashion world, her mother had been trying to dictate her life. With her father looking likely to become a Member of Parliament, Chloe's future was fast becoming tied to the murky world of politics. It was a world which seemed even seedier than the modeling and acting world she'd just escaped.

Her father had secured Chloe a place at the law firm where some of his buddies worked, though it seemed they would have been happy to employ her even without his connection.

"Hey, did you hear about Mr. Simmons?" Jenny aid

"What the geography teacher?"

"Yea I heard they found him in his garage in the car. Gassed himself."

"Shit no way," Chloe said. "I liked him too. At least you could goof off in his lessons. He was a bit of a perv though."

"Not as bad a Mr. Hudson." Jenny laughed.

"Don't remind me. Why did we do that? Even we should have known he wasn't allowed to take pictures of us like that."

"Helped us out though didn't it. I doubt we would have got the jobs with did without his free portfolios."

"That's true." Chloe pushed her hair back behind her ear feeling creeped out as she remembered the photo sessions in the art room where no one else was around.

"I'd give anything to get back in the game if I could," Jenny said.

"Yes, we both know what you mean by anything." Chloe laughed at her friend's wistful look. For a time, after leaving school, they had lived the high life, having both used portfolios made by their old art teacher to get their way into small-time modeling agencies that had then led on to some success for a few years. It was Jenny who always achieved that little bit more because it was Jenny that was willing to go that little bit further.

"Ooh you bitch," Jenny said. "I'll have you know I'm planning on becoming a big hit in the legal world."

"And how are you expecting to do that?"

"You should see the new skirt I'm going to buy," Jenny smiled.

She'd returned to Oakwell six months after Chloe. It hadn't been hard to get her a secretarial role in the same office, once Chloe had them told them about the friend she used to work with in London that was looking for a job. It turned out a glance at her modeling portfolio was all the recruiters in an organisation filled with middle aged men needed to see before offering Jenny a role. There didn't even have to be a vacancy.

"Hey, I thought this trip was for a new outfit for tonight, not your career." Chloe had been looking forward to the Bruno Mars concert ever since she had bagged tickets from one of the partners, who had been given them by a client. The partner had no idea who Bruno Mars was, and was only too pleased to pass them on. One thing Chloe missed about the London scene was the easy access to the best concerts.

Tonight, she was planning to have a good time, despite her mother lecturing her on how she should conduct herself to make sure she acted with the decorum expected of a politician's daughter. Though if history had taught Chloe one important lesson, it was that a combination of drink and Jenny tended to lead to nights of regret. Which was why it was probably a good idea she'd volunteered to drive to the Birmingham venue.

"Well, that as well. Come on, let's get started." Jenny slipped her arm under Chloe's as they stood and steered her towards the nearest clothes shop.

Chloe shook her head. "Why do I feel this will be a long afternoon?"

6

LIAM: OMG where did you get these?

Liam leaned his bulk closer to his keyboard as he typed into the chat window.

ALEX: Everything is out there if you look in the right places.

Liam knew what Alex meant; his old friend had told him that before, but these were sensational pictures. What had Chloe been thinking? When Alex had said he had a surprise, Liam had no idea it would be as good as this, and he'd already given Liam a treat he would never forget when he'd taken Liam on a night out.

LIAM: Amazing pics.

ALEX: She'll be yours soon. Think about that.

Liam had thought of little else since Alex had first told him. Alex, his timid friend at school, his buddy who had tried to survive against the bullies while they'd consoled themselves in their friendship. A sad little pair doing sad trivial things while others were living the high life of popularity.

The day Alex had simply vanished off the grid was one of the worst of Liam's life, and now Alex was back offering Liam the chance to have Chloe, the girl Liam had dreamed of since school. The Alex that had returned after fourteen years was a powerful man. Everything Alex had written online when he got back in touch was backed by a strength of mind and body that had Liam scarcely believing it was his old friend.

There was already a collection of 'Chloe' images on Liam's computer. Many he'd created himself, usually of her cowed down, humiliated, abused, exposed to his every whim. Some were based on pictures Alex had found when they were at school, having hacked into the school network and found pictures of some of the girls in their underwear on a teacher's computer drive. Others Liam had made from her modelling pictures he'd found online.

Hacking through a school's dodgy security was nothing compared to what Alex seemed capable of now. Liam clicked through the new gallery of pictures Alex had sent. There was nothing fake about these.

LIAM: I didn't know she'd been such a slut.

ALEX: It's amazing what a girl will do when desperate for money. After these, she packed up and came home.

LIAM: No wonder. What would her precious mommy and daddy say if they knew about these?

The pictures were under a different name, but it was clearly her.

ALEX: I know :)

LIAM: What are going to do?

ALEX: Drive her straight into your arms.

Liam liked the sound of that.

He'd been good friends with Chloe in little school. Then the lure of the cool clique had seen her hang with a different crowd, and Liam had only been able to admire her blossoming beauty from afar while others fawned over her. She hadn't wanted to know Liam anymore because knowing someone like him meant mixing with the social outcasts. Even acknowledging his existence would have brought derision from the rest of the clique.

It was, however, because of the previous friendship it hadn't seemed strange when she'd approached him for help with some tough maths assignments. Of course, Liam had said he'd help. Having dreamt of being close to her, perhaps touching the lovely blonde hair that bounced on her shoulders as she walked between classes, or breathing in the scent of jasmine, turning down the chance of spending time with her was impossible.

Twice a week, meeting in secret after school, they'd worked on her math and Liam had found she was far brighter than the dozy blonde she pretended to be in class, breezing through the work with him once he'd explained. It had drawn him in even more. They had chatted online, sometimes using a webcam with Chloe sharing her screen so he could see the school work problem. The best times were when the webcam was on her face, and they had simply chatted.

So well had they been getting on that Liam had dared to wonder if there was a chance their friendship could be more. When they'd talked about their hopes and dreams for the future Chloe had shown him her portfolio of modelling pictures, the clean ones with her modelling normal clothes, not in her underwear. She spoke of her dreams of modelling and Hollywood stardom. Her parents, she'd told hold him, wanted her to follow a different path. Chloe would sit next to him, close to him, close enough that he could feel the warmth of her skin against his.

Then she'd promised a special surprise for his fifteenth birthday for all the help he'd given her.

It was the worst day of his life.

LIAM: I could use these to get my own back. Send them to

her father.

ALEX: Maybe. Let me deal with the details. Have you found the information I need?

LIAM: Sure, all too easy with your software. Where did you get it?

ALEX: I'll send you an address to upload the info to.

It was usual for Alex to be evasive about what he did, or where he acquired the software tools that opened networks with consummate ease. He wouldn't even tell Liam where he'd been since dropping out of school and vanishing.

It had taken Liam a while to accept it was his old friend when Alex had contacted him a few months ago. Liam knew enough about the murkiness of the online world that meant people were not always what they said they were and it was only when Alex had revealed things about their childhood, that only he could've known, that Liam accepted him. Alex said he'd been travelling and finding himself, having returned so those that had wronged them could learn the error of their ways.

Alex had taken him out to a swanky bar in the city, the type of place Liam had never been to before. It was the introduction to a glorious white powder that had filled Liam with a confidence he'd never known before. A trip to a place where there were girls who would do all sorts of things if the price was right, even to hulking fat boys like Liam.

It was a night Liam remembered vividly, desperately wanting to visit the place again, but scared to even think about going through the door without the white powder that made him feel invincible. All at once the virtual world that had given him so much joy had paled in comparison to what the real world had to offer. In a single night, Alex had demonstrated there were some pleasures you couldn't simulate in pixels.

When he looked at the pictures of Chloe, he thought back to the amazing feelings that had burst through on his first night with a real woman. The memories of one of them writhing under his hulking torso while moaning with pleasure.

Alex offered the chance to have the same with the girl of his dreams. Lining up the white powder, Liam had come to love he snorted down the raw power and thought about the things he would do to her.

7

The thumping beat of the music that had been pulsing through her body all night was starting to give Chloe a headache. That and the incessant nagging from Jenny that she should let her hair down because Jenny had found a bloke and he'd spoken about a party. But Chloe didn't feel she wanted someone else tagging along.

"Come on Chlo babe." Jenny was hanging off her arm. "Let's live it up like we used to. I smell the money on this one, and I bet he's got loads of rich mates."

inghloe knew her friend had a good nose for men that would give her the high life. Jenny's wardrobe was full of designer dresses and shoes she hadn't bought, and Chloe had to admit tonight's choice was excellent, well-groomed and carrying himself with a confident manner that bordered on arrogance. She was sure she'd seen him before; it turned out he'd appeared on a few TV programs as minor characters before becoming a producer. The way he'd managed to drop a few industry names into the mix had impressed Jenny. Not that it took much for a good-looking man to impress her friend. The way he'd managed to drop a few industry names into the mix had impressed Jenny. Not that it took much for a handsome man to sweep Jenny off her feet.

The concert had been all Chloe had expected and it hadn't

taken much for her to be persuaded to hit a club afterwards. It had been good to get back on the dance floor, even if she was sober, and it was still nice to savour the admiring looks they both garnered from the men.

"If I wasn't sober, I might be tempted." Chloe leant against the bar where Jenny was greedily slurping down another expensive cocktail. The temptation was there to see if it was a real party and to let herself go. But she could see the disappointed looks on her parents' faces if she turned up hungover tomorrow for another round of door-knocking her mother had signed her up to; though she had graciously excused Chloe from the morning shift.

The people in the club were beginning to thin out. Chloe decided it was time for her to head home.

"Let's get fucked, babe." Jenny swayed over, leaning against her friend. "I'm sure we can both find a bed there. Sounds like a blast of a party."

"You know I have to be with my parents again tomorrow. It's bad enough without being hungover."

"Then sack 'em off honey. Give them the finger." Jenny demonstrated what she meant theatrically. Chloe grabbed her shoulder to stop her falling over.

"Christ Jen, it might be better if you came with me."

"No way. Do you know how long it's been since I've been laid?" Jenny said.

"You've been telling me all night."

"Three weeks, that's how long. And what about you? It's been months."

"Thanks for the reminder, but I'm good." Chloe swallowed the last of her Diet Coke. There had been the odd fling at work but nothing serious since she'd been back in Oakwell.

Something else her mother would mention whenever she went around for dinner. Chloe wondered whether her mother thought her being single was not good for the campaign.

"You've changed," Jenny continued. "I remember when you would be right up for this. You're becoming a boring little cow."

Chloe bit back a retort. Jenny didn't like it when people refused her and Chloe normally went along with what her friend wanted, which was the reason Chloe had ended up doing some of the stuff she regretted. She might not have any idea where she was heading in life but, unlike her friend, Chloe had no intention of trying to rekindle a career that was clearly going nowhere.

Even if it meant she was boring in Jenny's eyes.

"Darren was right about you. You're holding me back." Jenny pulled away from her.

"He said what?" Chloe raised her eyebrows towards the man returning from the cloakroom with Jenny's coat.

"Because I came back from London to look after you. I could have made it. Darren says I still could."

"Oh, did he now?" Chloe didn't know what to say. She knew the drink was talking and knew how Jenny could be when she was in this state. Jenny was quick to blame everyone else for her failure to make the career she'd always wanted.

Chloe wondered whether she should let her friend go off with someone as drunk as she was. They had both done it in London often enough, but it seemed different when Chloe was sober.

"Yes, he did. There's still a chance, you know. Darren said he might be able to get me some auditions. You'd have to let me go, though. You'd have to look after yourself."

"You fill your boots, honey. Don't worry about me." Chloe clenched her fist and concern over Jenny's well-being evaporated. "I guess I'll be on my way, so I don't cramp your style with Darren." Clutching her silver handbag, Chloe slid from the stool and smoothed down her black skirt.

"Come on, Chlo." Jenny grabbed her arm. "Come to the party with me. Darren says they'll have the best coke there, some TV people too."

"Not my scene any more darling, and that will mean I'll be the only boring bitch at the party. Ah, here's your knight in shining armour."

Pulling away from her friend Chloe strode away while trying to keep the tears from tumbling down her face. Chloe left the nightclub and headed toward the car park.

8

"Should we go after her?" Alex tried not to smile as he watched Chloe walk away from her friend. He'd hung back just enough to hear their row.

"No way, she's in one of her moods. What I want to do is go to this fucking awesome party you've been telling me about." Jenny threw an arm over his shoulder, leaning on him for support. One look into her eyes showed she was clearly on her way to oblivion. Making a show of getting his phone out of his pocket, Alex pretended to check his messages.

"Sounds like the perfect time."

Linking his arm through hers Alex led Jenny towards the exit, careful to walk slowly enough so as not to catch Chloe. The adrenaline flowed through him at the thought of what was ahead. It had gone so smoothly. The buzz he'd felt at approaching the two women and them not recognising him was astonishing. Worth the time spent at the dumb concert so he could follow them out in the hope of approaching them. A visit to a bar had been expected. The fact they went to a nightclub had made it almost too easy.

Alex had seen a glint of recognition in Chloe's eyes when they met, but his bullshit story of appearing on a few low budget programmes seemed to satisfy. After all, he looked so different from the awkward, geeky boy they had known in school. His blond hair dyed black as was his trim beard, and the contact lenses that made his eyes brown had made him look a stranger even to himself in the mirror. The skin and bones of his teen body had been replaced with tight, lean muscles, with the years of training he had put in.

"Wow, this yours?" Outside the club, they approached his car, and Jenny ran her hand over the sleek bonnet of a silver Porsche.

"Only the best ride for the best girl in the club," he said in his most arrogant voice to go with a flash of his perfectly white teeth. The car had all the gadgets and a luxury interior. Alex hadn't driven one before tonight. It was part of the reason he had chosen it when he'd seen it in the car park.

"That sounds good to me, darling." Jenny hesitated for a minute while Alex unlocked the doors. "Are you okay to drive?"

"No problem at all." Alex had only been drinking water, despite what she might have thought. Jenny shrugged before sliding into the cream leather seat, obviously not caring her skirt was riding high up her thighs. Alex wondered how many times the slut had gone with a man like this to ensure she got what she wanted.

They didn't talk much on the drive as Jenny's head lolled from side to side with the motion of his driving, as well as the beats from the stereo. Alex didn't know the songs. It wasn't his playlist.

"Seems a long way." Jenny murmured. Slumped in the chair she was curled up, her head resting on the spacious backrest.

"Soon be there, my lovely," Alex smiled down at her. "Soon be there." Running his fingers along her smooth bare thigh, Jenny moaned and opened her legs. Not wanting to be distracted from the road Alex pulled his hand away and allowed himself to anticipate what was to come.

As they hit the motorway, he let loose the powerful engine, revelling in the tight controls as he weaved through the traffic while always attentive for police or cameras. It wouldn't do to get caught that way. Five years of planning was not going to be thrown away by some lucky cop with a speed camera.

Despite all his training he still had a weakness for speed and beautiful women. After all, what was the point of life if you weren't going to enjoy at least some of it?

He glanced at his passenger, aroused as he pushed the accelerator further to the floor until he swung off the motorway and into the countryside.

By the time, they had reached their destination Jenny was, as expected, barely coherent. Alex helped her out of the car and into the farmhouse. He decided he would let her sleep for a while before he began. She would feel it more if she was lucid.

A shame that she would never know that he had virtually brought her back home.

9

"Hey, Dad I've been invited to a party."

"Jesus Miles, I'm in the shower."

"Oops, sorry." Zack heard the bathroom door close. "It's a proper party, Dad. Can I go?"

Zack could hear the excitement in his daughter's voice. "Where is it?"

"At Charlie's house. His parents are away, but they've given permission."

"Who's going? And who's Charlie?" Stepping out of the shower Zack slipped the towel off the hook. Drying himself he was already getting a sinking feeling about the conversation.

"Everybody. He's in my class."

"Everybody?"

"Well everybody who counts. And it means I count now, Dad."

"And who judges who counts?" Zack rubbed his body vigorously, trying to avoid his reflection in the mirror shouting to him that he needed to start an exercise routine again.

"You know what I mean. I never get invited to parties."

"You went to lots of parties when you were younger."

"Er, like when I was a child, and you still got party bags. This is the real deal, Dad."

Zack laughed, but she was right. Mary had organised all the

parties when Miley was little. There hadn't been any since Mary had got sick and faded away. Birthdays were quietly celebrated with a meal out.

"These are the kinds of parties that will end up with all sorts of people there," he said. "I don't want you getting mixed up with the wrong crowd."

"Neither do I. Give me some credit, Dad. I'll be going with Emily, and she's one of the sensible ones."

Zack had no idea if that was true, but while he trusted his daughter, his protecting instinct, his police instinct, a father's instinct, screamed for him to send her away to live with nuns until she was at least thirty. While clearly not a reasonable proposition Zack was sure he knew what the party would be like, and he would be sure to check with Nadine what sort of boy Charlie was.

Wrapping the towel around his waist Zack opened the door to a hopeful looking daughter. "I'm sorry, I just don't think it's right. You get to know these things-"

"When you are a copper," Miley finished, her face going a bright shade of red. "It's not for you to judge who my friends are."

"I think it is in this case, love. Think about it Miley, why all of a sudden do they want to invite you?"

"Maybe it's because they have noticed I'm a nice person they all want to get to know." Miley folded her arms.

"Or that you have blossomed into a lovely young lady with all the curves in the right places."

"Dad."

Zack could see that he had embarrassed her. "It's the truth, Miles; boys are fickle. Trust me on that one. Maybe the next time there's a party when you've got to know them a little better."

"There may not be a next time after this." Miley threw out some air quotes before switching to a more pleading tone. "What am I supposed to say? Sorry, I can't come to the party because my cop dad doesn't trust you not to be a bunch of perverts."

"I would word it better."

"Oh, my happiness is all a joke to you, isn't it?" Miley stamped her foot on the carpet

"Now that's not true." Zack held up a hand.

"Really? Then why don't you make some decisions that would make me happy? I never wanted to come here; you made me come here, and now all I want to do is make some new friends like you've been asking me to."

It wasn't entirely true Zack knew, but he let it go. "I do want you to be happy, Miley, but I want you to be safe as well."

"I can look after myself you know, Dad. Who was it taking care of us when Mum died? Or when you were in hospital?"

"You did, darling, but I'm not letting you go to an unsupervised party."

"Dad please, I promise I'll come home early." Miley switched tone again.

"I've said no, Miley, and I mean no." Zack moved to close the bathroom door.

"I hope you'll be happy when no one at school will talk to me anymore, and you've ruined my fucking life." Miley spun on her heels before she stomped to her bedroom, slamming the door shut behind her.

"Miley." Zack made to go after her but stopped himself. The only thing that would mollify her now was his permission to go, and he wasn't about to grant her that. He went back into the bathroom and stared into the mirror, imagining Mary looking back at him.

"I'm stubborn, aren't I?" he said. "But she's still our baby; it's just that she's grown up suddenly and I'm not ready for it. I'll make it up to her, I promise." He touched the mirror. "She's just like you were."

10

The phone vibrated on the bedside table. Blinking at the sun streaming through the open curtains, Chloe regretted being so tired she hadn't removed her make-up when she'd arrived home. Flapping hands knocked the phone off the table as Chloe leant over to where it lay on the floor and prodded it to life. There was a message from Jenny.

I think I have a keeper. Going to London for a few days. Then maybe Paris. Ciao.

"No way," Chloe took hold of the slim phone and scooped it off the floor before rolling onto her back.

You not bothering with work then on Monday?

They'll get over it gtg train to catch.

The annoying thing was Chloe could believe it as she threw her head onto her pillows and laughed. Jenny didn't care much about anyone except Jenny, and she was right about work; they'd get over it when she returned smiling sweetly and flashing her long legs. A trick especially successful when you worked in an office full of older men willing to hang off every word if it meant your skirt kept riding higher.

Still grinning Chloe realised it was gone ten, only an hour until her yoga class. She threw back the duvet and grabbed her robe from the back of the door, before padding barefoot down to the kitchen. Glorious sunshine bathed the large room in a warm glow, helping keep her mood bright as she investigated the fridge.

She considered sacking off the yoga in place of a lazy day. Maybe catching a few rays with a cocktail in the garden. After all, the Indian summer could be the last hot days before Autumn brought them down to earth.

Placing her hand on her stomach soon changed her mind. There had been too many missed exercise sessions in the last few months, with body parts not feeling as firm as they should. She needed to get back into a routine. That was always the problem when Jenny was around with her whirlwind persona that made routines a thing for other people. Chloe would be thirty next year; while she might not need the figure of a model anymore, she still wanted to be in some sort of shape.

After pouring a berry smoothie, she drifted into the lounge and settled on the couch before pulling her iPad from its shelf beside the blue sofa. Flicking it into life, Chloe checked Jenny's Instagram page to see if she'd already posted selfies of her latest exploits, but the last entry was from their shopping trip the day before.

"If she goes forty-eight hours that would be a new record," Chloe said to herself.

A message popped up as she was flicking through other Instagram posts. Chloe didn't recognise the number.

You were a naughty girl at school, Chloe Evans. What became of the photographer who took these pictures?

Chloe felt a knot in her stomach as she read the words. Was this a scam? There was a link in the message but she knew enough about the internet not to click on a link from someone she didn't know.

The words had her transfixed.

What became of the photographer?

Was the message talking about Mr Hudson? Gary Hudson, her art teacher at school? He'd put together her first portfolio.

Taking a deep breath Chloe selected the link and a new page popped into her browser, showing photo thumbnails. She gasped, realising what they were images of her in underwear and skimpy swimsuits, or where her hands were covering her breasts. Most of these pictures hadn't made the portfolio. Mr Hudson had persuaded Chloe to pose for them in case the agencies needed glamour shots.

Chloe felt sick. Had he put these on the web? She looked at the date of upload, and it had been fourteen years ago, about the time she had posed for them.

"Bastard," she said out loud.

Another message popped up.

Hello Chloe. You were naughty posing for your teacher like that. I bet you didn't know he'd kept these.

There was another link which Chloe selected. More pictures of her younger self, only this time she was topless. They were the extra special ones he'd taken, even ones with only her hands covering her privacy. Chloe had asked him to get rid of those straight after that particular shoot.

He'd promised he would.

"The fucking arsehole," she screamed. "Dirty fucking pervert."

"Fuck." Chloe pushed the iPad onto the coffee table, running her hands through her hair before burying her head in her palms. She grunted in frustration at how stupid she'd been letting him talk her into the riskier shoot. Chloe hadn't realised at the time how inappropriate it had been for a teacher to take those sorts of photos. Instead, she'd jumped at the chance of getting a free portfolio. What he'd created had impressed the first agency who looked at it, and kick-started her career.

Now she knew he was really a dirty pervert who got his kicks from taking pictures of the girls. She wondered if there were pictures of Jenny like this too.

Her iPad pinged again. She gave the screen a venomous prod with her finger.

Don't be too upset Chloe, you look very sexy. Be in touch.

Chloe looked around the room, shivering despite the heat, feeling as though someone was watching her. Jumping from the sofa she went to the large patio door, making sure it was locked, before pulling the curtains tightly together. Not satisfied, Chloe made her way around all the rooms checking each window was secure, and closing the curtains.

After sliding the bolts across the front door, Chloe ran up the stairs and threw herself under the duvet, letting the tears flow at the car crash she'd made of her life.

11

"What's the story?" Zack passed under the tape to where Detective Sergeant Nadine Morris was talking to a uniformed constable. As Miley had slammed the door of her bedroom Nadine had called him.

"Arson." Nadine broke off her conversation to face him. Zack liked his partner who shared his sarcastic sense of humour and view of the world. Nadine had lived in Oakwell all her life, worked her way up from a beat rookie, and had an encyclopedic knowledge of the town.

As a volunteer at the local youth centre, Nadine had her ear to the ground on all the teenage goings-on around town. It was Nadine, after all, who had fed Zack's paranoia on the antics of the other teens in Miley's school.

"Forensics?"

"On-site," Nadine said, "but it was a good burn, so we are not expecting to find much. The fire inspectors are on the way from Peterborough and should be here soon." Nadine and Zack were standing just inside the police tape, but far enough back not to piss off the fire crews completing their clean up. Considering it was a builder's merchant, and overflowing with various sizes of wood piles, Zack thought it strange only the offices had taken the brunt of the fire. The smell of scorched brick from the blackened walls still hung in the air as Zack eyed the devastation. With the building roof collapsed and no doubt extensive water damage from where the fire crews had fought the flames, there was only going to be work left for the bulldozers.

"All about the motive?"

"Pretty much," Nadine said. They both knew with a crime like this all they could do was shake the tree and see what fell out. "The owner has certainly pissed someone off, as he's had his tyres slashed and house broken into over the last few weeks. He's also the son of one of our esteemed candidates for the election. The father was also using this place as his campaign headquarters."

"Ouch," Zack said. "Coincidence?"

"Do you believe in them?" Nadine smiled.

"No, and so this makes it more likely the other one was arson?"

"I guess so. Here comes the owner now."

Zack saw a young man approaching them with his fists clenched and a determined look on his face that spelt trouble. A quick examination of the man's stance and body shape gave Zack confidence he could be handled if things got rough.

"Are you going to do something now, Nadine?" The man stopped a little too close for Zack's liking."

"It's most likely arson, Elliot, so of course we'll be investigating," Nadine responded taking a small step back to allow the police tape to be a barrier between them. The man looked down at it, as though contemplating whether it was a line he should cross.

"Then why didn't you investigate when the fuckers keyed my car, or when they trashed my house? You could have stopped this." He waved his hand towards the devastation in his yard.

"Officers took your statements and we asked around." Zack could tell Nadine was keeping it professional but had little love for the man.

"And that was all. No actual investigating? Fucking hell Nadine, I could be ruined. My dad's stuff was upstairs."

"There's no need to take out your anger on Detective Sergeant Morris." Zack stepped across Nadine, just enough to send a message to the irate man. "We'll be on this, pal."

"Oh yes, after the Right Honourable Mister Evans' fire I bet. My dad said you were all on his side. It's why people like us don't stand a chance in this town."

For the second time that day Zack was greeted with the back of someone stomping away from him. "Friend of yours?"

"Elliot Reed, Oakwell born and bred," Nadine said. "Made some money in house clearance after he left school. He then took over the yard when his old man decided on politics. It doesn't look like Mr Reed Senior has a cat in hell's chance of beating Thomas Evans though."

Zack glanced at what was left of the office buildings. Not a bad gig for a twenty-something. "Local business rival, do you think? Or linked to the burning of Mr Evans' offices."

"He had his rivals, but to be fair he's pretty well liked. He was a bit of a tearaway as a teen, but who wasn't?"

"I thought you were brought up by nuns?"

"Oh, yes I was quite the little convent girl," Nadine said, "Never touched a drop of booze until I was twenty-five."

Zack smiled, knowing how untrue that was if the station's social outings were anything to go by.

"Be interesting to see how much of his affairs he'll let us investigate," Nadine continued. "His old man has a few skeletons in and out of the closet. It's the main reason he hasn't done so well in the polls."

One of the reasons Zack knew they were often unable to get far with some investigations was the victims preferring seeing crimes go unpunished rather than risk their own wrong doings being uncovered. It was something he'd found all the time in the city.

"We have a list of names?"

"Being worked on right now. Elliot's right though, it's behind Councillor Evans' campaign fire in priority. He is going to be our MP after all."

"Just don't tell Elliot that and we'll be fine," Zack said.

"Sounds like a plan." Nadine laughed. "You look rough this morning."

"Gee thanks." Zack couldn't say the same for Nadine. Whatever the time of day she always managed a perfunctory layer of makeup, and to tie her strawberry blonde hair into a neat ponytail. She also seemed to be able to manage a friendly smile whatever was happening in her life or whatever time of the night it was, while Zack was often lucky to produce a welcome scowl before his morning coffee. "A row with Miley. She wants to go to a party."

"Whose?"

"Charlie Conner."

Nadine sucked in a breath. "Could be worse, but if I told you about him then it wouldn't help. I take it she took it well."

"Apart from the shouting and slamming doors, like an angel. Apparently, I'm stopping her having any happiness. Thing is, I've tried to get her to be more social, to make friends in this town, and when she does." Zack shrugged.

"She picks the wrong crowd. I've met your daughter Zack,

she's a tough cookie and not one to be bowled over by the clumsy charms of horny teens. Even Charlie's mates."

"You're probably right," Zack said. "But I don't think I'm tough enough to take the chance, even if it does mean I lose her for a while." Zack stepped back to allow two weary-looking fire crew to pass.

"Well, I don't envy you," Nadine said. "I've got all that to come from the other side with my boys. Come on, let's get this investigation started. Maybe we'll make a big hit in the detective world, proving this is an insurance scam which is part of an international terrorist ring."

"And I hear I've got to hunt down a missing ginger cat this afternoon."

"Say again?" Nadine said.

"A friend of the Chief." Zack shook his head. "Some old biddy in desperate need of her friend. Hadn't you heard? Obviously, the boss wanted his top detective on the job."

Zack ducked away neatly from Nadine's punch.

12

"A bit of breaking and entering," Dave whispered to himself. "Nothing you haven't done before. A piece of cake." Gathering himself Dave crept down the final part of the road, staying in the shadow of the hedges, until he slipped over the fence of the target house.

Stopping again Dave looked for any reason he could to back out. Maybe he could come back tomorrow, or never. Then a picture of bolt cutters crushing his fingers came into his head. Not doing this wasn't an option. What fucking idiot would turn down the way out of his shit situation the stranger had offered him?

No light emanated from the house. Dave had been watching for the last couple of nights, to confirm the old man's routine. At this late hour, he was long asleep. Taking a tighter grip on the crowbar he'd brought Dave sucked in some warm night air.

"This is it, Dave. Make it count."

Shoes crunching on gravel, Dave crept down the edge of the path until he reached the back door. He stopped and listened. In the calm, humid night there was only the distant noise of cars mingled with the occasional dog bark. He stepped up, jammed the crowbar in the gap between the door frame and forced it until the door swung open.

Fumbling in his jacket for a torch, Dave passed through the kitchen and entered the front room. The beam of the torch bounced off shelves with ornate religious figures, the dust glistening, but Dave was searching for a memory stick. Once he'd given it to the stranger then his life would be his own again. Heart racing as he searched the room, Dave's instincts screamed at him to get out of there.

For the millionth time, Dave promised himself he'd never gamble again. Once this debt was cleared, he would start afresh. There was no future for him in this town anyway. He'd considered going to London to see if he could make it there. Or maybe further afield. With the money he was promised, as well as his debts being wiped out, the world would be his oyster.

The stranger had jumped into his taxi, like any other punter Dave might have expected to pick up on a weekday afternoon. He'd talked about Dave's gambling, drinking and then the debt. Dave's hands had trembled on the wheel while his own questions of how the man knew went unanswered. Had his debts been sold on to this stranger? But he already knew the price of not paying back the lenders he'd taken from. They were the sort of people that made it perfectly clear when they handed over the cold hard cash. It was easy to imagine all sorts of horrors being inflicted upon his pathetic body.

Yet the stranger had offered a way for the debts to be paid off. All Dave needed to do was find a memory stick with all the evidence the police needed to put away a sick priest who'd been preying on his choir boys. A pervert living in a community ignorant about his past crimes. It had curdled Dave's blood to think such a man was living among them, allowed to move there by the Church who'd wanted him to go away without a scandal.

If the stranger was a vigilante seeking retribution for ruined lives, then Dave was all for it. A little bit of sneaking around in the sick fucker's house to get his own debt's cleared was almost an act of community service. Not that Dave had believed the stranger was for real at first, thinking he was being played until after the man had left three grand in cash on the back seat.

The search of the ground floor proved fruitless. Trying to be as quiet as possible Dave made his way upstairs, wincing at each minor creak his movements caused, convinced the old man would wake at any moment. Dave searched the two empty bedrooms first, hoping not to have to look in the one the man was asleep in.

After striking out, there was no option.

Taking some deep breaths, he turned off his torch and stepped towards the half-open door, hoping for the sound of snoring to mask his movements.

There was no noise from within.

Pushing the door further open Dave stepped inside the room as his eyes adjusted to the darkness.

His feet struck something on the floor.

Trying to steady himself Dave's other foot hit part of the same object. He fell forward, hands reaching out into the darkness. Crashing onto the floor he expected to hear the old man wake.

But as Dave lay on the floor there was nothing; not even the sound of breathing.

The hairs on the back of Dave's neck rose as a shiver of fear rippled across his body. There was something very wrong. He pushed himself to his knees and flipped the switch on his torch, slowly directing its beam to the object h'd tripped over.

It was the dagger sticking out of the old man's right eye which made him scream the most.

13

There is a parcel being delivered to your parents' house at nine o'clock. You may want to open it first.

A jolt of terror ran through Chloe. She almost dropped her phone as she leant against the back door trying to catch her breath. Locking up the house on her way to work, she'd almost ignored the text as she wrestled with the sticking door.

It didn't take much working out what was going to be in the parcel. Finding her mum's number Chloe hit the call button.

Voicemail.

"Shit." She clicked off. She'd have to go round, and that meant being late for work again.

Wrenching the keys from the door she ran to her red Mini, trying her mum's mobile again as she climbed into the car.

"Hi, Mum it's Chloe." She spoke as calmly as she could manage. "There might be a parcel delivered to your house by mistake. I should've sent it to work, but you know how blonde I can be. It's pretty important so I'm on my way to get it now."

She would have to come up with some other crap later. Her father would be out at the new campaign headquarters, if not already knocking on doors, but it would be a couple of hours before her mother left to join with her own team in drumming up support.

Her parents lived on the opposite side of town in an area Chloe hadn't been able to afford since moving back. Chloe's last modelling job had just given her enough to pay off her debts and put down a deposit on her own place to rent. While she could've moved back in with her parents, it would mean putting up with her mother's officious fussing over what Chloe was doing with every minute of her life. So, while normally the distance between their homes was a blessing, it meant Chloe had to fight through the rush hour traffic with sweaty palms and a pounding heart to stop her mother seeing those photographs.

Calling the office, Chloe told them she was running late with tummy trouble. It was the kind of topic that an office full of men tended to avoid. More than once she'd used it with Jenny for an impromptu shopping trip to the city.

Stopped at lights, she sent her mother a similar message to the voicemail.

"C'mon. C'mon." Chloe seethed at each red light or slow driver until the traffic allowed her to hurry through the leafier suburban lanes, eventually pulling up onto her parents' spacious drive.

Running to the front door Chloe unlocked it with her own key and pushed her way in.

"Hi Mum," she used the calmest voice possible.

"Hi dear," her mother was upstairs.

"Did you get my message?" Chloe's heart was thumping.

"Yes, love it's on the kitchen table. Would you have time to talk about your outfit for the fundraiser?"

Chloe dashed into the kitchen to see the small package unopened on the table. Relieved she scooped it up before heading back out of the house.

"Thanks Mum, I put the wrong address down like an idiot. Sorry, I've got to go, or I'm going to be in trouble for being late. I'll drop by after work, yea?" She pulled the door behind her, drowning out any response.

Collapsing into the car seat Chloe steadied herself. The package was about the size of an A4 jiffy bag; the perfect size to hold the contents she emptied out onto her lap. Copies of the pictures she'd seen on the Internet.

Her phone sang out.

Did I mention the package for your grandmother too?

14

Having slowed his pace enough to message Chloe, Alex increased his stride feeling full of energy. It was always hard to sleep well after a kill and the death of the old priest had been particularly satisfying. While the old man hadn't been part of his initial plans, Alex prided himself on the ability to improvise when things proved interesting.

Gary had mentioned him in passing, as some busy body who came by the hostel preaching 'the word' and then Liam had found out more about him while snooping around the council records. Then it wasn't long before the true nature of the sick bastard had been uncovered, and it was not something Alex could leave others to deal with.

Following the path as it reached one end of the park, Alex turned and slowed again to make sure his timing was right. The girls had entered at the top of the park, near the town hall, as they usually did. No doubt they were gossiping about some poor wretch who'd bought the wrong top or brand of shoes. He wondered why she'd decided to join a group of such small thinking girls when everything else about her was like Angel, and Angel would never have been part of such a group.

A few minutes later Alex reached the same entrance the three school girls had used to begin their walk through the park towards the high school. A dog nearly tripped him as it darted across the path, its owner oblivious as her eyes were glued to her phone. For a moment, his blood raged, but Alex calmed his mind, flashing a smile at the woman as she realised what had happened and tried to apologise.

Rapid beats filled his ears. Alex loved to run to all kinds of music, blocking out the world as he pounded the paths and worked his plans over in his mind. He would pass other runners whose runs were as aimless as their lives, blind to the true reality of the world around them. Blindly running as if it was doing them some good.

The wonderful sun bathed his skin in a warm glow as Alex accelerated to ensure he'd passed her before the three girls reached the end and turned away. He smiled inwardly at the thought of being on a tropical beach with Miley beside him. She would share his favourite place on earth. Together, as they always should have been. Holding her soft hair the way he had done with Angel so long ago when he was not yet a teenager. Maybe Miley would reach out for him in the dark and seek the comfort of his arms so he could make her feel safe. The last time he had held Angel's hand was when the final breath had hissed out of her battered body.

While he knew such thoughts distracted him from his mission, Alex had never expected there would be another girl like Angel in the world, never mind the same town, and maybe he could save this one from the horrors of life. Maybe Angel had come back in the body of the young girl walking ahead of him. Maybe his angel had returned to the earth. Maybe his love for her had transcended the very laws of nature. He knew he should scoff at such irrational thoughts. But every time he saw Miley he felt the same love he'd felt for his childhood sweetheart.

"Oh, Miley you are as sweet as any angel," he muttered after passing the three girls. "How many men go to bed with you on their minds? You tease them, don't you Miley? Offer them glimpses of delights they will never get to sample. They would never treat you like you deserve to be. You should be with someone who will love you, respect you, and worship you forever. We should be together forever my angel. You and I."

15

"**B**astard, bastard, bastard." Throwing the photos on the passenger seat, Chloe buckled her belt and started the engine. Her nana was on the same side of town, but she had no mobile and rarely heard her landline. Chloe slammed the steering wheel in frustration as she screeched into the street and moments later was back on the road.

"I don't know who the fuck you are, but I'm going to find out," Chloe screamed at the windscreen as a light flashed from a speed camera. She felt sick again. Tears welled up at the thought of her sweet nana opening the package to see the horrid pictures of her granddaughter she thought the world of.

Why had she been so stupid? Why was she always so stupid? Doing those pictures for the teacher had been stupid. There'd been enough in her portfolio to get her an agent, and most of the glamour ones had not even been good enough. Some of the girls had talked about him being some sort of pervert, who just wanted to get their clothes off, but Chloe's obsession with making it as a model had meant she'd believed everything he told her.

Perhaps she'd been more willing to do the glamour shoot because it defied everything her prim and proper mother believed. While her mother was always trying to get Chloe to behave more like a society lady of some throwback era, Chloe had been stripping down for the camera. Her mother had even been talking about the type of person Chloe should marry to further the family. Jane Austen was mandatory reading in the Evans' household.

And the reality was the portfolio of good pictures had managed to get her into agencies which had led Chloe to the bright lights of the London model scene, and for a while, she'd lived the dream. Though it was modelling on the fringes while others, including Jenny, were getting the better shoots. There'd even been the odd acting parts, mainly as extras, but Jenny had got a major part in a TV pilot, although it never got commissioned.

It wasn't just these pictures that sent shivers down Chloe's spine; there were others out there too. They may not have been done under her name, but they were far worse than the ones her sick tormentor had. She was always afraid some porn viewing guy at work would find them and realise it was her and she'd go into the office one morning to find the guys sniggering as they looked at her. Then there would be the lewd comments. As if they weren't bad enough already.

Chloe parked her Mini outside a small neat bungalow on the outskirts of Oakwell. Since Pops had passed away five years ago, nana had become more withdrawn from the community. Instead, she spent much of her time keeping the garden in the same perfect manner it always had been by her husband. Wondrous late-blooming flowers filled the borders with colour despite many other gardens having wilted in the heat, and the still lush grass was trimmed to perfection.

Chloe walked up the short drive while swallowing back tears at the memory of her pops and the great times running wild around the large garden that held so much mystery for a little girl. There were never the shouts for her to behave like a lady when she stayed with her nana and pops. Just the sound of laughter and smell of baking cakes. At least her pops would never know the truth of the girl he'd always called his sweetest flower of them all.

After ringing the doorbell there was an agonising pause before the gentle tap of her nana's shoes on the other side of the wooden door. As it swung open Chloe braced herself for the worst.

"Oh Chloe! How lovely to see you and thank you so much."

Chloe stared open-mouthed at her nana.

"Come in, come in." A broad smile spread across the weathered, wrinkled face as her nana pulled a thin maroon cardigan tight and led the way through to the kitchen. Chloe followed meekly, her breath coming too fast.

"They came about twenty minutes ago, such a lovely thought, Chloe. I was going to wait until you got back from work to ring you."

On the kitchen table Chloe saw a box of Thornton's chocolates next to a bouquet of colourful flowers. Stepping closer she saw a printed card on the table next to the chocolates and picked it up.

To a wonderful nana from her beloved granddaughter. I hope I will always make you proud.

"That you do Chloe, that you do." Still shocked Chloe found herself in one of her nana's famous hugs.

When Chloe eventually dragged herself away from the house, she was filled with terror and relief as she climbed back into her car. Closing the door, she buried her head in her hands.

This was so messed up.

The phone went off again.

Hope she enjoyed the gifts. Be in touch soon.

16

"Hi Zack. Sorry about this morning." Nadine perched herself on the edge of Zack's desk. "I hear you got the call out?"

Zack pushed his keyboard away and sat back stretching out his shoulders. "Yes, a sorry to disturb you Zack, I know we told you this was a sleepy town where nothing happens but we have another dead body to go and investigate. How did you avoid that pleasure?"

"I was already on a hospital run with Ben."

"How is he?" Zack knew her ten-year-old son had diabetes.

"He's coping, and we are hoping to get him a pump soon, which will make his life a whole lot better." Nadine tucked a strand of strawberry blonde hair behind her ear. "The worry still keeps me awake though."

"I bet it does." Zack wasn't sure what else to say.

"Long time since we've had a real murder." Nadine started to look through the photographs of the scene Zack had printed out. "And rumour has it there could be a serial cat killer."

"Very funny. That was not a fantastic way to spend an afternoon. She insisted we look for fingerprints. I mean I know whoever did it was pretty sick, but come on." Zack had found the cat nailed up a tree in the old woman's back garden. She'd told him of other cats in the neighbourhood that were missing, and made sure Zack had written it all down before leaving.

"Bit different this morning?"

"The real deal," Zack said. "Pensioner dead in his bedroom with horrific knife wounds to his face and body. Looks like the fatal blow was when his killer drove the knife into his eye. Autopsy is in a couple of hours."

"I hear they've dug Arthur out of retirement again for it." Nadine put down the photos and turned Zack's screen towards her, so she could start reading his report.

"Yea the new guy is sick again. Arthur should get onto it today. He always grumbles when we call him, but I know he loves it really."

"He misses not being in the game," Nadine said. "Burglary that went wrong?"

"There are signs of the place being searched, but then the old man's keys, wallet and even a tub with what looks like bill money were untouched. My first theory was that they were looking for something specific and, unable to find it, had tortured the old bastard until he told them."

"Sounds like you've got a second theory?" Nadine turned away from the report on the screen.

"Sure, when we got a full ID on the dead man." Zack pulled out a freshly printed sheet from the printer next to his desk and handed it to his partner. "One Casey Damon who moved here twelve years ago, after being defrocked by the Catholic Church for alleged breaches of discipline and ethics with his congregation in Ireland. It appears there were accusations about his over-familiarity with some of his boys. Nothing was proven, the Church moved him away and moved him out to prevent a scandal. And so, the nice old gentlemen was getting to live out the last of his days in this little town."

"Shit, and no one informed us."

"The Church has friends in high places," Zack said. "It's only more recently this sort of stuff became public. It appears our Reverend Damon was shuffled on before all that. There's a document sat over in the town hall, but it wasn't deemed important enough for the police. Until now."

Nadine shook her head as she read the document detailing the crimes the priest was accused of. "So, your second theory is someone found out about his old antics and decided to go all vigilante."

"That's about the size of it," Zack nodded. "Though it doesn't explain why they searched the place, which I think was done before the murder. We'll have to wait to see what forensics can tell us about that."

"Looking for some evidence? Or trying to make it look like a simple break-in that went wrong." Nadine slipped the papers back on Zack's desk.

"Maybe, but if they were going to fake that I would've thought they'd have taken more stuff. We've done some door knocking, and no one had a clue he was a retired priest, let alone any rumours about his unsavoury history. They all knew him as a kind, gentle old man who kept himself to himself most of the time and helped at the homeless hostel. I've asked Adam to trawl online and see if there's anything out there someone might have found."

"Our resident boy wonder," Nadine said. "Has he found anything yet?"

"Not come back to me." Zack knew Nadine was amused by his obsession with gathering and analysing all the data he could. The coppers at Oakwell, while not Luddites, had yet to embrace the world of data mining to eke out nuggets of information that could point to the guilty. For Zack, that had been his way of life in army intelligence.

Even in London his fellow detectives had been sceptical of how much time he'd spend sifting through seemingly unrelated information as part of an investigation. But they didn't argue when it paid off. While helping plan missions in territory held by Iraqi insurgents, Zack had learnt the importance of paying attention to the details.

"If there is anything there, Adam will find it." Zack had been impressed with the intern who'd started with them a few weeks back. Not just with his computer skills, but he seemed to have a knack for finding patterns in the information others couldn't see. Zack had already told Adam he'd make a good intelligence officer if he ever fancied the military. Adam hadn't seemed too keen.

"You got anywhere with the arson attacks?" Zack said.

"Zip. The fire investigator has confirmed the accelerant used at the builders was petrol. There are even remnants of the petrol canisters we're looking at. It wasn't conclusive at the campaign office."

"Insurance scam? Trying to cash in on the other fires."

"Difficult to tell," Nadine shrugged. "Could be. The family is supposed to be in a bit of financial bother."

"Ah my two favourite detectives."

Zack looked past Nadine, who rose from the edge of his desk, to see Detective Chief Inspector Rashid Sterling walking to towards them with his hands clasped firmly behind his back. The DCI was sporting the sort of smile on his face that made Zack realise his day was about to go south.

"Morning Sir," Nadine said.

"You get the notes on the priest case?" Zack asked. He knew the DCI would take the lead.

"I did, thanks Zack. We're setting up the incident room in the main briefing hall. First meeting after the autopsy. I hear Arthur has been called out again."

"He still has a steady hand." Zack nodded.

"However, there's another matter I'd like to speak to you about." Rashid shifted his weight from foot to foot. "There's a charity fundraising event in the town hall this evening. All the candidates will be there. I'd like you both to be as well."

Zack couldn't think of a worse way of spending the night. "To make up the numbers or do some detective work?" Zack winced at his tone. The DCI was a good boss all told.

"To represent the service in the area and build some relationships with the community." Rashid brought himself up a little straighter, his tone more clipped.

"We'll be there boss." Nadine cast a warning glance at her partner.

Zack bit his lip and smiled. "Sounds like a real pleasure, Sir."

17

Smiling sweetly, regardless of how she felt inside was a skill Chloe had mastered in the modelling world, and she was using it well as she was kissed on the cheek by yet another dinosaur of a councillor, who was probably wondering if he could get away with a hand on the small of her back slipping further down. The blue dress she wore, chosen by her mother, at least gave her some protection from eyes that tried to undress her. It had taken long enough to tie up all the lacing and make sure the hem didn't drag on the floor.

Chloe maintained her poise while other relics cast their eyes over her body as they were introduced. It wasn't a surprise as the men on the political scene were as bad as those who would hover around the fringes of up and coming models. Always seeking to exploit innocent girls for either money or the favours they could reap for their false promises of stardom.

Charity events seemed to be the worst. Brazen men considering themselves of some significance and attractiveness, despite their broadening bellies and vanishing hair, as though they thought their benevolence entitled them to more. It astonished Chloe how bold they were, even with their wives present. She dreaded to think of her own father acting the same, as he pressed the flesh to drum up support for his parliamentary bid. He was, after all, excellent at eulogising on the splendid charity work he was doing.

All the main candidates were pushing their charitable credentials at the fundraiser. Even some of her slimy bosses were there supporting her father. The only positive was her mother seemed proud of the way Chloe mingled with the dignitaries, laughing and nodding in all the right places, carrying herself like a lady out of some costume drama. For once Chloe didn't feel she was a disappointment to her family.

"Aren't they our local detectives, Peter?" Chloe heard her mother say to a tall, slender man who'd been introduced as the treasurer of the charity this event had been organised for. She remembered her mother telling her he'd a lot of influence because it was the largest charity in Oakwell, helping children from the poorer districts get decent opportunities. "I didn't know they were supposed to be here."

"Boss' orders," Peter said from behind an enormous glass of red wine. "Maybe it's because of the fires at the offices. I heard a whisper they think it could be arson. They might be here watching a suspect."

Everyone in the small group looked around as if trying to decide who in the room was most likely to be an arsonist.

"I hear you had a lucky escape, Chloe." It was Chloe's mother's friend, Mrs Brown, who spoke. She'd dressed up for the occasion, but should have gone up another size or two in the dress she was wearing. "A real hero."

"The police haven't done a thing." Chloe's mother's tone was terse. "All the money they get from the community and they haven't found a scrap of evidence.

"Well, there are mysterious goings-on," Mrs Brown said,

raising her already prominent eyebrows.

"What around the election?" Chloe's mother said in alarm.

"No, in general. You must have heard about the old man."

"Yes, of course." Chloe knew her mother would never have admitted not knowing some gossip.

The woman leant into the group. Almost spilling her own wine in the process. "I have heard he used to be a Catholic priest. Excommunicated from the Church for, well you know what has been in the news."

"Really?" Chloe's mother said.

"That's what I've heard too," another woman wearing an oversize hat butted in. "They're not making it public yet, so keep it to yourselves."

Chloe thought there was little chance they would get to midnight without the entire room being aware of this so-called secret.

"And then there is charity money going missing," Mrs Brown said. "I almost didn't come tonight. Well, after the last ball, it seems all the money has disappeared. It's only because you are running this one I came along, Peter. It's hard to find people to trust these days."

Peter cleared his throat. "A terrible business, I agree. Rest assured I account for every penny."

"And again, the useless police in this town haven't managed to find anything," Chloe's mother said. "That's why my husband is going to shake up the policing in this country. It's time we stopped being so soft on people and started locking them up."

There were murmurs of agreement. Chloe saw Peter take a long drink of his wine.

"Too busy stuffing their faces at paid for events." Mrs Brown tapped the side of her now empty glass.

"Well, they look so out of place mixing with people of our standing." Chloe followed the finger of the large-hatted lady to see a man and woman standing near the buffet table. They both looked bored, and Chloe knew how they felt.

"Hardly Inspector Morse quality, are they?" Mrs Brown chuckled.

"I know, and does she think those shoes are appropriate for a function like this?" Chloe's mother said. "Ah, Thomas where have you been?" Chloe looked up and smiled as her father stepped up beside her mother, before listening obediently as the talk turned to politics and his prospects of victory. The latest opinion polls were showing a healthy lead, but he was warning against complacency.

While the huddle droned on, Chloe noticed the strawberry blonde detective was no longer with her partner, having moved into another small group to join the conversation. The male detective was picking at a plate of potato salad, not showing any interest in what was happening in the room.

Something about him intrigued Chloe. He had a rough, hewn look more appropriate on some Hollywood actor than a local police detective. A face chiselled with the stresses of the modern world. Handsome though.

"Ah, young Chloe. Always a pleasure to see you at these events. There are some people I would like you to meet who are fascinated by your modelling career." Chloe realised she'd become slightly detached from her mother's gossiping group and there was an unwelcome arm slipped around her waist.

"Mr Richards, always a pleasure. How is the car business?" She plastered on her best fake look of delight as she glanced up at Oakwell's premier car dealer and supplier of fine automobiles to its fine people. Or such was his blurb. To Chloe, it meant he wanted to have herself and Jenny in as few clothes as possible, draped over a premier car. She wasn't even sure if it was for an advert.

"Still hoping to recruit the town's top model." He gave her a lascivious grin.

Chloe had no doubt his smile was as fake as hers, as she felt his hand pressuring her to move towards his buddies. It also edged lower on her dress. "That's a shame, because Jenny is out of town."

"You know what I mean." He gave her a wink. "You were always my number one."

Before his hand could slip any lower Chloe neatly spun away. "I'm retired I'm afraid, Mr Richards. After all, I'm positively ancient in the modelling world." She looked across to where the detective was sitting and decided that she was hungry.

18

MILEY: He still won't let me go!! And now he's gone out again when the whole reason for coming here was so we'd be able to spend more time together. I could've still been in London with my friends.

ALICE: Where's he gone?

MILEY: Some stupid charity ball he said he couldn't get out of. Still, at least I can do what I want.

Miley took a swig of one of the bottles of beer she'd pilfered from the fridge, doing so as much out of defiance as to give her courage for being on camera later. She needed to earn some quick money for the outfit she wanted.

ALICE: I take it you're still going to the party?

MILEY: Hell yes. Not staying in just because Mr Do Goody says so. I can take care of myself. Just need to earn some cash.

ALICE: I can get us a good gig tonight.

MILEY: I've got my usual.

ALICE: He's a pussy. I'm talking about big bucks, baby.

MILEY: ?

ALICE: Wants two girls playing strip with him. A hundred quid each, easy money.

MILEY: I'm not sure about that.

Alice may have introduced her to the world of sugar daddies, where older men wanted to chat with them and were willing to pay, but Miley wasn't as inclined to go as far as her friend. A few skimpy clothes and a flash of flesh might be needed to keep them interested, but not stripping off completely which Alice admitted to doing.

She knew her friend didn't do it for the money. Alice did it for the attention because if there was one currency Alice could never get enough of it was male adoration. For a while Miley had dismissed it, laughing it off while disturbed at her friend's secret. Then she'd found out how much she was making for very little effort, and Alice opened a whole new world where Miley could make all the money she needed to enable her to fit right in with the coolest crowd in the school, and still have a big chunk left over. It turned out to be a lot easier than spending half the night coding at ten bucks an hour.

She'd read about the dangers online, watched the videos at school and listened to her dad. When he'd allowed her to have the computer in her own room, he'd warned her about the Internet being full of perverts and weirdos, but he never mentioned the good money they would pay.

ALICE: Stop being a pussy Miley and let yourself go. It's just a bit of harmless fun. I hear Josh really fancies you. He's not going to want you if he thinks you're an uptight bitch.

MILEY: He really likes me?

ALICE: That's what Maisie says.

Josh was fine. Without a doubt, the best-looking boy in the school and to think he was interested in her.

ALICE: So?

MILEY: I've already got someone tonight. He's already paying me a hundred.

That wasn't quite a lie. She would get a hundred to pay for a dress if she went topless and she hadn't decided about that.

But she did want that money.

ALICE: You dirty slut. I want some of that action. I gotta go. Customers waiting. CYA.

MILEY: Laters.

Closing the chat window Miley finished off the first beer as she read through her emails before buzzing a few of the global chat-rooms. She giggled at some of the comments about her, and cheekily replied to entice more. In her email was a hundred-pound voucher that would give her enough to buy the dress she wanted for the party. Presumptive, but with another beer Miley thought it would be okay.

HACKER BOI: Wot u doing?

Miley groaned as another chat window opened. She couldn't be doing with him today.

MILEY: Not much. Going to bed now. Feel tired.

HACKER BOI: Wot it's early. Thought we could hang out and check out some new code I've got.

MILEY: Not tonight hun, sorry.

Despite not wanting to lie, whoever was behind the username had got very clingy in recent weeks. It was as if he knew the times it was least convenient to speak and asked her on purpose.

HACKER BOI: You'll never get your dreams like that angel.

MILEY: I know, just not tonight.

There was another chat box flashing. A paying client. HACKER BOI had been good to her and been a good online friend in the dark days after she'd moved to Oakwell, but he was getting too much now.

MILEY: Sorry hun. GTG.

She closed the window and logged out of global chat before opening a private chat window, making sure her camera was in a perfect position. This was a sugar daddy she didn't get to see, which was fine by her. Having them on camera often meant seeing wrinkly old men with distorted faces as they played with themselves.

He accepted her chat window straight away.

WILLOW MOON: Hi baby.

SILVER WOLF: You are looking very sexy tonight. Stand up so I can see you better.

19

"You look pleased to be here," Chloe added some finger food to her plate, before moving near to where the detective was sitting.

"Not really my thing." He offered a smile Chloe knew wasn't genuine. She'd made enough of them tonight to recognise the difference.

"More into car chases and running down the bad guys in your bare feet?"

"That obvious?" Zack looked up, his smile spreading to his deep blue eyes. She wanted to see more of that smile. His eyes flicked over her, and she found herself hoping he liked what he saw.

"Well, it is to my mother and her cronies." Chloe waved over to her mother who'd been joined by a few more middle-aged women wanting to be seen with her husband, the man likely to be elected in a few days.

"I thought you politicians' daughters were right at home pressing the flesh." Zack winced. "Sorry, I didn't mean that how it sounded."

"Hey, you say it as you see it. I respect that." Chloe offered her first real grin of the night. Zack, looking a little flustered, opted for prodding at his potato salad while Chloe added a few more nibbles to her plate, waiting to see if the detective was going to further the conversation. It seemed he wasn't.

"They're wondering why you and your partner are here." Passing in front of him Chloe checked the jugs to find at least one had some coffee in. "Want some?" she said, after pouring herself a cup.

"No thanks. Not here by choice. I'd never be at anything like this by choice."

"Wrong type of people?"

"No, that's not what I meant. Jeez, I can't say anything."

Chloe laughed. "Detective, I know what you mean. But it's not the wrong type of people; it's what they become when they gather in packs. All fake teeth, fake smiles, and in most cases probably fake boobs."

"Which one are you?"

"That's very personal, detective."

"I didn't mean that you had fake, you know." He nodded to her chest area.

"Boobs is perhaps the word you are looking for. No, I'm still hundred percent natural. Except for the smile that is."

"Then why are you here?"

"Dutiful daughter I am, Sir." Chloe put on a common accent, which at least made him smile again. "My father being one of the candidates means I get rolled out to prove what a happy family we are, all supporting each other."

"I detect some cynicism," Zack said.

"Only the merest whiff. But, after all, you're a detective."

"So why do they think we're here?" Zack asked.

"Ooh, now that's what's so intriguing." Chloe perched on the edge of a seat near to Zack. "Rumours of strange goings on in the town, mysterious deaths. Defrocked priests slaughtered in their beds, young women escaping blazing infernos, strange lights seen across the moors. Which one is it, detective?"

"Call me Zack, not a car chasing, shoot out kind of detective I'm afraid."

"Shame, you could have wrapped it all up by morning."

"Yes, but I still haven't even found out who killed Mrs Wiggins ginger cat. The priest killer must wait."

"Cat killings? Why haven't I read about that in the news?"

"The media are keeping a lid on it." Zack tapped his nose. "Don't want to cause a panic."

"Yes, I can see why." Chloe put her finger on her lips. "I promise I won't tell anyone."

"Good thing, for your own safety." There were a few more minutes of silence as they both picked at their food. Chloe wondered how old he was. His eyes looked young, but the wrinkles on his face and the occasional fleck of grey in his hair gave him the look of one who'd seen a few years. She couldn't help noticing there was no wedding band on his finger.

"How are you after the fire? I saw the footage."

"It received more views than the TV pilot I was in." Which Chloe knew was probably true. "No harm done, and the publicity has been outstanding my mother tells me. Sometimes I think she started it."

"Well, it's not been the only fire we're looking at, so maybe I should bring her in for questioning."

"Now that I would like to see," Chloe said, picturing the look on her mother's face as she was hauled into a police car. "So, no truth in the rumours of strange goings-on then?"

"Only what you've read in the papers."

"Nicely avoided. Your partner seems to be doing a better job of mixing with the cream of society." She watched the demure detective talking with a group of businessmen on the far side of the room. Chloe had spoken to her after the fire, which at the time no one had found any reason to call deliberate. She'd been friendly and business like and Chloe had liked her. She tried to remember if the female detective had been wearing a ring and couldn't help wondering if the two detectives were an item.

"No need to waste energy when they come to me." Zack winced again. "Now that sounded pretty bad."

"Absolutely and I'm deeply offended." Chloe stood and dropped the remains on her plate into one of the bins as her mother beckoned her over. "But I will forgive you if you bring the cat killer to justice." She held out her hand. "I'm Chloe by the way, not that you appear to care about such trivial issues of names when there are much bigger mysteries for you to solve."

Zack took her hand with a firm grip.

"Pleased to meet you, Miss Evans. Zack Carter, Cat Detective."

20

Peter felt sick as he sucked on a cigarette. Not just because it was twenty years since he'd last smoked, but because of the fraud he felt mixing among the dignitaries at the event. The nicotine surged through his body, giving him some small relief from the fear gripping him. He took a large gulp of wine and wished it was vodka. Even a few stiff drinks had failed to stem the stress being among people he felt could see right into his soul at the fake he was.

Before he shook every hand, Peter rubbed his palms against his trouser leg to wipe away the sweat he believed to be there. Peter plastered on a mask of sincerity to everyone he was introduced to, thanking them for their compliments at how much he'd done for the town with the way he ran the charity. Everyone was amazed at the fundraising he'd achieved because none of them knew where most of the money really came from. If they did, he'd be on his way to prison.

"Times have changed when you are alone in smokers' corner. In the old days, half of 'em would've been out here making their sneaky little deals. Mind if I light up?"

"No, not at all." Peter merely glanced at the man who'd joined him at the back of the town hall where all the bins were. Though as Peter was trying to get away from the crowd, the intrusion wasn't welcome.

"Cheers man. Can I bum a smoke? They don't let me have them on me when I'm working."

"Here." Flipping a cigarette out of the packet Peter looked the younger man over. He was wearing grey coveralls with some sort of utility belt.

"Got to make sure every thing's running good for the cream of Oakwell's society." The man shrugged. Peter nodded, offering his lighter.

There was silence for a while as they both stood under the night sky. The sound of the assembled dignitaries and their laughter drifted from the door the man had propped open with his mop. Peter sucked hard on his cigarette, feeling uncomfortable with the stranger beside him. He'd needed to get away and think.

"You got problems, dude?" The man's voice startled Peter from his dark thoughts. "We all got problems. Every one of those tossers has problems." The man jerked a thumb back towards the inside of the town hall.

"No, things are fine." Peter didn't want to be talking to the cleaner. He drew hard on the last of his cigarette and was about to flick it to the floor.

"Things aren't fine for you though, are they Peter?"

The cigarette paused in mid-flick. In an instant the man's manner, tone and accent had changed. "How do you know my name?"

"Folks have been calling you it all night." The man grinned as if it was some sort of joke.

"I'm sorry, I think I should be getting back inside." Peter dropped the butt onto the floor.

"What would they think if they knew it had all gone?"

Peter felt as though his insides had been ripped out. There was a pain in his chest. Was it a heart attack? He felt as if someone was clutching at his windpipe, stopping him from breathing. How could he know? How could a cleaner know?

"What would they think if they knew how you invested the money to make such good returns? You don't run a charity; you run a money laundering service for mercenaries. You are such a good man Peter, helping all those poor kiddies of this town. But you weren't always such a saint, were you?"

"Who are you?" Peter hissed.

"I'm someone who makes it his business to know the past and someone who holds the key to your future, Peter. I can make all your problems go away."

"I don't know what you're talking about." Peter looked down at the cigarette and crushed it under his polished black shoes.

"I think you do, Peter. It's why you're so nervous in there because you think at any moment one of them might find out the truth that all the lovely money has vanished."

"I haven't taken it."

"Oh, I know that." There was that grin again.

"Then how can you possibly make my problem go away?"

"Because I took it."

Peter stared incredulously at the so-called cleaner leant against the wall, his own cigarette burning down to the filter. "What have you done with it, you little fucker?" Peter darted forward. Pushing himself up against the man, and taking him by the front of his coveralls until he was pressed tightly up against the wall. "You put that money back now, or I'll fucking end you."

"And lo, the real Peter is revealed. The demons inside you rise once more. You can never send them away you know, they'll always be in you."

Staring into the man's eyes, Peter didn't see any fear. "Listen, friend; I know people who will make your life a living fucking hell if I tell them about you. Now, what have you done with the money."

"But you won't tell them, will you? Your friends are not the kind of people that take failure lightly. It's why you shat your pants and got out, wasn't it? Because they didn't give a fuck, who got hurt on their operations. How many children do you help now all because of those who died at your hands? You've been a shit your whole life and you think you can redeem yourself by running a fucking charity."

Peter let go of the man and slumped against one of the bins feeling sick. Images of the young bodies crushed under the rubble of buildings his devices had destroyed flashed through his mind. The screams of the mothers trying to find their little ones. The laughter of the members of his team because they saw all the brown skins as a waste of life.

"You've still been happy to use the money though, haven't you?"

"I use it for good," Peter whispered.

"Don't be a fucking hypocrite."

"What do you want?" Peter needed a lot of drink and fast. He needed to forget.

"Just some of your time. And some of those skills you had when you were a naughty boy."

21

Chloe kicked off her heels and wriggled out of her dress before flopping onto the sofa. Had the remote not been on the other side of her coffee table, she would've clicked on the TV to see what mindless drivel she could unwind to. Chloe realised she should get herself some water if she wanted to avoid a nasty headache but it all seemed like too much effort.

As the evening progressed more drinks had been pressed into her hand, and she'd felt her mother was trying to line her up with potential suitors. Any councillor with an eligible son was introduced, and Chloe thought her mother would marry her off tomorrow if it would get them a few more votes.

Reaching into her purse, she pulled out a bunch of business cards handed over during the night and glanced through them with amusement. Most were given on the pretence of a job offer because someone as talented as Chloe was surely wasted as a mere receptionist. All with the subtext of a date and never handed over in the presence of her parents. Still, she'd accepted them with a smile, a flutter of her eyes, and a promise to contact them should the need the arise.

One of the few people who hadn't handed her a card was the detective. Her ego noted he hadn't drooled over her like so many of the older men, putting it down to him being on duty. Something about his rugged handsomeness kept him in her thoughts, even though she was concerned at already thinking about an older man as date material.

Tossing the cards onto the table, Chloe flicked her phone to life. There were no messages. She'd still not heard from Jenny, who was probably in Paris right now without a care in the world, and Chloe missed her presence in the house. Jenny would have put her straight about fancying the detective, or then again, might have told Chloe just to fuck him.

Why was it always her friend getting to swan off with no sense of responsibility holding her back? It always seemed to happen for Jenny, always managing to squeeze that little bit more out of life than Chloe. Perhaps it was because her friend was willing to take more risks than Chloe to do what it took to get on.

Chloe knew of at least one television role her friend had bagged by being very friendly on the casting couch. There'd been chances for Chloe too, more than enough, but she'd stormed out, determined to make it on merit and not because of how far she was willing to open her legs.

Even then as the work began to dry up, the photo shoots became more sordid, and she'd been desperate for money when an offer came in from an agency she'd turned down in the past for being almost pornographic. About to be thrown on the street with nothing, she agreed to a shoot she regretted as soon as she walked out of the door clutching her cheque. The morning after, Chloe had paid her debts and fled home, leaving her shattered dreams and pride behind.

With an urge to speak to her friend, Chloe dialled Jenny's number, disappointed it went straight to voicemail, but she didn't leave a message.

Chloe stretched out, resting her head on the back of the sofa, wondering if she could be bothered to go up to bed. Closing her eyes, the image of the detective came unbidden as she imagined his arms wrapping around her body.

Her phone jolted her awake. An unknown number.

It looks like there are lots of men who like you, Chloe. I wonder if any of your father's supporters have seen what you are really like? Be a good girl, Chloe.

A cold, icy feeling gripped her as she saw pictures of herself at the charity event. Her stalker had to have been there. It was the only way he could have done this. She thought back to all the people she'd met, trying to work out who it could've been.

"Who are you?" She screamed at the phone, before throwing it onto the sofa in frustration. Then almost immediately she picked it back up and replied to the message.

Who are you? Why are you doing this to me?

The phone pinged with a message from Jenny's number.

Heart racing for joy Chloe opened the message, expecting to see her friend's face smiling at her from in front of the Eiffel tower. She would ring her, tell what was happening. Jenny would know what to do.

Instead, she saw Jenny's body.

22

"Looks like you picked up a fan last night," Nadine said, raising her eyebrows as she walked in front of Zack's desk.

"A fan?" Zack looked up from his computer.

"The blonde bombshell you were chatting up when you couldn't be bothered to mingle with me. I couldn't help but notice while I was doing the community relations exercise the DCI asked us to do, that you'd decided to chat up the best-looking girl in the room, and no less than a prospective MP's daughter. Very impressive. Did you use the old Zack Carter charm?"

"Very funny. What does she want?"

"No idea, she only wants to tell her sugar daddy," Nadine sucked on the top of her pen giving a girly giggle.

"Well, maybe it's because she wasn't too impressed with the last detective she spoke to, who can offer no results on her case."

"Ooh, you bitch. Or maybe she wants to slap you for being a misogynist pig."

"Hilarious. Where is she?" Zack rose from his desk before others in the office overheard Nadine's banter.

"In reception. Do you want to book a private room?"

Zack gave Nadine the finger as he headed towards the

main reception. He couldn't help being intrigued by Chloe's appearance, after all, she'd been the high point in an otherwise dull evening. Even when he'd watched her after they'd spoken, she managed to be part of the event while remaining slightly above it.

Chloe sat in the reception area hugging herself with her arms. With her hair tied back in a simple ponytail and devoid of any makeup Zack thought she looked stunning. He told himself to get a grip but still opted for one of his winning smiles as he approached her.

"Miss Evans. How can I help you?"

"I need to report a murder." Chloe blurted out.

"Murder?" Zack was stopped in his tracks.

"My friend Jenny. Look." She rose from the seat, thrusting her iPhone in front of him to reveal a picture of a woman lying on the ground. Zack took the phone to make a closer examination. While he couldn't confirm whether the woman was dead, she appeared in a bad way.

"Who sent you this?"

"It came from her phone," Chloe said. "She met a man the other night when we were in a club in Birmingham and went with him to a party. I've had a few messages saying she was in London then off to Paris. Then last night I received this."

"Have you spoken to her?"

"No. When I ring it goes straight to voicemail, as if it's switched off."

Zack turned to one of the uniforms behind the reception desk. "Can you prepare an interview room and ask Nadine to join me?"

There'd been times in his life when Zack sensed something was wrong before it seemed apparent to anyone else. It was an instinct Zack had learnt to listen to over the years because he realised it had saved his life and his brother's more than once. When three seemingly unconnected events happened in quick succession, Zack never assumed coincidence. It was why he'd been rated so highly as an intelligence operative in Iraq and Afghanistan. A skill that saw him save a lot of soldiers lives.

As he walked into the interview room with Chloe, he knew something was seriously wrong in the sleepy town of Oakwell.

23

"I'm just having an off-day Mum; I'll be fine for the rally tomorrow." Chloe wasn't sure how much her mother was concerned about her health or that she wouldn't be with them canvassing. She'd taken the day off sick to go to the police, and the thought of going to work with Jenny missing or worse was out of the question. At least there was some hope Jenny could just be lying drunk at a party and it was all a joke.

"Are you sure there's nothing wrong?" Her mother persisted.

Her mother's voice seemed even more shrill than usual, forcing Chloe to hold the phone away. "I'll be okay I promise. Just going to curl up on the sofa and watch some crap TV."

"If you're sure. I can come around, you know."

"No Mum, I'll be fine." Her mother fussing over her was the last thing Chloe wanted.

"Okay. You sure it's not because of the fire. Smoke can do funny things. I've read it online."

"Look, mum, I've gotta go, I'll speak to you later." Chloe cut her mother off. Shoving her phone across the table, Chloe looked at the empty coffee maker. As badly as she needed a caffeine hit, Chloe lacked the energy to get out of the chair. Folding her arms on the table, she rested her head, feeling the urge to cry at the mess of her life.

She kept going over the interview with the two detectives. They'd been nice, listened carefully, taken notes and asked her questions about Jenny's normal social activities but they'd been clear it could be nothing other than a missing person case as it stood. She might just be off her heads on drugs and booze. Something Chloe had said Jenny had been prone to do in the past. Zack had said they'd run a trace on her phone, but it would take a few days.

While giving her some hope, Chloe knew they didn't know about the other messages she'd been receiving. If she'd told the police about them, then how long before her past revealed? How the press would lap it up so close to the by-election.

She'd intended to tell them. Convinced herself it was the right thing to do while sitting in the waiting area. Then the detective had walked out with that great smile reminding her of her favourite film star, Matt Damon, and she'd known she didn't want him to know how much of a slut she was.

In her sun-baked kitchen, it seemed such a stupid decision and maybe if they didn't find anything she'd tell them. If it was after the election. While she may not have bought into the whole politics thing like the rest of her family, she certainly didn't want to be the one to ruin it with her sordid past.

"Get a grip of yourself, girl." Looking out of the window Chloe decided a drink and some sun might just bring a little cheer to her life. It would be stupid to waste a day off, especially during probably the last heat wave of the year.

After going upstairs to change into some cut off denim shorts and a sleeveless top, Chloe checked her fridge for anything to mix with the remnants of a bottle of vodka she'd found in the cupboard. Remembering the night, she and Jenny had smashed through most of the bottle made her smile. Jenny had just moved back from London after finally calling her own career a dud. But she still had tonnes of stories about what she'd been up to and which celebrity was secretly shagging who.

"Where are you, Jen?" Chloe poured the last dregs of the vodka into a glass. Slipping on her sandals, Chloe went to pick her phone up from the table when she noticed a missed message.

Was today a good idea? I thought you might like the below; I think it could be very popular. Maybe your family would like to know you are becoming an internet sensation.

24

The angle of the camera captured Chloe's expression perfectly as she selected the link in the message. Alex could see her browser being directed to the site Liam had set up in dedication to her beauty. The main screen in the dining room Alex was sitting in displayed everything Chloe was viewing. Alex lifted his bowl of muesli off the long central table, spooning the contents into his mouth as he watched. Another screen showed the visual feed from the hidden camera in her kitchen and captured the exquisite emotions on her face in high definition as she clicked on the pictures.

Page after page of images of her life, interspersed with her modelling pictures, were revealed to Chloe as she browsed the site. There were other users on the site as well as Chloe, Alex could see the popular pages. Pages of her last photo shoot where she was naked and compromised appeared to be a favourite, though it was a close run thing with the gallery of images Liam had created. Fake bondage picture seemed to be a speciality of Liam's. The site itself used a fake girls name, but all the images were of Chloe.

Alex thought it would be interesting when Liam finally got to have his way with Chloe, partly because Alex doubted his old friend would have the guts to go through with it. Alex found most idiots who spouted off online about what they would do if they had the chance were too chicken shit when the opportunity presented itself. Perhaps the copious amount of coke Alex was giving Liam would make the difference.

The horror and rage spreading across Chloe's face pleased Alex because he liked to see strong emotions in others. It was a sign of people no longer in control. Angry people were not rational people and prone to make things worse with thoughtless stupidity. A stupidity Alex often exploited. He especially liked the moment she reached the page showing live streams and saw her own face live on the site.

Chloe's next actions were quite rational, however, and inevitable given what she had seen. One by one his visual feeds vanished as she rampaged through the house seeking out and destroying the hidden cameras. Alex finished his muesli while she searched, and considered whether to go and make himself a milkshake. She nearly found them all, but Alex was too smart for the likes of Chloe, he was smarter than everyone because he knew this would happen. In anticipation, two of the cameras had been hidden with such expertise only blind luck or sophisticated surveillance detection equipment would reveal them. Coverage of the lounge and her bedroom had been maintained.

It had been so easy to gain access when neither of the girls had been there. Lazy people who couldn't be bothered to do their own cleaning were such easy targets because they employed cleaners with no idea about security. Chloe's wasn't the only house he'd gained access to while spending a few weeks working for a cleaning company. It had also amused him that he was cleaning Chloe's house for her. Alex had done an excellent job too, much better than the normal people who had worked at the company. Alex always took pride in his work, even if he was faking it.

Chloe collapsed on the sofa, hugging a cushion and rocking as she kept looking round. Then she jumped to her feet, slipped her tablet into her handbag and stormed out of the room. Alex deftly manoeuvred his mouse to bring up another software program. His tracker showed her car on the move. Across other screens, he hooked into the town's CCTV network, allowing him to see her progress.

"Where are you going, Chloe? Are you going to see mummy?"

Alex watched her pull into the main town car park next to a Costa Coffee. There was a glimpse of her entering the shop. He dragged the screen of her tablet back onto the main view when it had connected with the WIFI, bringing it back onto the grid. Again he could see everything on her screen.

He watched her browsing Facebook before she began looking through profiles on LinkedIn.

Alex smiled and opened a chat window.

25

LIAM: I can't do it.

When Alex's message came through excitement had rippled through Liam. Then trepidation as the thought of going outside on his own to meet with Chloe took hold. The last time he'd gone out the nerves had been soothed by the coke Alex had brought, and then the rest of his body had been consumed with ecstasy under the guiles of the women of pleasure. Cocaine was an instant cure to agoraphobia.

ALEX: It's what you've wanted. We can use this for you to get to her.

LIAM: I know. I'm nervous.

ALEX: You getting cold feet?

It was one thing acting out all manner of perversions in his fantasies, creating fake images of Chloe enduring torture and humiliation, and another when he thought that it might happen. Liam had dreamed of revenge for how she'd treated him, even agreed with Alex about going through with it in the real world, because at the time he thought Alex was bullshitting. Only he wasn't. Alex didn't bullshit about anything. It was like Liam's visions of being a real hero in the online games and always getting the girl. Pure fantasy that had no place in the real world. Only Alex seemed to be able to make those fantasies come true.

ALEX: Remember what she did to you. She didn't have second thoughts about your pain. She looks down on the likes of you and me, Liam. Their type always do. Make her your bitch now. Make her pay for what she did to you.

Liam clenched his fists as he recalled the vivid memory of the night he thought she was going to play a crazy strip tease game with him over Skype. He'd believed it when she'd said it was a cheeky little birthday present for all his help. He'd wanted to believe what she was saying was true, because the thought of Chloe performing for him meant all rational thinking had taken a vacation.

The game was obviously rigged, and he'd been the one who ended up naked. Chloe sitting in her lacy underwear had excited him so much Liam hadn't cared about his clothes coming off. He was only reluctant to push off his boxers until she'd said that if he was willing to go all the way then so was she. At the same time, she'd unhooked her bra, teasing as though she was going to slip it off and reveal all. Then his pants had not been able to hit the floor quickly enough.

The laughing faces were still etched in his memories as vividly as the moment it had happened.

All Chloe's cool buddies were there on the screen having known about the game all along. The next day everyone at school had seen the recording and especially found funny the part when he'd tried to get off the chair, only impeded by his pants around his ankles he'd gone tumbling to the floor adding his naked white butt to the show.

ALEX: When you think of what she did to you, how do you feel?

LIAM: I hate her.

ALEX: When you make those pictures do you feel better?

LIAM: Yes.

ALEX: Do you think when she sleeps she dreams of someone like you next to her?

LIAM: Never.

ALEX: The only way to get what you want in life is to take it. I've told you that.

LIAM: Yes.

ALEX: You want the better life I've shown you? You want the life I lead?

LIAM: More than anything.

Liam lay in bed at night alternating his fantasies between Chloe and the woman Alex had taken Liam to for his night of sexual pleasure. It was easy to imagine it was Chloe riding him and not the prostitute. According to Alex, there were women all over the world willing to be fucked by all manner of men, provided they were paid enough. Alex had given Liam a glimpse of a life where he could be the master of people and never have to cower before them again. It was the life he'd always wanted. What Alex was teaching him was that he could be the master in his games. If only he had the balls to make the right moves.

ALEX: What do you do with your dark thoughts, Liam?

LIAM: Channel them into hate and onto those that have wronged me.

ALEX: And who has wronged you, Liam?

LIAM: Chloe Evans.

ALEX: Who do you hate?

LIAM: Chloe Evans.

ALEX: Go and meet her Liam. Lead her to the truth of who she is.

LIAM: I don't know what to say to her.

ALEX: Let her come to you. Just go in there, buy a coffee as though it's what you do every day. She's looking for someone Liam. She's looked at your profile. She's looking for someone with the skills to help her.

She'll come to you. Then she can be yours.

26

Chloe wasn't sure how long Liam had been in the line for coffee before she noticed him. He may have been much fatter than when she last saw him, but she could still recognise his face. There were dark patches under the arms of the large T-shirt that tried to conceal his bulk. Grey joggers and some horrific looking flip-flops finished off his outfit.

His appearance surprised Chloe, not just at being in the coffee place, but the fact his LinkedIn profile talked about a successful computer expert who seemed to be doing some major freelance gigs. There was no picture, and Chloe had imagined him as a successful businessman, dressed every day in a tie and shirt and probably not the type of person that would be willing to assist a washed-up model with a stalker. It was why she'd moved on looking for others that might help her.

The last message from her stalker had chilled Chloe to the bone after she'd seen the website filled with her pictures, some in her own home. It made her physically sick, and she'd raged around the house finding and crushing each of the cameras, terrified at how they came to be in her home.

She had to get out of there and find someone who could help her. What if there were more cameras she couldn't find?

It seemed even harder to go to the police now, the site looked as though it was hers even if it wasn't under her real name. The galleries were even named as if she was keeping it as a video diary. There was even a blog which had been filled in with her daily antics. She could imagine how many people would see it if she went to the police, how quickly it would get out there into the press. How quickly her life would be torn apart, and her father's campaign destroyed

Chloe wanted to ring Zack, not just because he was police but because she thought he might help her off the books, give her some advice. They probably weren't allowed to do that kind of thing, and though she'd picked up her phone a couple of times she'd lost her nerve. No, this was something she had to try and sort out without the police.

Finding someone to help her hunt down the location of the site and shut it down was her number one priority, and maybe the same person could help her locate who was doing this. The problem was finding someone. Most people she knew were back in London and would revel in her trauma. There were the IT guys at work of course, but again she could imagine their faces when they saw the site. How soon before they shared the images with their friends while telling her they were doing everything they could to shut it down.

She'd looked up Liam on LinkedIn because Jenny had spoken about having seen him on the site. Jenny had talked about having a reunion of the old-school year, talked about it as though everyone would be so pleased to get together. Jenny seemed oblivious to the way they'd treated some of the people in those days. People like Liam. Would he even talk to her? But she needed help, and at least Liam was someone she knew even if it was from her school days.

Taking a few deep breaths, Chloe rose from her chair.

27

"Hi Liam, it's been a long time." Chloe had been about to add the usual "you're looking good" until she realised how crass that would have sounded. Liam was not looking good, and his bulk was something he seemed to carry around with difficulty.

"You look nice, Chloe."

Chloe felt herself smoothing down her T-shirt, suddenly conscious of him looking her up and down. "Thank you; I hear you're doing really well in computers."

"I get by." Liam finished ordering his drink before standing at the end of the counter while it was made. "I heard you were into modelling."

"I was, now I'm into being a legal secretary."

"Didn't quite work out?" Liam thanked the barista for his coffee.

"Not really. Look do you want to come and join me."

Liam put his head down and shuffled his feet as though he was thinking about her offer. He then looked up and smiled. "Sure."

They moved over to the couch, Liam taking the seat opposite. He stirred sugar into his drink. Chloe watched him, trying to picture the young boy she'd been friends with at junior school. His change had certainly not been for the better, and would he want to help her after the way she'd treated him?

"Someone is stalking me. Cyber-stalking me." Chloe could only think of a direct approach to say what she needed to.

"And you think it could be me?" Liam stopped his stirring.

"It could be anyone. That's why I need help. Somebody with your skills." Chloe was rather taken aback by his relaxed manner. She remembered him as a nervous wreck around her, around most people he'd considered part of the cool gang. "They've set up a site with my pictures on it. I want to get it shut down."

"You any idea who it is? "

"No. Every time I see someone I know I think it could be them. It's driving me crazy."

"So, you think it could be me?" He stopped after adding four packets of sugar to his drink.

"Yes." Chloe was surprised at his manner.

"Very honest, which is remarkable for you." His eyes seemed to bore into her.

"I know I did wrong by you Liam, when we were at school, I treated you like shit. I just want to say I'm sorry, I truly am." Liam only nodded. "I know I have no right to ask for anything from you. I was wrong, there was a lot that I did that was wrong back then, but I've changed. I'm not that cruel bitch you knew. I'm not the person who was mean to you. Do you understand that?"

"Why did you do it?" For the first time, Liam's cool exterior broke. Chloe could see the pained expression.

She turned her head, looking out of the window at the people walking by lazily, not wanting to rush in the afternoon sun. "I don't know, Liam. At the time I saw other people, those that were not part of our group, as some sort of sport."

"But why me? We'd been friends, and I was helping you." He shrugged his shoulders. "Not that you needed it."

"I suppose it was because I had known you before. I thought you would be easier to..." The words caught in Chloe's throat. She had been such a bitch. "Manipulate."

"You destroyed me."

Chloe looked back at Liam and thought she could see tears in his eyes. Was that why he was so obese now? She wanted to dismiss the thought because he'd always been a chubby kid. Only it wouldn't go away. She remembered him getting even fatter after that night. Just a pudgy kid who hid himself away whenever he could so the rest of the school barely noticed him anymore.

"I'm so sorry."

There was silence between them. Chloe wanted to speak but didn't know what to say.

"What is it you want from me?" Liam finally asked.

"I need someone to find the site, shut it down and find whoever is behind it." Chloe took a deep breath. "They may have killed Jenny."

"What?" Liam leant forward, a look of alarm on his broad face, and it was that moment Chloe was sure that he wasn't her stalker.

"I don't know for sure, but she went off with a man when we were out in Birmingham at the weekend, and I'd heard nothing until I was sent a picture of her body. The police say we can't be sure it's her. But I know it is. I'd try and trace him myself," Chloe said, "but I don't have a clue what I'm doing. I hear people can pretty much trace anything these days."

"Most of the time that's true, but if someone doesn't want

to be found, then it can be almost impossible to do so. There are ways though; people make mistakes we can exploit." Liam looked as though he was regaining his composure. "If there's a site, then there is a physical location, so I can start there."

"Will you try for me? I can pay you, as a consultant, for your time." Chloe felt a glimmer of hope.

"What makes you think he's stalking you too?"

"I found hidden web cameras in my house. And he sent me pictures."

"What kind of pictures?"

She could tell from his look he already suspected. "You know, the kind that a girl wouldn't want the rest of the world to see."

"Interesting." Chloe could see he was enjoying having the upper hand. He was probably eager to see the pictures for himself. She considered walking out but then whoever was going to assist her would see them.

"Will you help me?"

"I'll need access to everything you've been sent; you realise that?"

"I know." He'd returned to being cold and aloof again. "But it has to be done in the strictest confidence. It's a crucial time for my family, so I can't have any of this getting out."

Liam nodded. "I understand. I can try to help you. I can add software to your devices which would help trace things that you open. I'd need access to your computer and any other devices you have been contacted on."

"That's fine, can you come around mine and do it or do I need to bring them to you? Can you check for any other cameras in my house? I see on TV people have gizmos for that."

"I can't look for the cameras themselves, but I can look for the signals they might be sending. I can come around yours to do that."

Chloe saw there was an eagerness in his expression that fed the nagging doubt inside her. She couldn't believe she needed help from someone who would clearly get a kick when he saw the photos. "Tonight?" If he was going to see everything that was going on, she was keen to get it over with.

"It will take me a little while to get together what I need, but tonight should be good. Send me the link to the site now. I can start trying to trace that as soon as I get back."

She couldn't help picturing the look on his face as he clicked through the images. Or imagine what he would be doing while looking at them. Chloe swallowed down her disgust before grabbing a pen out of her purse and writing on a serviette.

"Here's my number. Text me when you're ready to come over."

"Okay."

"You don't know how thankful I am. And I'm sorry again Liam, for what I did. I truly am."

As she left the coffee shop, Chloe wondered if it would be enough to keep him from spreading her pictures around some geeky computer forums.

28

"Hi, Dad." Miley snapped the laptop lid down and jumped off her stool, giving her dad a hug and a peck on the cheek as he walked into the house. The kitchen smelt of the chicken pie warming up in the oven. There was a glass on the table, ready for his favourite beer.

Miley had prepared for another assault on her dad to get permission to go to the party. It was time to work on his guilt, a trick she'd used more than once. One of the problems with having a policeman for a dad, and him mixing with some of the worst scum in society, was his distrust of everyone. She was proud of what he did if it didn't interfere with her social life.

"Hi hun, good day?" Zack dropped his keys and phone on the side before going over to the oven.

"I received another commendation for my maths work, Mr Cravat keeps trying to persuade me to join the maths club."

"You don't want to?"

"I've tried hard to get the friends I have Dad; I don't want to ruin it all by engaging in social suicide."

"But you do computer club, don't you? Isn't that a den of pale-faced geeks?"

"We're not in the dark ages now. Everyone's getting into computers." Though it was true, most of them were still pasty in the skin colour department.

"I shall leave that one to your judgement." Zack started to get the plates from the cupboard.

"Let me do that." Miley hopped across the kitchen, taking the plates off him. "You grab a beer and sit down."

"Okay." He duly took a cold bottle from the fridge before taking his seat at the table.

Miley dished up the pie and chips, continuing to soften him with talk of how well she was getting on at school. "Anything new at work today?"

"A missing person." There was an agreement between them that her dad would talk about some of the things he was involved in, providing she told no one else. "A local woman on a night out in Birmingham."

"I thought this was supposed to be a quiet town." Miley thought it might be wiser to steer the conversation away from that topic. "There seems to be a lot going on."

"How do you mean?" Zack sipped his beer in between mouthfuls of pie.

"Fires, murders, even a cat killer. For the first six months you were here you spent most of your time visiting old folks in their homes."

"Maybe it's just a mini crime wave. I blame the youth of today."

"Ha very funny." Miley flicked one of the peas off her plate at him, before deciding to change the conversation to the holidays. "I still think Florida this summer."

"Aren't you a bit old for Disneyland?"

"Dad there's a lot more there than just Disneyland, other theme parks and water worlds."

"Sounds hot, busy and expensive." Her dad pushed away his

plate.

"Probably all three, because it's good." Miley smiled. "You did promise me when I was little."

"Yes, I know, but that was back then." Miley knew what was unsaid, her dad had always talked about taking her as a family, and Miley knew his reluctance was because it was hard to think of going on the trip without mum. It would be their first proper holiday with just the two of them. They'd been away since mum died, but with her grandparents.

"She'd want us to go, Dad." Miley reached over, resting her hand on his arm.

"I know," Zack smiled, placing his hand on top of hers. "This weekend we'll go down to the travel agents and see what there is. I promised you a big trip next summer, and if that's where you want to go then, that's fine."

"Thanks, Dad." Miley leant forward and kissed him before gathering up the plates. "You know you won't always have to go everywhere with me if you need a break." She began stacking the plates inside the dishwasher. "You could just relax by the pool with a few beers sometimes. I'm old enough to look after myself, you know."

"I know you are hun, we'll see when we get out there."

"So, you agree then?" Miley moved back to the table, resting her hands on it by the side of her fathers.

"Agree with what princess?"

"That I'm old enough to look after myself?" Miley steeled herself. So far it had gone well.

"On most occasions, I think you are."

"Then I should be able to look after myself at a party."

"That's different, Miley." She heard the change in his tone.

"How is it?" Miley protested. "I'll be there in a house where they'll be from my school."

"Unlikely. These parties get out of hand and have older kids come along who you won't know. We've already been over this."

"But you don't know that Dad, and if it did get out of hand I'd ring you to come and get me. I'm sensible like that."

"I know, but Miley."

"But what Dad?" Miley raised her voice in frustration. He was just being stubborn.

"Look, you're not going, and that's final. I've already said no, and I'm not arguing with you again."

"For fuck's sake Dad, see reason." Miley regretted the outburst as her father's face went red.

"Don't you dare use language like that around me, young lady." His voice was calm and composed, a danger sign for Miley. "Thank you for dinner, but I think you should go to the room for the rest of the night and study."

"I can do my work without being told to." Miley went sullen.

"Then go and clean out your filthy mouth," he snapped, and she knew it was over. Fighting back her anger Miley turned and stomped up the stairs, making sure she slammed the doors sufficiently to signal her mood.

She threw herself on her bed. Frustrated at not being allowed the freedom she yearned for, guilty for putting her father in such a black mood, but still determined to go to the party and prove she could look after herself. She had already found the perfect dress to buy that would surely attract Josh's attention.

It only seemed like she'd been lying there for a few minutes when she heard her dad knocking.

"I'm sorry I shouted, darling. Are you okay?" Miley didn't

answer; she wanted him to think she was still pissed. "Look I've got to go out, someone has been hurt at the level crossing. Will you be alright?" Miley remained silent. "I'm sorry about the party but I know the sort of boys that will be there, and you're just not old enough yet. It's not you I don't trust it's them and sometimes you can find yourself in a position you're just not mature enough to handle. I'd rather you be mad at me than anything happens to you. I'll see you later. Love you hun."

"Love you too, dad," she whispered as he walked away.

29

With shaking hands Dave rolled the last of his weed into a joint. He'd need something else soon to take the edge off. He knew a shop around the corner that sold spice. You had to ask for it since the stupid government had banned legal highs, but Big Joe kept a stash.

This was something Dave had thought himself in control of, but now he needed the sweet oblivion more than ever. If he'd any cash, he would've gone to score something harder. Maybe then his troubles would just slip away, melting into a world where you didn't have to give a fuck.

Only going out meant seeing the papers and their glaring headlines about the murder of the old priest. While there weren't many people sympathetic to the old man's death, Dave knew the police would be all over it, and all over him if they found out he was in the house the night the old man was killed.

The smoke started to calm him. He'd rung in sick again, couldn't drive in this state anyway. The taxi was sitting in the drive, and though not working meant no money, all he wanted to do was get fucked up. The curtains were closed in his flat to shut the world out.

Dave had no idea what to do. How the hell had this gotten so out of control?

He'd nearly done it; got clean, and had been so close to getting his money back. Then he'd gone and fucked up again, and when you borrow money off people like he had you don't get fucking stupid unless you want to end up in a world of hurt. You end up taking jobs from strangers who get into your taxi. All because they say they can solve your problem.

The job to get the evidence had been so simple until he'd found the dead fucking body. He might have bolted but what evidence had he left for the cops to find? To cap it all he'd not recovered the memory stick he needed to pay off the debt. Not that it would have done any good anyway, now the dirty old prick was dead. But a deal was a deal, and Dave would've been able to collect his money.

There was the noise of a car engine outside. Dave tensed. Every time he heard a car he was convinced it was the police. He waited to see if there would be the sound of the buzzer or even the battering on his door. The engine faded, he sucked in another lungful of sweet weed.

Maybe he should hand himself in. He could come clean and explain that he had been after some cash and then found the body. After all, he hadn't killed the old fucker so his prints wouldn't be on the knife. But Dave didn't trust the coppers. They wouldn't believe a scum bag like him, and Dave knew they would think he was guilty whatever he said; he knew what bastards they could be when they thought they had their man. Walking into the cop station, protesting his innocence, would be yet another stupid thing to add to his long list of fucked up things he'd already done.

Another suck on the joint. At least that was helping ease the stress. Dave looked for the ashtray, finding it among a pile of chip wrappers.

His phone vibrated on the table. Dave shoved wrappers and cans out of the way until he found it.

Two jobs I need you to do, and all of this will go away. There will be enough money for a new life, in a new country, where no one will find you. Two jobs and you are free.

Dave quickly typed out his reply.

What the fuck happened at the old man's house?

You failed to get there in time.

I think you set me up, you prick. Who are you working for?

Dave wasn't going to piss about. He didn't trust this guy.

You have one more chance. Do it right this time, and you will be free.

And what if I don't?

Then the next time there's a knock at the door you won't know if it's the police or those you owe money to.

"The goddam mother fucker." Dave wanted to hurl his phone across the room and smash it into tiny bits.

Two jobs and you'll be free. There is money in your account.

Dave flicked off his messages and logged into his bank. This morning it had been in the red. Now he was looking at a cool thirty grand. Shit, he could just up and leave right now.

If you try and leave without doing the jobs, then the money will vanish.

Could this prick do that? Probably, after all, he'd made it appear. This fucker seemed to be able to do anything.

Are you in?

Did he have a choice?

30

"That was an excellent speech Mary, your husband is certain to win, and quite right too. It's time this country was locking up lazy layabout criminals." Chloe stood dutifully by her mother's side as Mrs Brown spoke. The well to do woman still looked a little flustered from arriving late, though a large glass of wine seemed to be allowing her to regain her composure.

"Why thank you, Enid. I hear you got caught up in the trouble at the crossing." Chloe's mother said.

"If it's not idiot drivers causing problems, it's idiot people. Oh, maybe that's a little harsh but why would someone do such a thing?"

"You have to feel for the family really," Mary said.

"And the poor train driver. No, I'm sorry, I've always thought that people who throw their lives away are very selfish." Chloe knew the thin stern woman who spoke as Mrs Woodsman, a patron of her father's campaign and rumoured to be considering running for Mayor of Leicester city in next year's elections. Her face reminded Chloe of the bad witch from *The Wizard of Oz*. She was someone who would steal candy from a baby if it furthered her ambitions.

Chloe was in shock from the news. At first, it had just been a young man who had thrown himself under a train that was passing through the station by the crossing. Then she heard the rumour it was Toby, the very Toby who'd been on the periphery of her crowd at school. Never quite good enough to be part of the cool clique, but always invited to the parties, always cracking jokes with a permanent smile on his face.

Now he was gone.

Chloe saw her father making his way towards them, but that would take a while with the amount of people who wanted to shake his hand. Some, Chloe knew, were opposed to him a few months back but now they knew a winner when they saw one. If she'd thought the modelling world was superficial and fickle, it was turning out to be nothing in comparison to politics.

His speech had been on law and order. How the country was too soft on the criminals, to the point where they were gaining the upper hand. Over the years, she'd often heard her father ranting at the breakfast table at some lenient prison sentence he'd read about in the morning papers. Chloe wondered what Zack would've made of the speech.

"They're sure it was suicide?" Chloe asked.

"I hear the police are still investigating, but it almost certainly was," Mrs Woodsman continued, obviously revelling in the rapt attention. She then looked at Chloe. "Are you okay dear? You look awfully pale."

"He was in my class at school." There was a small set of gasps from the group.

"I'm so sorry my dear. Were you close?" Mrs Woodsman asked the last question a little too eagerly for Chloe's liking, putting her on edge. No doubt the old bat was after a few titbits of juicy gossip.

"Not since school," Chloe noted the disappointed sag of the

woman's face.

As the conversation progressed into a wider discussion about suicide and mental illness, Chloe found herself thinking about the boy she'd known, trying to understand why he would have thrown himself under the train? Was it really suicide? Greg had been killed in a car accident, Elliot's yard had been burnt down, and there was still nothing from Jenny.

Chloe checked her friend's social feed all the time, but there was still nothing. Having reached out to some of their old London mates, Chloe had drawn a blank there too. Was she even still alive? The image of her body Chloe had been sent sprang into her mind forcing her to push it away before the tears came.

They had to be connected, these things happening to her old school friends had to be linked with whoever was stalking Chloe. Was she next on the list? Perhaps she was being pushed to see if she would break like the others. A cold chill swept over Chloe and she began to feel sick at the thought. What if she wasn't pushed over the edge by him? What would the stalker do then? Would she end up having some sort of accident too? She thought about Zack, should she go to him to tell him everything?

Pushing these thoughts aside she got out her phone to text Liam. Could he find out more about what had happened to their old school companions?

"Not here Chloe, dear." Looking up she saw her mother staring, a deep frown on a face entrenched with makeup. Chloe wondered why her mother wore so much when she was still so beautiful for her age. Slipping the phone back into her purse Chloe forced herself to engage with the conversation. At least it might take her mind off her worries.

"And what do you think, Peter?" Mrs Woodsman turned her attention to the tall man on her left. He didn't seem as keen to take part in the discussion as he had the other night and Chloe had caught him glancing around somewhat nervously. Perhaps she would have Liam check him out as well. "Should these people who kill themselves be pitied or condemned?".

"We can't ever know what drives people to do such a thing," Peter spoke in a measured tone, but Chloe noted he didn't look anyone in the eye as if he was talking to himself. "We can't know the depths of despair which consume some people, making them think the only escape is to end it all. We never know what secrets they have that not even their closest family know about. I, for one, certainly will not condone people in such pain. I would just hope they get to seek help so they can be guided back onto the right path."

31

"What's the scoop? Hey, Adam, right?" Zack looked up from the screen as Nadine entered the briefing room. He'd messaged her about coming in early after stumbling back to his own house later than he should have. After watching the body of a young man being peeled off the rail tracks the offer from two of the uniforms to grab a pint seemed a perfect way to escape from the horrific reality he'd witnessed.

A decision he regretted, and not helped in the morning with Miley deliberately banging about the house while refusing to talk.

Sat in the pub on his third pint, Zack had remembered Miley talking about some of the nasty things happening in the town. She'd also spoken of another recent suicide, and something had clicked in Zack's brain the way it used to in the past. Something which usually meant he'd just found a connection between things that had all seemed unrelated.

"Pleased to meet you, Detective Sergeant Morris." The young intern was sitting in front of the screen next to Zack. Sweeping aside his blond fringe Adam turned and offered his hand to the detective.

"Please, call me Nadine." Zack's partner pulled a chair from another desk across the room to join them. "Seeing two men staring at a screen this intently means it's either porn or you actually have found something interesting."

"Wow, funny as well as an average detective. The whole package."

Nadine thumped Zack on the arm behind the intern's back. "Seriously, what've you got? You caught the short straw again last night, but I heard that it was a jumper."

"That pretty much sums it up from what the train driver could tell us. But it was something Miley said last night about there being a sudden increase in stuff going on when this was supposed to be a quiet town. When I came here it was pretty much a sleepy hollow, only in the last few weeks things have gotten interesting."

"How so?" Nadine frowned. "Okay, there was the murder of the priest, which is big news for us, the arson in the last few days. But apart from the savaged cat, which I hear you still haven't solved, there hasn't been much beyond normal."

"And the missing, if not murdered, friend of Chloe."

"Unconfirmed. But I'll concede likely. A blip, though. We've had it before in our sleepy hollow, and Chloe's friend may have been killed in Birmingham not here."

"He's right." Adam pointed to a chart on the screen. "Crime has risen over the last few weeks. Most of it is small scale, some burglaries and car break-ins which can often be put down to someone operating before they get caught."

"So statistically not significant," Nadine said. "Then how is he right?"

"On its own, you'd have to say nothing out of the ordinary. If we went back, we'd see a similar blip. A particularly bad one about twelve years ago." Adam moved the mouse across the screen, bringing the graph for that period into view.

"Yea that was when I was a probationer. For a few weeks, it was like watching a TV cop show there was so much going on."

"Were they in black and white?" Zack realised, being five years older than Nadine, that was not the best of lines.

"No, that was your rookie year." Nadine pulled her chair closer to Adam and leant in so she could see the screen more clearly.

"Anyway," Adam continued, "as you say, on its own nothing to get excited about, but I've introduced other elements into the equation and look what happens."

Zack had seen the chart before when these new stats were added in, but he was pleased to see Nadine's reaction. The chart rose like a mountain peak.

"Wow, what did you do there?"

"Factored in other anomalies, not necessarily crime related at first glance, fatal accidents and suicides for one," Zack said.

"Both unprecedented against the normal curve. Look, the red line shows the mean over the last two years." Adam pointed to another line on the screen, which emphasised the spiking of their main plot point. "I've not got all the data for the last twenty years to match the crime stats, but I should be able to do that today. If Detective Inspector Carter's right, I suspect we will see that this is a statistically significant moment in the town's history."

"And this doesn't even include the dead cat," Zack said.

"Interesting, but I still don't get where this is going." Nadine turned to look at Zack.

"I think we'll find something which links these anomalies. I want to examine the suicides in more detail."

"Are you talking about something or someone being behind

this?" Nadine asked.

Zack nodded. "Yes. I can't prove it yet. But if we look hard enough I think we'll find something."

Nadine glanced back at the chart. "It's a pretty big leap of imagination."

"I know." Zack shrugged. "It's what I did for a living."

"Can we get their computers? The ones who committed suicide? Find out what was going on in their lives?" Nadine said.

"It's already being done for Toby Henderson," Zack said. "His parents have given approval. We're trying to work on the old teacher's, but as he'd no relatives, it might have already been tossed or wiped."

"I'm on the case with that," Adam said. "I'll get it tracked, though I might need authorisation."

"I'll make it happen." Zack nodded before stretching back on his chair so he could see Nadine better. "What do you think?"

"I think you may have stumbled on something here, boys. I'll get us some coffee."

32

Peter turned the key in the brand-new padlock. "Look, honey, let me pick up a takeaway on my way home. Text me what you and the boys want and I'll order it before I leave." He pulled the door of the lock-up open, and after a quick glance around the yard to make sure it was empty, he slipped inside. "I'll try not to be too late, babe, but I gotta get this work finished."

Closing the door behind him, he hung up and pocketed his phone. His wife wasn't happy about him working late, she never was, but she'd be happy enough once he'd brought home a slap up takeaway meal complete with ice cream dessert. It might even gain his sons approval for once.

It shocked Peter how easily he'd slipped back into covering his actions with lies and deception. At work, they thought he'd left early for a doctor's appointment. At home, they thought he'd be working late on an important project. Neither knew his true intention nor had any idea of the darker aspects of his past. For years, they'd seen him working on spreadsheets and drumming up support for the town's children. For the last few nights, when the rest of his family had been sleeping, Peter had drawn up the notes and diagrams that were folded up in his trouser pocket. Sketches of devices he used to build in those darker days.

Peter knew he should be appalled at what he was doing.

He was angry at himself for regressing into his old thought patterns as easily as someone slides on a pair of their most comfortable pyjamas. Yet he felt excitement at the prospect of once more building a perfect device. After the days of worry, it'd been such a relief to know there was a way out. Even Janet had commented on how vigorously they had made love last night, after days of him telling her he was too tired.

Not many people managed to do what Peter had, giving up a life attached to mercenary units around the world. It'd all gotten too intense in Iraq when the war was supposed to have officially been over. There was still money to be made by his unit, but he'd begun to wonder who the good guys were when he'd realised the devices he'd been building for their covert missions were killing or maiming so many children. An ambush that had been meant for an insurgent truck had destroyed a school bus. After meeting one of the kids, and watching his struggle to move through the rubble-strewn streets of his hometown with no legs, Peter had vowed never again.

He'd stashed away enough dollars to have a good crack at a decent life when he returned to England. After working for a few charities decided to set up his own to help children with disabilities as he'd seen in Iraq. But the money was scarce, and when his old pals came calling and offering to throw money into his funds if he would launder their cash through the system he decided his skills with numbers could be used. Justifying his actions with the good he could do for the children of the small town of Oakwell.

Working with charities was his way of trying to give back to the world he had taken so much from. So what if some of the money was from the illicit goings-on in the most corrupt countries in the world. If children in need could benefit from it, then what was the issue?

It'd given him a lot of joy seeing a child's face when a new motorised wheelchair arrived to change her life. Or the parents' expressions as they clutched each other in their modified house which could finally be a home for their special child. He felt the difference he made to those lives far surpassed anything that went before, and when marriage and family followed, the old memories were only present in the darkest of nights.

He'd suffered the political part of running a charity with a heavy dose of scepticism, spending nights around dinner tables with those who knew nothing about the real pain in the world; pontificating from their position of wealth and privilege as if their opinions mattered. There were so many he thought could use a real lesson in suffering, but the same people often had heavy purses they wanted to unburden themselves of, so they could look better in the community.

The stranger had already returned half the money to the charity's accounts as promised, and when the devices were complete the rest of the money would be there, Peter was sure of that. Something about the straight-talking man meant Peter could tell he was on the level. He'd promised no children would be hurt and only the pompous idiots who thought themselves so important would suffer.

Peter had no problem with that. Sometimes society needed a bit of a spring clean.

All the items he'd requested were there. Every piece of equipment needed to build the three identical devices. It had been so long since Peter had dirtied his hands he turned over the small metal items slowly, marvelling at their feel in his fingers. He was already putting them together in his mind, connecting the wires, tuning it to the right frequency so they could be triggered by old-school mobile phones.

Moments later his hands were moving smoothly as the first device took shape. Sparks flew as he soldered the parts he needed. Despite the copious plans he'd drawn, there was no need for him to refer to them. It was all in his head, and he created minor refinements along the way.

There was the faint sound of a car engine as he stepped back from his workbench. Stretching his back Peter looked at the devices on the table with satisfaction. Checking his watch, it was later than when he said he'd be home. No amount of ice cream would appease them tonight.

Leaving the lockup, Peter pulled out his phone and sent a message to a number he'd been given, as the sound of sirens raced by on the main road.

It is ready.

33

"So, what has kept my two detectives from the murder inquiry they're supposed to be working on?" While Zack was pleased the DCI had come to their conference, he could tell his boss was pissed they'd been out of contact for most of the day.

"Sorry Sir, but Zack had an idea this morning that might be relevant," Nadine said. "And you were kind of busy at the time, so we didn't want to bother you."

"Busy on a murder case, as well as all the other bloody things I have to manage at the station right now. Which is why I need my detectives on point and at the end of a phone. I've only got ten minutes because of some damn event tonight I need to attend. What progress have you made on the priest murder case?"

"This will only take five, Sir. Come and look at the screen." The DCI came over, taking the seat Zack offered which was closest to Adam. "Bottom line is we don't think this murder is a one-off."

"I'm sorry?" Zack saw Rashid's eyebrows shoot up at that suggestion.

"Chloe Evans," Nadine said, "our prospective MP's daughter came to us with what she believed to be a picture of her dead friend sent to her phone."

"I read the notes. But we have that as a missing person currently, as she sent a text she was going to Paris. Miss Evans couldn't even ID the picture, and that's not related to the case you should be working on."

"Maybe it is." Zack ploughed on. "Last night Toby Henderson was hit by a train."

"Suicide." The DCI glanced at his watch.

Zack nodded. "Elliot Reed has been the subject of vandalism, burglary and his yard was burnt down last week. His father, who is also a candidate in the by-election, worked out of those offices."

"Crimes yes, that Nadine is investigating, but no murder and no relevance to this case."

Zack brought up the next slide. "Greg Barrow killed in a car accident four days ago."

"Tragic, but no crime. Look what are you getting at here? All I'm seeing is lots of stuff the public could be saying we've made no progress on. But number one is the murder.

"Zack thought it was suspicious we had so many incidents so close together." Nadine cut in. "So, Adam crunched the data."

"And?" The DCI looked at them expectantly.

"What if we were to tell you that all of them were in the same class in the same school, even in the same social group." Zack brought up a slide with pictures of all four. There was an older man, in the middle.

"And this guy." Rashid pointed at the new image.

"A teacher from the time they were there. He committed suicide three weeks ago."

"Interesting and worthy of further inquiry. But not related, so I'm back to why are we not working on the main case?

I'll get asked about it tonight and, as yet, I have nothing to say. We're already getting mauled by our prospective new MP over our crime results. This won't help."

Zack understood where he was coming from. Since the DCI had to take over the day-to-day running of the station after the previous station head had retired early on short notice, it had heaped a lot of pressure on their boss.

"Adam, show him what else you have." Zack pushed his chair back a little, allowing access to the keyboard. He was happy for Adam to get the limelight. After all, he'd done most of the work through the day to get what they needed.

Adam cleared his throat. "Some other things we've found are a little more tenuous but still relevant. Another girl of the same year was reported missing in London six months ago, though it's thought she has upped and gone off backpacking from a scribbled note. Another is serving time in prison in Spain for drug smuggling, though still protesting her innocence that she had no idea they were in her bags. There is one of the male pupils inside for murdering his next-door neighbour in Liverpool. Some of the others I'm still trying to track down."

"How does this all relate to our current murder enquiry?" Rashid was leaning forward, staring intently at the newspaper cuttings Adam was bringing up.

"Well, at the moment, there is no direct link," Nadine said. "But we started looking at this because of the increase in unusual activity recently. Adam."

He brought up the chart showing the overall increase in minor crime and accidents. "And the last time we had a spike like this was twelve years ago."

"Not a period we would want to relive," Rashid said. "Okay,

I get there are some statistical anomalies here which are coinciding with Oakwell's first murder in a long time. But is this all you have?"

Zack saw Nadine looking at him to answer, which was fair considering he was the one who wanted to go out on a limb on this one. "I think there's someone behind this, someone with a particular grudge against a certain group within the town."

"And you have reached this conclusion how?" The DCI turned a face of diminishing patience towards Zack. He glanced at his watch again, as if emphasising the point.

Zack took a deep breath. "When a series of seemingly random, unconnected events occur, which push the standard curve out of shape, you look at why. When you find connections between some of the data points which indicates an order, then you need to start working out why. You need to look deeper.

"We received permission from Toby Henderson's mother to examine his computer. It appears Toby was gay but was hiding the fact from most of the outside world. Only someone found out, and they'd been messaging him that he should be disgusted with himself, that he should kill himself to spare his parent's shame. Apparently, his parents are extremely religious and do not approve of homosexuality."

"It's pretty horrific stuff," Nadine added, as Adam brought up a slide with screenshots of some of the messages.

"He didn't just commit suicide Sir," Zack continued. "He was driven to it."

"Do you know who sent these?" They had Rashid back on track.

Adam shook his head. "The Facebook profile used appears

to have been set up for this purpose alone, and it's been deleted. We'd have to go through a lot of channels to get any further on identifying who it was and my guess is that it would be a wild goose chase."

"Not your average troll," Nadine said.

"No," Adam agreed. "This person knew exactly how to use the system to stay off the grid."

"And it means this was tantamount to murder," Zack said. "It means Jenny Mabbut is not just a missing person in my eyes. Sir, we could be looking at three murders here, not just one."

The DCI glanced at his watch again. "Okay. It's thin, but there's something here. Keep on it, let me know the authorisations you need. Find out more about the other suicide, and I want another briefing close of play tomorrow. But I do need a report on the priest murder by the end of today. If I don't tell the press something, we'll be hung out to dry."

As the DCI left, Nadine turned towards Zack. "If the people in the same group at school are being targeted, then I think we need to have another chat with your new girlfriend."

34

ALEX: Did she suspect anything?

LIAM: No.

ALEX: Are you watching her now?

LIAM: Yes.

The remaining camera in Chloe's bedroom was displayed on Liam's monitor as she was settling down for the night. It was hard to imagine he'd been in that bedroom earlier. Though easy to think of things he might do with her in there.

ALEX: She still needs teaching a lesson.

LIAM: I wanted to take her when I was there.

ALEX: It was good you resisted, Liam. Your time with her will come. When she considers you her hero, you will show her the power you now possess.

LIAM: I've made some more images. Should I post them on the site?

ALEX: Sure. Maybe I'll send her message so she can see them.

LIAM: When will it happen?

Liam felt a bead of sweat roll down his face. He was excited at the prospect, despite the fear of pushing things on to the next level. It was as terrifying as it was exhilarating.

ALEX: In a few days Chloe and this town will learn what it means to cross those who hold real power. We hold that power Liam, people like you and me. We reveal the secrets people try to keep hidden.

LIAM: What else will happen?

ALEX: :) All will be revealed. How are you getting on with those tasks?

LIAM: I'll be finished with the hostel soon. The town hall should be compromised by morning.

LIAM: What do you want the hostel for?

ALEX: You remember Mr Hudson?

LIAM: The old art teacher.

ALEX: Well, Mr Gary Hudson will be causing some fireworks in the town tonight. You might particularly enjoy one of them.

LIAM: He's at the hostel.

ALEX: A dirty old man reaping what he sows. Still, he has been of use to our cause.

ALEX: I have work to do.

ALEX: Let me know when the hostel is compromised.

LIAM: OK.

Liam wondered if Alex knew he wasn't as far along on the tasks as he was making out. A line of coke and a few beers meant he'd spent more time making the images of Chloe than he should have.

There was little choice but to get on with it now because Alex wasn't the kind of person you let down. Tonight, Liam had to make sure he'd broken the security of the town hall and the local homeless hostel. The hostel would be easy, he'd already had a peek, and though it was a newish building with new security, that security was wide open to someone like Liam. With the town hall, however, his friend wanted to know when he had full control of the security systems and cameras.

Liam couldn't figure why he would want the hostel's systems disabled. Then again Liam struggled to work out much about his enigmatic friend since he'd returned. He knew Alex had an agenda against the town and could understand why after the way he'd been treated.

The way they'd all been treated.

Lifting data from the archaic systems in the town hall had been easy, a piece of piss compared to what Alex was asking now, even with the software he'd provided. Hacking into a system was usually not the problem, hacking in and staying undetected was the real skill, as every moment your software was on a network there was a risk of detection. The longer you left it in their systems, the more likely you were to be caught.

Some of the jobs Liam had already done for his friend had revealed the sick nature of many of those considered influential in the town. Hacking into their private accounts proved simple once Liam knew how, and the secrets these people were keeping from the rest of the town were astonishing. Alex promised once this was over he would publish it all across the internet, as Liam wanted all the world to know their nasty little secrets.

Suspecting his tasks would take him through to the early hours, Liam was prepared with sufficient energy drinks and high sugar snacks, settling his bulk in the extra-large computer chair he'd bought. He'd thought about looking after himself better if he was going to be spending time with Chloe, but if Alex delivered her as promised, Liam would be able to treat her how he wanted regardless. Maybe it would do her good to have a fat sweaty body on top of her instead of the hunks she was probably used to. He imagined Chloe bound face down as he whipped her perfect backside while she begged him to stop.

Liam shook the thoughts from his head.

There was work to do.

35

Gary had waited until the other guests in the hostel had settled. There were still the night wardens, he knew, but the two on shift would soon be snoring away in the television room. They didn't care about the people in the hostel anyway. He'd heard them calling most of them "gold grabbing immigrants" who should be "shipped back to their own country". A sentiment Gary agreed with especially as there wasn't a word of English spoken among the other guests.

Gary was sure they were stealing his stuff from the fridge, even from his room. A few days ago he'd confronted them, only to be subject to a tirade of abuse in a foreign language. The implication of the words was clear enough, and he wasn't going to challenge them again. Instead, he tried to hide his stuff the best he could.

Not that the staff treated him any different, his friend had been right about that too. No one cared about people like Gary. They were just an inconvenience, a burden on the hard-working taxpayers of the country. It wasn't people like Gary his friend said were the problem, after all, it wasn't Gary's fault the establishment had fucked him over. It was the damn immigrants that didn't follow the rules while being happy to take the free money. They needed to be eradicated.

Gary saw how the system favoured the immigrants, just as his friend said. Two of the families were being given homes when Gary hadn't been offered anything, and he'd been born in this rotten country. His friend said they needed to be driven out by making this country a place where they wouldn't want to live anymore.

And Gary was going to do his bit.

Taking another hit of Spice, Gary controlled the urge to scream with animal fury at the feeling of awesome power coursing through his veins.

"Tonight is my night you mother fuckers."

He had two jobs. Two raging infernos to inflict upon a town that had kicked him into the gutter and kept stamping on his head to keep him there. Then there was his little task he could complete along the way.

Revenge against the bitch who'd started it all. It would be even sweeter since Gary managed to score some of those little blue pills off one of his dealers. After making the bitch scream in pain as he raped her, then watching the high school reduced to ashes, would be the icing on the cake.

It was Chloe who'd told them about what he was doing. Even though the photographs had given her the career she wanted, the little bitch had run to daddy about the perverted teacher who'd taken advantage of her innocence. It was because of Chloe his life was so fucked up.

It was his turn to return the favour.

Gary didn't care that he'd been told she was off limits. He was fed up with people telling him what he couldn't do.

Gary pulled a large canvas bag from under his bed, which smelt of the cheap aftershave being used to mask the true nature of the contents. Retrieving the device, and a small mobile phone he checked both were switched on. The rest of the items were for later. Things he'd put together himself.

At the door, Gary looked back at the room he'd lived in for two years. A squalid space that showed how worthless his life was, and how much it was controlled by the council that ran the hostel because everything had to be on an approved list. It could all stay and burn. Gary was done with this life.

There were still noises from the other rooms as he made his way to the top of the stairs. A few foreign words of an argument Gary couldn't understand, spoken low enough not to disturb others at this hour. Not that the occupants cared about anyone else, but because the night wardens got seriously pissed if they had to deal with incidents in the night. It wasn't unknown for the wardens to throw out anyone who fucked them off, and they'd just make up some bullshit in the morning about finding the person stoned.

Downstairs Gary heard the wardens' snoring above the sound of the television. He still closed the door to their room, making sure it would be as late as possible before they realised something was wrong. Walking through to the kitchen, Gary found the gas pipes and began fixing the device to the outside of the main pipe as instructed. There were even Velcro straps to make his work easier. His friend thought of everything.

Having set the switch, Gary slipped out of the side door, found one of the garden benches the others used to sit on and smoke their drugs, and dragged it to the door. Had there been enough time he would have blocked the other exits too. The main door of the modern building was electronic. His friend said that one would be taken care of. Gary saw no reason why any of those inside the hostel deserved to survive the night.

There was an empty house near the hostel. It had been

abandoned since the hostel had opened and its owners had moved out, desperate to either rent or sell. A small stone wall surrounded the overgrown garden, and Gary hopped behind it, before crouching down into the shadows. He lit the screen of the mobile, licking his lips with anticipation. Then he dialled the only number in the phone.

The first noise worried Gary. A muffled sound like a damp firework failing to shoot into the sky. What had he done wrong? He'd followed the instructions to the letter.

Then it happened.

A fireball ripped from the kitchen, engulfing an entire side of the hostel in a brilliant orange glow. Gary felt the heat on his skin, turning away as the initial blast passed over him.

His phone beeped with a message.

Beautiful. Now onto the school.

Gary would go to the school, but there was a little sideshow along the way he wanted to attend. He dry swallowed one of the blue pills before moving out from behind the wall. It was time to visit little miss Chloe Evans.

36

SILVER WOLF: I would love to see a little more.

WILLOW MOON: Ooh, that's naughty.

SILVER WOLF: I know. But I could get you that perfume you always wanted. The real expensive one.

WILLOW MOON: That sounds nice. What would I have to do?

SILVER WOLF: I would love to see what was under those silk panties.

WILLOW MOON: That would be very naughty. You know how old I am?

SILVER WOLF: You know I horny I am?

Miley hesitated over the keyboard. There was no way she wanted to go that far. Something she'd told him already. Only he was her best client, and she'd barely had to do anything for the gifts so far.

WILLOW MOON: Maybe if you are a good boy.

SILVER WOLF: :) That would make me a very happy man.

For a moment, Miley thought her window was going to explode as an explosion shattered the night. Darting across the room, she pulled back the curtain to see flames reaching into the sky from a building in the distance.

"Miley, did you hear that? Can you see anything?"

She heard dad on the stairs. "Shit." Miley realised what she was wearing. She'd started the night in the shortest of white skirts with a bright yellow top which showed off her flat belly, an outfit which guaranteed a good payday. The skirt and top were both on the floor by her chair.

Panicking as she heard her dad running up the stairs, Miley flicked off the monitor, before grabbing her bathrobe. Scrambling into it, she kicked her clothes under the bed only just reaching the door to twist the lock open as her dad reached it.

"There's a big fire too." Miley opened the door her heart hammering.

"Can you see it?" Her dad pushed inside, going over to the window to witness the orange glow. "Something went up, but I can't tell what it is." He watched for a minute or so while Miley shifted her weight from foot to foot, hoping he would leave.

"What are you doing?" her dad asked, as he turned back into the room. He walked closer to Miley, inspecting her face. "Are you wearing lipstick?"

"I was just trying some makeup on." Miley buried her hands in her robe pocket so he couldn't see them shaking.

"Why? What are you up to?" Her father glanced over at the computer screen. She could tell something had stirred his suspicious police mind. It was rubbish living with a detective when you had something to hide.

"I've been working on my YouTube channel." Miley produced a story she had ready for this sort of occasion. "Maisie, from school, has nearly a thousand subscribers to her makeup videos, and Zoella is famous because of her vlogs and she started by doing makeup. Now Zoella's mega-famous, and she was on Radio 1 yesterday." It wasn't a total lie, as her friend

Maisie did have her a channel.

"Who the hell is Zoella?"

"Come on, dad millions of people watch her fashion vlog now. she's everywhere.

"Who watches these videos anyway?" He was looking out of the window again which was a good sign for Miley. It meant he was already losing interest in the conversation.

"Other girls like me."

Her dad's phone rang.

"DI Carter, yes I can see it. Okay, I'm on my way." Killing the call her dad turned back to Miley. "Looks like I'm going to get a better view of that fire. It's the homeless hostel."

"My God, is anyone hurt?"

"Not sure and I don't know what time I'll be back so lock up after me." Miley followed her father out of the room, waiting dutifully as he changed shirts before they both went down the stairs. Miley was always concerned when he was called out. She still remembered another night when the call came that dragged him away and he didn't come home. The knock on the door later that night had been a policewoman with a tale of how her dad was hurt.

Before he left, she wrapped her arms around him. "Be safe, Dad." And when the door closed, Miley made sure it was locked as she had promised.

Back in her room, she didn't bother to see if Silver Wolf was still online, as she turned off the computer. Sitting at her dresser to wipe off the makeup, Miley felt awful lying to her Dad. She hated that she was having to sneak out to the party because his overprotectiveness stopped her moving forward with her life.

She'd learnt how to look after herself when he was in

hospital eighteen months ago. They'd wanted to put her into care, but Miley had been determined then that she could cope on her own and look after her dad when he came out. Granny and grandpa had come to live with her at first to help. It was enough to keep the social worker at bay.

Miley had learnt to be self-reliant.

Now all she had to do was prove that to her dad.

37

Chloe breathed in the black cherry scent of the candles as she sank deep into the bubbles, allowing the warmth to ease the tension from her body. Soft pan-pipes floated through from the Bluetooth speakers in her bedroom and the three glasses of wine she'd consumed while in the bath had taken the edge off nicely.

Having been through the house Liam was convinced there weren't any more cameras. He'd even fitted some extra bolts for her until the locksmith could come around to change the locks on the front and back door, and he'd advised her to get a burglar alarm.

Detective Sergeant Morris had called asking if she could come down to the station to answer some more questions in the morning. Nadine wouldn't tell her what the questions were. Had they found something out about Jenny? Was she okay?

The tension the water had soaked away for a moment returned. Reaching out Chloe drained the rest of the large glass of red, and looked despondently at the empty bottle.

Chloe was disappointed it wasn't Zack who rang and found herself thinking about him as the warm water lapped over her bare skin, wondering what he was really like. Maybe it was a childish fantasy that she wanted him to be the hero, coming to save her in her hour of need. In a world where she always seemed to be surrounded by powerful older men, or at least those who had managed to convince others they were powerful, Zack was the only one who'd exuded a raw power that came from who he was and not what he was.

She pinched her thigh.

"For God's sake Chloe Evans, he's got to be a least forty."

Trying to get him out of her thoughts she considered Liam's visit again. He'd examined all her devices to clear them of any exploits her stalker might be using to control them, and he said he was close to finding the hosting company of the wretched web site.

She'd seen the desire in Liam's eyes; the same puppy dog looks he'd given her when they were young. Though now and again she'd felt a darker more sinister gaze that had made her realise she'd have to be careful. After giving him a peck on the cheek when he left, Chloe felt him linger, trying to drink in her smell. Still not certain he wasn't her stalker, Chloe wasn't sure letting him into all aspects of her life was one of her best decisions, but he seemed to be helping her, and there were glimpses of the old Liam she remembered from before Chloe had screwed him over.

When they'd been working together on the homework assignments, she'd enjoyed his company as it had been nice to talk someone intelligent for once and not have to pretend to be dumb because being smart wasn't considered cool. She nearly hadn't gone through with her group's little game in the end. Wished she hadn't.

It was good to know the house was clear so that she could relax again. The locksmith would be around in the morning to change the locks. She'd even stopped the cleaner coming around. It was a luxury she could never really afford anyway. It had been Jenny who had insisted they get one.

There was still nothing from her friend. Chloe kept checking social media, desperate for some silly post telling her it was all okay. Every day that went by convinced Chloe her friend was dead. What if that was what they wanted her to do tomorrow? To identify Jenny's body?

She wondered if Toby had been stalked before he'd killed himself, and what about her other old friends? Hadn't Greg died in a car accident? Chloe hadn't spoken to him since they'd left school, but Jenny had heard about the wreck. Her mother had told her about the other campaign office being hit by an arson attack after Chloe's lucky escape from the flames. Didn't Elliot own that yard now?

She sat up in the bath.

How many of her old friends was she still in touch with? How many were still alive? Was that it? Was that the reason? Because she and her friends were nasty when they were at school, this was revenge for the way they'd treated people? Chloe dreaded to think of the number they would've pissed off as she recalled the group's antics. What they'd done to Liam was the tip of the iceberg.

She'd tell the police the truth tomorrow. Tell them about her stalker. It was close enough to the election now, Chloe was sure they'd keep it from the press until the results were declared. Then she would face the pain it would bring, maybe go abroad and seek a new life.

Blowing out the candles Chloe stepped out of the bath. After drying her hair, she slipped into a silk nightshirt before sliding beneath the duvet and flicking on her iPad to begin the task of tracking down her old friends as the soft pipes still played in a valiant effort to soothe her soul.

38

"Sorry, my wonderful creation. There is another beauty I need to see to tonight." Gary heard sirens closing in on the devastation. People were spilling out of their houses around him, despite the lateness of the hour, to witness his work.

Melting into the shadows of hedges and trees Gary moved unnoticed by eyes turned towards the fire. In his bag were the tools to wreak more havoc on the town, rags and lighter fluid, which may not have been as sophisticated as the device he'd just used, but in his hands, would cause as much damage.

The thought of Chloe's house suffering the same fate stirred Gary's loins. It wasn't just the burning of the house; it was knowing he would be violating her on his terms. Destroying her in every way.

He'd been by her house a few times and was nearly run over by her the other day when she sped away from her drive, not even noticing him. That was the thing about bitches like her. They ignored people like him. The homeless didn't exist in their world. Gary saw it all the time in the shopping centre. The young girls and boys would just pass by and not even look at him sitting there hoping for a few coins so he could have a coffee.

A fire engine passed urgently screaming its alarm, blue

lights reflecting off every window on the street. Neither it nor the police car that followed paid him any attention. He was invisible. Gary had been invisible since the day he was sent to prison, and all because the prim and proper bitch had blabbed about who did her portfolio. He still remembered the day the police knocked on the door and seized his computers.

The day his life ended.

Gary hurried through the streets, slipping down alleys and through shortcuts only those who walked the town at all hours of the day knew. The sirens became distant, though if he glanced back, he could see the orange glow of the fire in the clear night sky as he made it to the backyard of Chloe's house. Pausing for a moment, he savoured the anticipation of what was ahead.

Walking up to the back door while pulling his coat over his hand, Gary smashed one of the four glass panes in the upper half. He then reached in and pulled back the bolts. It still took a couple of shoves to open the door. Perhaps he was getting weaker. He took a roll-up of Spice from his pocket and used his lighter to allow more of the strong, sweet smoke to fill his lungs and energise his blood. There was nothing he couldn't achieve. No one who could stand in his way.

The surroundings, her home, fuelled his rage at the injustice. Why should she get to live in a nice house with wonderful things when she'd fucked his life? He expected all the girls lived like this, profiting from the start he'd given them in school while he'd spent his years in prison and on the streets.

His friend was right. The people that wronged him deserved to be punished.

Stubbing out the joint, Gary closed the backdoor before turning on the gas hobs. Some of the gas would leak out of the broken pane, but it wouldn't make any difference. The house would still become filled with gas.

He went into the front room, pulling a bottle of lighter fluid from his backpack and sprinkled it over the fabric sofa and carpet. After casting the empty container aside, he considered lighting the fire and letting the house burn with her in it while he watched from a distance. He could listen to her screams as the flames seared her soft flesh. Perhaps she'd run screaming from the house her clothes on fire, hoping someone would save her. He thought of pissing on her to put out the flames. Pissing on her face because it was the kind of thing people like her did to him.

It had happened to Gary more than once when he'd tried to sleep under a bridge down near the canal. Drunks that were staggering back in the early hours needing a leak and thinking how funny it was to piss on the poor homeless fucker curled up under some wretched cardboard. More than once Gary had woken to feel the warm fluid spurting against his face to the backdrop of cruel laughter.

While Chloe had been tucked up in a warm bed with her soft skin covered by the finest sheets the world had been pissing on Gary. The thought of her naked body stirred an erection which urged him into action. Grabbing the top of his jeans, he ripped the buttons apart to release the nakedness beneath. The warm air felt good, and Gary took hold of his cock thinking about how good it would be to force it into the bitch. Peeling off his T-shirt he looked towards the stairs leading to where the she would be asleep.

A light came on.

It was good she was awake now.

He would teach the bitch a lesson she would never forget.

39

Chloe jolted awake.

She lifted her head from the pillow, listening in the dark. She'd fallen asleep with the music still on, and the sound of the pan pipes still filled the room. Reaching across Chloe stabbed the pause button.

There was silence.

Then a noise from downstairs.

Was it next door's bloody cat trying to get in again? She'd had words but how can they control a cat? She'd been through her lock up routine, checked every downstairs window was closed and secure. But the mangy ginger cat had a habit of finding its way into her house anyway and could scramble through the bathroom window. More than once Chloe had shut the cat inside as it had quite happily strolled in and curled up on the wash basket.

Pushing the duvet back she climbed out of bed and, still listening for further noise, she padded across the carpet in her bare feet to the landing. Or was it the stalker? She cursed herself for not bringing a knife. Her rape alarm was in the drawer by the bed. Maybe she should go back and get it.

But it was probably that damn cat.

Chloe turned on the landing light.

She froze.

A figure, a man, was standing at the bottom of the stairs staring at her.

"Get out of my house," she shrieked as loudly as she could. She might not have a rape alarm, but she could at least scream the place down.

"I just need somewhere to sleep." The figure was a naked, emaciated man with an unkempt beard and pale skin. But there was something familiar about him. "I won't be any bother."

A crazy look in his eyes glinted in the light. Chloe couldn't help noticing his erection. "You can't stay here," is all she could think of saying as she moved back.

"I won't be any bother."

"I'll give you money. I've some cash in my purse in the kitchen, and food too if you need some. Take what you need." The man certainly needed food. She'd never seen anyone looking so thin.

"I just want somewhere to sleep, somewhere I won't be alone. I've nowhere to go." He moved onto the stairs.

"Look, I'm sorry you've nowhere to go." Chloe backed up some more. "If you take some money you can find a place to stay; there are hotels." Chloe tried to think if she had something she could use as a weapon. All that came to mind was the sharp heels on Jenny's shoes.

"But they won't take me, will they? They won't take someone who looks like me, and I'll be forced to sleep under a bridge again, I can't stand that. What if a bunch of kids find me?" He came two more stairs closer to Chloe. "They would poke me with their sticks. They would set me on fire. It's what they do to people like me you know. Because we don't matter."

Chloe could see his fists clenched; his body was virtually

shaking. His erection almost mesmerising.

"You've got to help me, Chloe. It's your fault I've ended up like this."

"What do you mean? How do you know my name?" That recognition again, as he stepped further into the light that was coming from the landing.

"You knew me well enough when you posed for me at school when you wanted those pictures."

"Mr Hudson." Chloe swallowed back another scream. It was him. It was her old teacher who'd been stalking her.

"You told them about me, Chloe, you told them I was a dirty old man. They sent me to jail with the scum of society; then they threw me onto the streets. But you did alright for yourself, didn't you Chloe? You got to live the high life. Daddy made sure that happened, didn't he?"

"Oh my God." Her legs almost gave way as memories flooded back and she leant against the wall to steady herself. "That's not what happened. My parents found the portfolio and asked who took the pictures. I told them because I didn't think there was anything wrong. They said you'd moved to another school."

"You must have told them more than that, Chloe. They came after me and fucked me proper."

Chloe couldn't understand what he was talking about. There hadn't been any of the glamour pictures in the portfolio they'd found. Her father had gone off with a grim look to make some phone calls, but nothing further had been said to her. Afterwards, she'd heard about Mr Hudson moving on to another school. Nothing about prison. She'd thought her father might have helped push him out of the school. Stupid now when she thought about it.

"I never knew," she said.

"Still the pure, innocent Chloe, aren't you? Batting your fucking eyelids to get everyone wrapped around your finger. Getting Daddy to have me fucked over. You burnt my future Chloe Evans, and now I'm going to burn yours."

"It's you, it's always been you." Behind the fear, Chloe started to get angry. "You put those pictures online. You knew what you were doing was wrong. You deserve everything you got."

"Fuck you, Chloe." The man sprang up the stairs.

40

As Gary grabbed Chloe's nightshirt and pulled her towards him she lashed out with her foot, catching his belly and forcing him back down the stairs. He grabbed the bannister to steady himself.

As Chloe attempted to scramble away along the landing Gary rushed her, leaping up the stairs until he was over her, and ready this time when her foot came out again. Catching her ankle, he yanked her down the stairs taking pleasure in her squeals as she bumped her backside on each step and her white silk shirt fluttered up giving him a peek of the cream panties beneath.

A furious desire consumed him. He wanted to rip those fine panties off her body, force her down, and make Chloe look at him as he entered her. The look of disgust on her face would make it even more delicious as he made her suffer.

"Kicking isn't very nice," Gary spat, delighted when his spittle landed on her face. "I was being friendly."

"Please. I'm sorry for what happened to you, but don't do this." Chloe gripped the bannister, trying to stop herself being dragged further down the stairs.

"Do what? Treat you like the slut you really are? You were happy with the life I helped you get." Gary let his hand slide down the back of her leg, savouring the look of horror on her face. "But what will happen to you when it's all taken away? What will happen when I've torched your house and left you bleeding on the streets? How will you survive Chloe?" He flicked the lighter from his free hand up so Chloe could see it. "I suppose you'll go running to Daddy again, won't you? Isn't that what you always do?"

He could see the beauty realised his intention, if she'd not noticed the pungent aroma of gas in the air before, she surely did now.

"Please don't. I never meant any harm. I never knew what happened." Chloe's terrified eyes were trained on the lighter.

"You know I actually believe you, Chloe. You were so naive back then, so intent on being a star you didn't know what happened to people like me if they were caught taking photographs of the students. I think if I'd told you that fucking me would help your career, then maybe you would have. Would you fuck me now if I promised to spare you? Would you do anything I asked of you?"

"I really am sorry. I'll do anything you want, just don't hurt me."

"That's nice; I think I'd like that." He relaxed his hand for a moment as the rage dimmed and allowed him to dwell on the possibility of waking up next to Chloe every day. Perhaps he could hold her firm body in his arms before watching her move around the kitchen as she cooked his breakfast. He could feel the soft touch of her skin as he smelt the bacon cooking. Maybe he would wrap her in his arms and make love to her. Live a normal life again.

Gary fell back as Chloe threw herself at him, sending them both crashing to the bottom of the stairs. Chloe reacted first jumping to her feet and darting towards the kitchen. Gary's hand snaked out, grabbing her leg with such strength he spun her around, knocking her forward into the kitchen. There was a crunch as her head hit the tiled floor.

"You don't learn, do you?" Climbing to his feet, Gary stepped over and slapped the side of her face. "It's time I gave you a proper lesson." Gary seized the front of her nightshirt, ripping it as he pulled her back into the lounge and thrust her onto the sofa where he pushed her face into the cushions.

"No, please, no."

"You've been a bad girl Chloe, and bad girls need punishing."

Gary took hold of her panties and tore them from her as his whole body burned with desire, marvelling at the invincibility he felt. Twisting her legs, he flipped Chloe over exposing her sweet sex. Maybe he would flick on the lighter while he was inside her so they could both burn in a deadly embrace. Maybe for a moment, he would be able to smell her lovely flesh burning.

The future had so many possibilities as he forced her thighs apart.

41

Liam flicked his gaming headphones onto his neck and pushed the chair back. Reaching across into his mini-fridge he pulled out another tin of Mountain Dew before opening a chat window.

LIAM: The town hall is yours. I'll send the link for the control program.

ALEX: Excellent work. You did well on the hostel too.

LIAM: That software is cool, you gotta tell me where you got it?

ALEX: I have my sources.

LIAM: Ha, I could make a fortune using it.

ALEX: Money is not something you'll need to worry about again Liam.

LIAM: That would be great. I have a tonne of projects I'm supposed to deliver for clients.

ALEX: Ignore them.

LIAM: Really?

ALEX: We've seen what we can do together. Why do you want to be a slave to others?

LIAM: I don't.

ALEX: This is just the tip of the iceberg. I've been places, done things and fucked women that most men only dream about. And didn't I used to be just like you?

LIAM: Yea, a school nerd.

ALEX: And now those that looked down upon us bow to us.

LIAM: Sure.

ALEX: Don't you want to have the woman of your dreams doing everything you want?

LIAM: Yes.

ALEX: Then tonight it looks like you might need to be her hero.

LIAM: What do you mean?

ALEX: Are you watching Chloe's house?

LIAM: Yes.

ALEX: Then look closer.

Liam glanced at the screen displaying the two cameras in Chloe's house that were still working. The last time he'd looked she'd been in bed, her soft hair spread about the pillow. He frowned seeing she was still there but switching to the lounge camera he could see a shadowy figure. It looked as though the figure was removing its clothes.

LIAM: Shit, who is it.

ALEX: Our friend Mr Hudson.

Alex brought up a picture of their old art teacher on the screen.

LIAM: No way. What the hell is he doing there?

The figure in the room didn't look anything like their old teacher.

ALEX: He's already had a busy night.

A video covered the chat window for a few moments showing a building on fire. Liam recognised the hostel.

LIAM: Fuck. He did that?

ALEX: He likes to burn things. He's supposed to torch the

school next, but I guess he's decided to settle an old grudge first.

LIAM: What's he going to do?

ALEX: Burn her house down probably. Rescue her Liam. Stop him.

Liam saw Chloe's head spring up from the pillow and was sure he could see the man moving towards her stairs on the other screen. Could he get there in time? What could he do?

LIAM: Shit I'm going.

ALEX: Be her hero Liam.

42

C hloe tried to resist him turning her over, but his strength belied a scrawny body.

"Don't do this." She felt him force her legs apart with ease. The smell of gas was getting stronger, and she knew he was still holding the lighter.

"I've wanted to do this for a long time, Chloe. Every time I looked at the pictures I'd taken of you I wanted to fuck you. I wanted to fuck you back in school, and I would've if I'd known how you would betray me."

He crawled on top of her. Chloe swung her right arm, connecting with the side of his head but he just looked at her and smiled.

"Do you want to burn, bitch?" He flashed the lighter at her, toying with the lethal catch. "Do you want to feel the flames scorch off your flesh? You'll smell it as you burn. You'll smell the flesh like cooking meat."

Chloe saw the madness in his eyes and knew there was no reasoning with him. He wouldn't be satisfied with raping her. He was going to kill her. He'd probably already killed Jenny. The only person who could do anything about it was Chloe herself because she didn't want to die.

"Fuck off," Chloe screamed as loud as she could. She gathered all her strength and pushed against the sofa while throwing her arms forward just as Gary was straddling her. For a moment, he was off balance, the hand holding the lighter forced to reach for the back of the sofa to steady himself.

Chloe pulled one of her legs as far back as it would go before smashing into his face. There was a satisfying crunch, and when she pulled her foot back Chloe saw blood spurting from his nose. Striking again she sent him crashing to the floor.

Even as Chloe rolled herself off the sofa, Gary was up and coming at her. Pain ripped through the top of her head as he grabbed her hair and this time Chloe aimed her foot at his exposed groin.

Gary staggered back, but she could see he was recovering again. Taking advantage of the respite, Chloe scrambled to her feet and sprinted into the kitchen, expecting him to be racing after her. Instead, Gary stood, smiled and walked towards the doorway raising his arm.

"Come back to me Chloe so that we can burn together."

Chloe threw herself across the kitchen to the back door, slamming the bolts back and yanking at the handle. Glass shards ripped at her bare feet from the broken window and gas filled her nose, choking her breathing.

The door stuck.

It always stuck.

"Fuck no, not now." Chloe pulled the door handle as energy sapped from her body.

"Stay with me, my Chloe. Stay and watch the fire as it consumes us. I've learnt how beautiful it can be. Share that beauty with me."

Chloe turned and saw the naked man stood with his thumb ready to flick the lighter into life, and she knew she was going to die.

43

W ILLOW MOON: Are you thinking about me? Arthur hadn't been expecting his phone to light up. He was lying next to his sleeping wife when a chat message arrived from Willow Moon. She might not have known who he was, but there was rarely a moment when he didn't have a picture of Miley Carter in his head.

While doing the post-mortem on the old priest, Arthur had been conscious of her father's presence in the room. The Doctor got on with the DI, he was a good man, but knowing he was watching the DI's daughter online meant it was a struggle to keep his ageing hands steady as he'd cut into the priest's body. Zack had even talked about them both going out for a drink again soon. Arthur didn't think he could anymore.

SILVER WOLF: It's late. I'm in bed.

He hadn't been asleep when the message came through. Since seeing Miley's father on the webcam when he'd burst into her room, Arthur had felt sick to the stomach. Though she'd shut her screen off, Arthur had still been able to see her talking to her dad, and he'd expected to see him stride across the room to find out who she'd been speaking to.

He'd shut down his computer before hurrying to bed and had been waiting for the sound of cars pulling up outside, or lights flashing through the curtains before the full force of the police smashed through his door. His betrayal discovered.

Twice he'd staggered to the bathroom, certain he was going to be sick. One time there was such a pain in his chest Arthur was convinced he was having a heart attack.

Despite the pleasure of watching Miley, he always found himself in the bathroom after each session, trying to avoid his own gaze in the mirror because the reflection condemned him for the weak-willed pathetic creature he was. Sometimes he tried to justify his actions by considering Miley almost a fully-grown woman. But he couldn't hide from knowing how he loved to watch young girls perform. It wasn't the first time, and he knew it wouldn't be the last.

WILLOW MOON: I bet you're thinking about all the naughty things you would like me to do. We could do them now?

SILVER WOLF: I'm not at my computer.

WILLOW MOON: I'm downstairs.

SILVER WOLF: Where?

Arthur's chest tightened. His breath became ragged.

WILLOW MOON: Lying naked downstairs on your white leather sofa. I know who are, Arthur.

Arthur nearly dropped his phone in shock. He looked across at his wife, convinced the sound of his racing heart would wake her. She was still sleeping.

SILVER WOLF: Is this a joke?

WILLOW MOON: Come and see for yourself.

He heard a noise downstairs. Miley couldn't be down there could she? Yet how else would she know he had a white sofa? He strained to hear anything more.

SILVER WOLF: Are you really there?

WILLOW MOON: I'm waiting for my Wolfie so that I can

do naughty things with him.

Arthur swung from his bed, taking care not to wake his wife. He knew she was a heavy sleeper, rarely disturbed when Arthur needed his regular nocturnal bathroom visits. Slipping his feet into his comfortable brown slippers, he reached for his robe. Confusion clouded his thinking, but if Miley was down there, he had to see her.

Not bothering with the lights, he crept onto the landing before pausing to listen again. There was no sound, but he thought he could see a faint glow at the bottom of stairs. Arousal gripped him at the thought of the young girl in his house waiting for him. Arthur slipped down the stairs and entered the lounge.

There was a shape on the sofa.

Excitement surged through him.

"Miley?"

"Or someone who cares for her very deeply."

Shock jolted through Arthur's body as he heard the man's voice.

"Shit, I'm sorry Zack. I deserve everything that's coming to me," Arthur said, convinced it was Miley's father in the shadows. He thought of his wife sleeping peacefully upstairs. What would she say when she found out what her husband had been doing? Stomach clenching in fear of the future, Arthur knew the good life he'd known was over. He'd got away with watching a girl like Miley before. But not this time.

"What are you sorry for, Arthur? Your sins now or sins of the past?"

The voice didn't sound like Zack's.

"I don't know what you mean," Arthur said.

The man rose, moving towards him, and Arthur could see

his face obscured by a mask. Arthur felt a dampness in his pyjama bottoms as his bladder let go. Even in the gloomy lounge he knew he was looking death in the face.

"For when you stood by while others took advantage."

"I still don't know." Arthur stopped as he realised the man's meaning. Other images came to him he was ashamed of. "I wasn't strong enough; I never did anything."

"No, you just watched and kept your silence. And now you are watching again."

Arthur remembered when he'd watched some of the films as they were made. He recalled the face of a girl who was called Angel and looked like an angel. She'd been the most exquisite creature he'd ever seen. She'd never seemed to mind stripping down in front of them. Always smiling, always teasing. She had touched him once, and Arthur had nearly exploded with pleasure.

Miley looked so much like her. How was he supposed to resist when he'd seen Miley's photo on the web? When she'd been one of those he could pay to talk to?

"Who are you?" Arthur tried to back towards the stairs and catch his breath.

"Her friend."

The shadow leapt forward with a cat-like grace and Arthur was sure he saw the glint of a blade. There was a pain in his neck, a searing, burning pain, but as Arthur raised his hand to feel, darkness took him.

44

Liam barrelled into the kitchen door, smashing through and almost sending Chloe flying. In the kitchen, he saw a naked man in the other doorway holding a lighter and grinning like the Joker. Liam smelt the gas and knew they didn't have long. He grasped Chloe's arm, yanking her into the night, and having pushed her ten yards down the garden path something told him to throw themselves both to the floor. He then scrambled to get them behind a large evergreen tree.

"We'll all burn in hell," came a screech from behind them.

The explosion that followed ripped through the trees and bushes. Even behind the largest tree in the garden, Liam felt the heat sear his bare skin. Chloe screamed as the rattle of the explosion died out. Thick smoke emerged from the kitchen now engulfed in flame.

The intense heat kept them both cowed down against the cool grass. But Liam knew they needed to move before the fire it spread to the dry bushes that surrounded the garden.

"Are you okay?" Liam shouted as he came to his senses. There was a dull ringing in his ears.

"I think so. Liam is that you?" Chloe pushed herself to her knees.

He put his arm around her back and under her arms. Chloe

grabbed him to help steady herself. She still looked dazed.

"We should go to the hospital," Liam said as they stumbled through the back gate.

"No, just get me out of here," Chloe said. "I'm not hurt."

"What happened?"

"I think I found my stalker."

Liam didn't say anything more as they made their way to his car, but he became acutely aware of how little Chloe was wearing. Her white nightshirt was ripped open with nothing covering her bottom half. Had she been raped? Had the old teacher already had her? There was a surge of anger at the thought of someone else taking Chloe. Wasn't she supposed to be his prize? He wondered if Alex had been honest about Mr Hudson and his instructions. Had the old teacher been told to come here by Alex? Was his friend trying to deny him his prize?

Reaching his car, Liam helped Chloe into the passenger seat.

"You should go to the hospital or at least the police."

"No hospital." Chloe buried her head in her arms. "But you're right about the police. They'll be on their way. Can we get to yours first, Liam? I don't want to them to see me like this."

"I've got a jacket in the car." Opening the back door, Liam retrieved a dark blue coat he sometimes wore on the rare occasions when he ventured out. Chloe wrapped it around herself, offering a weak smile as she climbed into the car.

"Thanks, Liam. And thank you for rescuing me."

"All part of the service." Liam offered a smile. He'd only just made it in time, tearing across the few streets between their houses, his engine racing and adrenaline pulsing through him like never before.

"At this time of night?"

"I've found where the website is being hosted." Liam climbed into the driver's seat. "I came to tell you I can get it shut down."

Tonight, he was her hero.

45

Zack was surprised to see Nadine's number when his phone rang, having already told his partner to go to back to sleep because there was little she could do. The fire crews had the blaze under control at the hostel, but by the time they'd have it extinguished and safe, Zack thought it would be mid-morning.

"I told you there's nothing to do here," Zack answered the call.

"There's been another one," Nadine said.

"Another what?"

"Explosion."

"Fuck me, where?" Zack glanced around the horizon, expecting to see more flames leaping into the air.

"Chloe Evan's house."

Zack was stunned. "Is she okay?"

"Yes, she got out. It's not all, Zack. She was attacked by an ex-teacher, a Mr Hudson. He blew himself up using a lighter when the house was full of gas."

"Christ and there's all the hallmarks here of a gas explosion."

"He's been homeless for some years after coming out of prison."

"And I'm outside a homeless hostel."

"Exactly," Nadine said. "I'm with Chloe now at a friend's.

He pulled her out of the house just before it went up."

"You're not taking her to the station? Hospital?"

"She's not up to a full statement. Looks like she fought the guy off, but she's not hurt. Apparently, Chloe wasn't telling us everything when she last saw us."

"Go on." Zack backed further away from the fire to make it easier to listen.

"Someone has been stalking her online and by text this last week. Threatening to circulate pictures of her."

"Pictures?"

"It appears she succumbed to the more sordid side of the modelling scene before she gave it up. Taking part in a photo shoot that might create a few red faces among her father's campaign team. I think there's more and she's talking freely now."

"So, she's been blackmailed?" Zack could the see the fire was dying back as the fire crews kept a strong flow of water on the worst parts. If anybody had been caught inside, they wouldn't have stood a chance.

"Not as such. But there's more Zack. There were also pictures from when she was starting her career, which turns out to be at school. No prizes for guessing who the photographer was."

"Our homeless ex-teacher." Zack whistled, looking out over the fire. He was one sick man.

"Bingo. It turns out he'd taken pictures of several of the girls, including Jenny. It looks like we've got our man. He told Chloe that he'd set the fire at the offices she escaped from too. I bet you a month's salary he's behind the other arson attacks."

"No bet on that score." But something didn't feel right to Zack. The pieces seemed to be forming the picture Nadine was putting together, but his gut told him there was something still missing. As though they were building the wrong jigsaw. "Was he really homeless or just pretending to be?"

"We don't know yet. He did time after admitting the charges of taking indecent photographs, but it was all done discreetly to avoid a scandal. No doubt orchestrated by Chloe's father. I can't even remember it being mentioned in the press or at the station and I was a trainee here then. Why do you ask?"

"Just curious of how he had access to phones and computers if he was harassing her that way."

"You can get online pretty much anywhere these days," Nadine said. "I bet the hostel had internet access."

"Maybe, and maybe I'm just paranoid." Zack didn't think so. "Get the doc over to check her out anyway, and get her booked in for a statement in the morning. Her friend too, if he was there. It's going to make a hell of a splash in the media, so we better make sure we cover all the angles. I'll call the Chief now."

"Will do." Nadine cut off.

Zack hung up and had the desire for a strong cup of coffee.

"Just going to get a brew, Roger. You want one?" The other copper on the scene signalled with his thumbs up, and Zack set off on foot to the nearest twenty-four-hour Mcdonalds. It was a hike, but it would give him time to think things through.

His gut told him this was just the beginning.

46

Zack had known some crazy times at his old station, but nothing like the frenzy which accompanied the dawn sun that morning. The smoke in his clothes mingling with the stench of sweat as the heat continued its assault. He needed a shower, a good breakfast and some sleep, only they were luxurious that would have to come later.

He'd rung Miley letting her know he wouldn't be back, and to be careful. While everyone might be convinced it was a closed case, there was nothing which made Zack change his opinion that this was not over. Miley had already heard about both fires on the news and was full of questions. At least she took him seriously when he said he thought there was still someone out there, despite what the media were saying. His daughter wasn't stupid.

The DCI was all over them as soon as he came in trying to collate all the information he needed for a press briefing. Already the media machine was running with the story of how an ex-teacher had gone on a drug fuelled frenzy enacting a vendetta against his old school. The national papers, in the town for the by-election, were quickly on the story of the fire and the grim death toll. Zack was always amazed at how the press managed to get their information so quickly.

"I still can't get hold of Arthur." Nadine placed a steaming mug of black coffee onto Zack's desk. "We've sent a car round to pick him up. The DCI has arranged another examiner to come over. Oh, and we have a briefing in less than an hour. The Chief is calling everyone into the station before he makes a statement."

Zack looked over towards the DCI's office. "He's looking pretty rattled this morning. Not used to this and I've heard Chloe's father has put some pressure on."

Chloe had spoken to her parents before coming into the station to make the statement, and her father had already been on the phone to the DCI. Chloe's involvement was to be kept as limited as possible from the media, and if one word got out there about the pictures there was going to serious question of the department's conduct. Zack could tell the DCI was pissed at being dictated to.

"Biggest news in the town for years. I was still wet behind the years when we last had this much excitement. Plus, after his offices being torched and now his daughter's house, he's rightly not a happy member of the public." Nadine stifled a yawn. "Enjoying your new space, Adam?"

The student looked up from where he was perched on the edge of Zack's desk, his laptop occupying the only space that could be made, after pushing the rest of the crap out of the way.

"Not a problem." Adam gave Nadine a smile and pushed his hair aside.

"Getting anywhere?" Nadine said.

Zack had called Adam early. With his doubts about the official position on the fires, Zack wanted Adam to run down the list of names of people Chloe had initially thought might have been stalking her. Taking Chloe's statement had cemented his views, and he'd been surprised at how strong she was being, despite the ordeal she'd suffered. He'd ticked her off for not telling them everything when she'd come in about Jenny, but Nadine had stopped him being too harsh.

Like everyone else, Chloe thought the old teacher was to blame and had been surprised when Zack had asked for the list.

"I'm running down everyone I can." Adam leant back. "Then everyone in the same year as Chloe. I'll have a report on them soon."

"I want Adam to observe Liam's statement," Zack said. "Chloe said he'd been trying to track the stalker down via the messages she'd received. I want to see how far he'd got. I need Adam to verify the truth in what he says about tracking her stalker down."

"Looks like she was no angel," Nadine muttered, looking at her fingernails. "Like father, like daughter."

Zack knew Nadine didn't have much time for Chloe's father's politics or his manner of doing business. Especially after the way he had called the boss that morning.

"I still can't see past the teacher though Zack," Nadine said, "and the DCI isn't going to be too pleased with us poking around elsewhere when we should be getting the teacher case together."

"He's not our man," Zack stated. In the interview, Chloe had told them about the pictures from modelling down in London when things were not going well, and while they were out there on the Internet they were not under her own name. "How did a homeless man with little resources come by them and make the connection? How was he able to seemingly know Chloe's whereabouts when she was in the car? She had cameras in her house Nadine, which meant he had to have had some way of getting them in and then monitoring them."

"Stolen them, and stolen laptop in the hostel," Nadine suggested.

"A cold, calculated drug-crazed homeless killer?" Zack looked at her questioningly. "What about the priest?"

"He could have been visiting the hostel. Pissed the guy off. We've found out he had been doing some charity stuff and working with the homeless."

"Fair point," Zack conceded. "It does provide us with a link to the ex-priest, but not a motive."

"Burglary would then come into it," Nadine persisted. "Or blackmail for drug money, if somehow he'd found out what the old man had been up to. I agree some questions need answering, but the boss isn't going to like it. Right now, he's got a closed case for the press."

"It's our job to be curious, Nadine," Zack said, taking a much-needed gulp of caffeine, "and I'm happy to be proved wrong."

"Well, you better have your story ready. He's coming over." Nadine nodded over towards the DCI who was approaching with a concerned look on his face.

"You need to get over to Arthur's house right away," he said.

"You got hold of him?" Nadine asked.

"He's dead."

47

"He always gets up in the night lately. I think I heard him again last night." Mrs Robinson dabbed the already soaked tissue to her eyes. "He had a weak bladder and sometimes when it wakes him he can't go back to sleep. I knew he wasn't there when I woke up, but I didn't think anything would be wrong."

She started sobbing again. Zack stood patiently, looking out of the kitchen window while Nadine held Mrs Robinson's hand at the family sized table.

Arthur's body had been stabbed and sliced with dozens of cuts. The forensics team would be a while yet. The Chief had called in assistance from a neighbouring force after the night's events.

"Has there been any trouble from anyone? Anybody being threatening?" Nadine asked.

"No, nothing. Arthur was such a gentleman, he didn't harm anyone, and he certainly didn't get into any fights. You know that, Nadine." Mrs Robinson looked up at the Detective Sergeant.

"What about his habits?" Zack asked. "Has he been doing anything different recently?"

"He'd been on the web thing more," Mrs Robinson said. "I'm not much for that myself, but it stopped him from getting bored."

"Really?" Nadine said. "He was always a complete Luddite with us, never typing up any of his notes himself and refused to do anything on a computer. What kind of things was he doing?"

"I don't know. He'd talk about all the fascinating things you could find on there, all the information. I never really paid much attention. I liked it best when we went bowling before his knee went funny. I think he used to chat with people on his computer. Text chat or something he said. It would keep him up after I went to bed." Her faced clouded over, and the tears returned. Zack looked at Nadine; the interview was over.

"Mrs Robinson," Nadine squeezed her hand, "would it be okay if one our boys had a look at his computer? We might find some clues as to what happened."

The old woman nodded."Yes of course. I'm sorry I need a minute."

Nadine squeezed Mrs Robinson's hand before the old woman stepped out of the room.

"Another knife attack," Nadine said.

"You know of anything that connects Arthur to the priest or school?"

Nadine shook her head. "I've known him since my rookie days and can't see anything that ties him to either."

"This isn't the work of a homeless man, Nadine. Arthur was murdered by somebody who knew what they were doing. Not some old art teacher fallen on bad times."

"I'm beginning to think you're right. What the hell is going on in my town, Zack?"

Zack turned back to the window overlooking the long, well-groomed garden. "I don't know, but we better find out before this gets any worse."

48

Liam felt the sweat roll down the inside of his arm as the recording device started.

"Interview with Liam Edwards, commencing at fifteen seventeen with Detective Sergeant Nadine Morris and Detective Inspector Zack Carter. Mr Edwards has declined representation." Liam liked the woman who'd started proceedings. He was wary of the detective inspector.

Liam may have had nothing to do with the deaths at the hostel or the attack on Chloe, but as his secrets would land him in prison his heart was beating so loudly he was sure they would hear it. It was the same way he'd felt on seeing the headmaster at school when he was younger, even if he'd done nothing wrong.

"Can you think of anyone who would want to hurt Chloe?" Nadine got straight to the point.

There was a moment Liam had wanted to blurt out everything, angry someone else could have taken Chloe away from him, but Alex had convinced him it wasn't like that. Gary Hudson was supposed to have torched the school not go after Chloe, and Liam had liked the idea of the old school going the way of the hostel. It was a shame it didn't happen.

"Until a few days ago, I'd no contact with her or most people from the school to be honest, so I've no idea of her friends or enemies."

"What about when you were at school?" Nadine said.

"She was part of a cool clique, very popular with most people."

"But not all?"

"Some thought they were cool and wanted to be part of their group. Others thought they were just bullies."

"How did you feel about Chloe in school?"

Liam hesitated. "We were good friends in primary school, but drifted into separate groups as we grew older. I was never one to be part of a cool gang. Never will be." Liam turned his hands towards his bulk and gave a rueful smile.

"Did your group harbour resentment?" Nadine continued.

"Yes," Liam nodded, "and envy, and dreams of having girls like Chloe as our girlfriends."

"Did you have those dreams about Chloe?"

"Yes." Liam thought was no point lying.

"Did you harbour resentment as well?" Nadine asked.

"Not until after they decided I was to be their next pet project and Chloe was the bait."

"How do you mean?"

Liam saw Nadine glance at her colleague with raised eyebrows. "She approached me wanting help with home-work, which I should've realised was stupid. You see Chloe pretended to be dumb in class, to fit in, but she wasn't, I knew that. She didn't need my help because it was an act to draw me into their stupid games."

"Why?" Nadine looked genuinely curious.

"To start flirting with me. To start making me believe I had a chance with her so that I ended up exposing myself to her on my webcam without realising everyone else was watching."

Liam could see the surprise on their faces. He was hoping his candour might deflect them from asking awkward questions where he wasn't as keen to be so open.

"Were other kids treated like this?" Nadine asked.

Liam shrugged. "In different ways yes, though the other kids got wise to it. I heard some of Chloe's friends got more reckless as they hit college but I'd moved into my own world by then."

"What do you do for a living?"

Liam noted Nadine's voice had gone a little softer, hoping it was a good sign. "I'm a freelance software consultant, taking jobs over the net and delivering them remotely. That way I don't even have to leave the house. It's easier for people like me." Liam looked down into his lap. "I'm not a people person."

"You can make a lot of money that way? Make a living out of it?" It was Zack who spoke. Liam looked up to see he had leaned forward.

"A lot of money if you're good, there are those that make far more than me. As your reputation grows so can your rates. It's a way of making money that suits loners."

"So, you're a computer expert?" Nadine asked.

"In my field, I consider myself okay. Expert may stretch it a little." Liam tried a smile and wished he hadn't.

"The way Chloe has been contacted," Zack said, "do you have the skills to do that?"

"No way, that's really hardcore. The sort of skills people like me dream of. Some of it I could work out in time, by reverse engineering. Masking your computer's identity is stuff you can pick up in forums but the rest, dream world."

"You tried to help Chloe in tracing who was stalking her?" It was Nadine.

"Yes. It's why she was back in touch with me. The messages came from one-time accounts and numbers. Impossible to trace. I dropped some software onto her devices for if he tried to contact her again."

"You think it would trace them?"

"Not sure but I needed to try," Liam said. "The messages were like ghosts that seemed to melt away as soon as you shined any light on them."

"Is the work you do legal?" Zack asked.

"Mostly."

"Why mostly?" Zack said.

"Sometimes the software we use isn't strictly legit. You know, if you want to use it but don't always want to pay for it, or maybe grab some passwords for sites so you could get into them for free."

"What sort of sites? Porn?" Nadine gave Zack a stare. Zack shrugged.

"Yea, sometimes." Liam shifted in his seat, feeling the perspiration on his brow as well now as the continual trickle from his armpits. He thought about his computers back in his house and how they might decide to go after them. He should have dealt with that possibility. There were programs installed to scramble the drives at the click of a button, but he hadn't activated them before leaving the house. He was stupid. He'd only thought about hiding his stash of coke. Alex wouldn't have been so stupid.

"The techniques used on Chloe were very sophisticated?" Zack asked.

"Very." Liam almost breathed a sigh of relief that the conversation had turned back to where he felt more comfortable.

"Not the sort of thing someone could do from an Internet

cafe?" Zack continued.

"Not in the modern world, detective." Liam looked at Zack who was pulling at his lower lip thoughtfully.

"You knew the old teacher too?" Back to Nadine. "Mr Hudson."

"I did. Again, I've not seen him since school."

"You think he would've been capable of harassing Chloe using the techniques you found? " Zack asked.

"I don't know what he'd been doing since our school, so I couldn't say."

"Why did you go back to her house last night?"

Liam tensed at the female detective's question, but he'd already talked it through with Alex and prepared his answer. "I'd traced the website with her pictures on it, which meant she could request to get it shut down."

"You needed to tell her this at one in the morning." Nadine raised her eyebrows.

"I thought she would be pleased I'd found out."

"I bet you did," Zack said. "Liam, are you the one behind this? Did you set up the website, which is why you knew where it was hosted?"

"No." Liam swallowed.

"But you can see why we could think it could be you?"

"I'm an expert with computers and was in school with Chloe. She treated me like shit, so I have a motive. Logically, if you don't believe our old teacher was behind it, then I would think you consider me your number one suspect."

49

A cool breeze ruffled the edges of the paper Alex skimmed through while other people in the park enjoyed their lunch hour. He'd dressed like one of them, white shirt, black trousers and cheap shoes. Just another office worker enduring a sad sandwich from a Tupperware box while appreciating the sun and a daily newspaper.

It was the hottest day of the year, the weather section said, and the hottest September day on record. The country was being warned of powerful storms on the way, heralding the heatwave's demise.

Alex liked storms and the chaos they brought with them. He liked people to see how weak they were in the face of nature. Even mighty politicians and rich oligarchs could find themselves stranded and homeless just like the rest of the people.

When you stood on a beach while a storm was raging around you and angry waves smashed against the rocks you were perched on, then you learnt about the raw power of nature. Alex was the storm now. Alex was the conveyor of chaos, and it was in that maelstrom of uncertainty his plans could be woven like intricate tapestries connecting people in a way they would never have expected.

Oakwell had it coming, and if the good folk thought last

night had been a tragedy, then they were in for a shock. Alex watched people pass in and out of the town hall, many still wearing suits despite the heat simply because they wanted to look important. They thought they ran the town, they though they were the ones in control.

They knew nothing.

The paper spoke of the ex-teacher who'd fallen on bad times, as they speculated on his reasons for revenge. There were reports of previous arson attacks they linked to Gary. The tabloids had their man and were busy ripping his life apart. A connection had already been made with the prospective member of Parliament's daughter, and Alex wondered how long it would be before the media found the pictures. Half the time they received their information from coppers who couldn't keep their mouths shut. He wouldn't be surprised if some of those involved had already stashed away copies of Chloe's pictures and were contemplating leaking them.

Although the world wasn't looking for him yet, Alex knew not all the police were convinced it was the action of the ex-teacher. The detective heading up the investigation, Miley's father, was smart. Something Alex appreciated. It added an extra challenge in reaching the end game. The fact he was the father of the beautiful angel sitting with a group of her friends on the scorched grass of the park, added extra spice. But Alex didn't want the truth coming out just yet, which was why he'd already taken steps.

Peering past the edge of the paper he appeared to be focusing on, Alex watched Miley, enraptured by the wonderful smile that encompassed her soul. Strands of brown hair fell either side of her face, framing her exquisite beauty. The detective's daughter was surely what Angel would have grown to be had she not been cut down by those filthy, worthless animals. Alex and Angel would've been together forever.

Alex knew he should rise above such thoughts. A life dedicated to teaching the world about the crimes being committed by those who masqueraded as the establishment, need not be distracted by such fancies as love. There were crimes against humanity perpetrated by the very people who were supposed to serve the common folk, and Alex was destined to exact retribution. Yet he couldn't dismiss Miley reminding him of happier times so easily. When Alex saw her, he wanted to be that boy again, together with Angel in the treehouse spying on the neighbour or having sleepovers where she would roll towards him in the night, and he could wrap his arm around her fragile body. He'd wanted to take her away from that place and care for her, give her a better life.

But the very town that should've been caring for such a sweet girl destroyed her.

Perhaps with Miley the dream could be reborn. She could be his to look after, to keep safe from the evils of the world, and she would need someone soon, Alex had seen to that. There would be no-one to look after her, and it would be Alex offering her solace and a beautiful future.

There were times when he thought he considered giving up his plans if he could have those precious moments back. If he could enjoy life again the way he did with Angel and see the delight in Miley's eyes when they visited the wonders of the world.

Miley and her friends rose from the grass. He watched her smooth down her skirt before passing close by his bench as they headed off towards the school. The smell of the chips she was still eating from a small cone masked her normal scent as she continued chatting with her friends, with no idea how her life was about to change.

A few minutes after they disappeared from view, Alex packed up his lunch box, fixed his fake ID and headed towards the town hall.

50

" Look at the map, Zack. In the time, it took our Mr Hudson to go from the hostel to Chloe's house; there was ample opportunity to visit Arthur. It's virtually on the route." DCI Rashid Sterling was pointing the map Zack had pinned to the incident room wall.

"I accept that Sir," Zack said.

"But you want me to accept that there were multiple murderers out in the town last night?"

"Yes. The murder of the priest and Arthur don't fit the pattern, Sir. Someone else did those, and I think it's that person behind everything going on."

The DCI shook his head. "What's your evidence to back up this conspiracy theory, Detective Inspector Carter? I've already had a mauling from the press who appear to know more than we do and our probable new MP never seems to be off the phone. We have a connection between the priest and Gary Hudson, and you should be looking at the connection with Arthur to tie up the case."

Zack glanced to Adam for help, the intern looked nervous at speaking up in front of the boss, but he cleared his throat.

"The skills used to hijack Chloe's devices were very advanced. The lads at Central are already drooling over some of the software, and using one time accounts the way he did needed specialist knowledge. Even if we got the logs from the providers of the Internet addresses of those who created them, we know it'll lead nowhere. It's not something that fits the profile of Gary Hudson. We can't even find any online presence for him."

"You're an expert on profiles now?" The DCI stared at Adam. Adam went red.

"You know what he means, Sir?" Nadine gave the DCI an intense glare. Zack knew the two of them had known each other since she was a beat cop in the town and there was respect between them that transcended rank. "You've read what Gary was doing after being released. He's just not got the skills."

"Look I'm sorry Adam, you've got a point." The DCI moved away from the evidence board, slumping into one of the uncomfortable plastic chairs. "Everyone wants this done and dusted with the by-election so close. The council don't want the eyes of the world seeing a town full of killers. Christ, Chloe's father is even being touted as a future Prime Minister, and everyone wants this one wrapped up in a nice neat little package.

"Okay, I'll accept that Gary Hudson didn't possess the tech skills. I accept there's currently no motive or evidence showing he killed Arthur, but he could've arranged others to do it for him? Isn't that what people like Chloe's friend Liam do? Isn't that what you're saying is a possibility, Zack?"

"It is," Zack agreed. "But to hire someone would cost a lot of money. How would he have financed it?"

"People on the web working for him. Maybe just to practise their skills." The DCI shrugged, and Zack thought he looked exhausted.

He'd sympathy for his boss. How many times had he seen good coppers only want to look at the evidence which suited their theory? He'd done it himself often enough, especially when the top brass was looking for a quick result and they already thought they had their man. The fact the suspect was a homeless bum with a shady past made things look good from a PR point of view.

"You mean they could've helped him out for a few small favours," Nadine said. "Like maybe some of the fires he started were to benefit them, rather than any revenge?"

"Something like that," Rashid nodded. "Though I'm not sure, that's the case here."

"Or someone was manipulating him," Zack said, "getting him to do their dirty work, while he worked from the safety of a console. Whichever way I look at this Sir, I see someone else behind it all. We need to keep digging. The priest's death looked frenzied, but the kill wounds weren't. Arthur was killed by someone who knew how to handle a blade. We need to rip apart their lives and find the connection. It's there, Sir, we just need to keep looking."

Rising from the chair, the DCI went back to the evidence board, taking a closer look and obviously mulling things over. Zack bit his lip, it was never easy for him to be quiet, but this was one of those moments.

"We need to keep any further investigations out of the press." The DCI eventually looked back towards them. "Our official line is we have our man. I can't be involved, you understand?"

Zack nodded. He understood the politics. "Thank you, Sir."

"You really believe something else is going on here?"

"I'm fucking certain of it, Sir," Zack said.

"I've read your reports, Zack, what you did for our boys

in the army. If someone is messing with us, find him and shut him down before this gets any worse." Zack saw the DCI glance at the pictures of what remained of the hostel after the fire. "If it can get any worse."

"We'll end it, Sir," Zack said.

"I'll authorise what you need." Rashid turned away from the board and picked up his jacket from the chair he'd been sitting on.

"I want to lean on, Liam," Zack said. "I think he knows more."

"Good." Rashid looked relieved at having made a decision. "I've got to go, ladies and gentlemen. Keep me in the loop. Keep this out of the press."

When the DCI had gone, Nadine shook her head looking at Zack. "He just put his arse on the line for you, cowboy. You better be right."

51

Chloe sighed as she followed her mother into another shop in their quest to replace her lost wardrobe.

"There's no good to be had moping. You need to move on quickly. When your father wins, it will be different for all of us."

"Yes, Mother," Chloe would be glad when the afternoon was over. There was a conservative edge in the clothes she could buy, and Chloe was constantly reminded how fortunate it was that the election night dress was safe at her mother's house. A dress Chloe hadn't even seen.

Every time Chloe picked out something with a skirt higher than her knees her mother was tutting, and Chloe could've sworn when she'd tried on a low-cut top her mother had been fanning herself, not with the heat, but holding back her outrage. There was a style that her mother wanted Chloe to wear, and it was difficult for Chloe to resist as her mother was fronting the money.

"And I don't know why you don't just move straight back in with us. I'm not sure I approve of you staying in that boy's house. No one has heard of him since school?"

"He works as a computer consultant. Makes good money actually." Chloe smiled at the startled look on her mother's face.

"I hear he never leaves the house, and when he does, it's all baggy T-shirts and joggers. It's not the sort of image you should be associating with now. Certainly not when your father wins."

"Yes, but at least he doesn't have the press camped outside, and has a spare room I can sleep in right now." Her mother tutted again, a sure sign Chloe was right. Her parent's guest bedroom was overflowing with campaign literature, and outside there was constant press presence in the street, which Chloe felt were good enough reasons to keep her distance. As yet, the media hadn't tracked her down to Liam's house.

The attack on her own house was public knowledge, and as the daughter of the leading candidate, it all added to a juicy story for the press. Chloe kept away from them as much as she could. Even her mother didn't know the extent of Mr Hudson's attack, and the longer Chloe kept that way, the better. She was grateful her mother hadn't allowed the campaign team to make her bravery a focus, though Chloe suspected her mother didn't want her daughter getting all the attention.

"You'll need to move in when this is over, and you can leave that job too. At least you've picked up skills with a law firm that we'll be able to use."

"Yes, Mother, I can make an excellent cup of tea."

"Don't be sarcastic, Chloe, it doesn't become a politician's daughter."

Chloe bit back another retort. At least they were in her favourite shoe store, and shopping therapy provided a welcome distraction from what was happening elsewhere in her life. Chloe knew she'd have to move back in with her parents after the election. Not only because there'd be no more excuses for not doing so, but there was something about Liam that made her uncomfortable.

He'd told her she could stay as long as she liked, but Chloe felt a simmering resentment and at times thought he watched her with a creepy, desperate longing. It was something she was used to from men, just not ones she shared a house with.

"Shh, don't say anything, but that's the detective's daughter over there. She's in Mrs Reynold's class, you know. Supposed to be very smart." Chloe felt her mother grab her arm, motioning towards a group of three girls coming out of a fashion boutique with their own haul. "The one with the brown hair. Apparently, there's some party tomorrow night everyone is going to. I bet they've all bought shocking clothes. You would expect better from a policeman's daughter, but that's just the problem with today's society."

One advantage of having a mother who liked to gossip about everything and everyone was that Chloe had been able to learn more about Zack. It seemed her mother was quite impressed by him, even though she thought the little of the rest of the police.

When Chloe had given her statement, there'd been a confidence exuding from him, a strength of purpose beneath the rough edges of his personality. Chloe knew he was widowed with a teenage daughter and that he'd come up from the city after being injured in a knife attack. An accidental search on Google had revealed honours received for his time in the Intelligence Corps in Iraq and Afghanistan.

Outside the station after giving her statement, he'd walked Chloe to her car, giving her a hot flush when she'd thought he was going to ask her out. Instead, Zack had told her that unofficially he didn't think this was over and to let him know if anything happened again. He'd placed his hand on her bare arm, but all she'd felt was horror at the thought her stalker could still be out there.

Watching Zack's daughter laughing with her friends across the other side of the shopping centre, Chloe had the urge to ring Zack, or at least message to see if there was anything new. Well, that could be the excuse.

Chloe's phone pinged with a message as she was trying on the first pair of shoes her mother disapproved of.

It was Liam. He'd agreed with the DI that the stalker might still be at large and promised to keep looking.

The site is being shut down.

That's great, Chloe messaged back, *quicker than expected?*

Yea, and have another lead. I need to talk to you. When are you back?

52

"What do you think about Liam?" Zack took a sip of his Americano. The morning rush had died down in the Costa Coffee, leaving only a handful of people. Zack was still yawning as he nursed his giant mug, with a fresh Danish on the side. He'd been tossing and turning all night, because of the insufferable heat and thinking the case through. More than once he'd risen to make some notes only to find his thoughts too muddled by exhaustion.

"He has the skills and motivation, but doesn't feel like it's him," Nadine said. She looked a lot fresher than Zack felt.

Zack nodded. "I know, but I can't shake the feeling he's involved. Do you think we've enough to get some boys round his house to see what they can find with his equipment?"

"Not even close."

Zack pushed the Danish around the plate. "I've had Adam poking around online, to see what he could find and if he could, ahem, accidentally find his way into Liam's accounts."

"Ah, the maverick cop who doesn't play by the rules." Nadine laughed.

"Hey Lady, I play by the rules, I fill in the forms. If Adam's able to find a way to snoop, it might bring us closer to this sick son of a bitch."

"Not disagreeing partner." Nadine held her hands up in

surrender. "Did he find anything?"

"Struck out. No way of getting close without Liam knowing Adam said. But what Liam said he does for work all checks out. He's pretty damn good at it apparently."

"His story about school was also true." Nadine stirred her cappuccino. "Chloe confirmed everything he'd said. She's pretty ashamed of what she did." Nadine had spoken to Chloe on the phone before they left the office the night before. Zack had promised to keep her up to date.

"Not quite daddy's little princess when she was younger."

"Ooh, do I detect the shine going off her now, Detective Inspector? She seemed pretty disappointed it was me who rang her," Nadine said.

"Never had a light on her, Detective Sergeant." Zack found his heart give a leap at Nadine's words. There was something about Chloe, and not just her stunning looks, which he found damned attractive.

"Ye sure, but whatever she did in the past she's going through a pretty horrendous time of it now. How many of her old gang have we managed to get hold of?"

"Apart from Elliot, who we already know has been a victim? None," Zack said.

"Seriously?"

"There's one we can't find any trace of; the rest are dead or in prison. Some of them have been involved in terrible accidents. Only until now no-one has treated them as suspicious. I want to consider Chloe's friend a murder case now. Her phone signal went offline at a cell tower down near the canal. She never went to Paris."

"We looking in the river?"

"The DCI is getting that organised."

"So, Chloe and Elliot are the last ones, and there's already been a swipe at Chloe? Ironic both their fathers are standing in the by-election."

"Exactly, though this group don't seem to be his only victims, it's as though he has a vendetta against the whole town. Something must have really pissed him off."

"Someone else from the school?"

"Would seem likely. I've put Adam in charge, as he's got a handle on it. Not everyone agrees as he's just an intern." Zack made some air quotes with his fingers. "But he's a grip on the data, and that's all I care about."

"Maverick cop again." Nadine smiled.

"Just get the job done anyway I can babe, and be damned with those goddamn suits and their rules." Zack tried a fake American accent. "Not really, just logical and the boss gave it the nod. We've got to go door to door around Arthur's house again to speak to some of his friends. See if they could shine a light on why someone would have him killed."

"Anything on Willow Moon?" Nadine asked. It was the name of the girl Arthur had been contacting online. From the conversations Adam had found on Arthur's computer she was probably a schoolgirl. "The obvious link."

"Nothing yet. Adam's on that too. I've even got Miley poking around on the forums to see what she can find out for me." Zack held his hands up again. "Yes, I know, not within the rules, but she can find out if any of her classmates have been contacted."

"You have a theory." Nadine sipped down the last of her coffee.

"That Willow Moon was an underage girl. Difficult to believe Arthur would be involved in that shit, but it would give whoever it was a good reason." Zack shook his head and looked out of the window. He noticed a black car parked in a lay-by up the road from the Costa Coffee. Had he seen the same car earlier near his house?

"We better get talking to his neighbours and see what we can find out." Nadine began to rise from her chair. Zack looked at his watch and then back to his Danish, which he didn't want to rush.

53

Dave was going to get his life back.

A dozen cigarettes were stubbed out in the driver's door. There was half a bottle of vodka under his seat. The courage he'd needed to get this far. His hands shook as they held the wheel, but he was as calm as he was ever going to be.

Parked up in a lay-by off the high-street, Dave sat in a stolen car. It was a pretty nice one too, black exterior with tinted windows and full leather trim; the sort thing he might get himself when this was all over. The stranger had chosen well and left the car where he said he would together with the promised tools. A shotgun, the barrels cut short, rested on Dave's lap. He didn't like to look at it, because then he had to think about what he was going to do.

Just two acts, that's all it would take. Two acts, the memories of which he would be able to drown in drink and drugs, on an exotic island enjoying the high life. Maybe he'd sample some of the pleasures he'd seen the rich fuckers in this town indulge in. It was time he got a slice of life's sweet pie. He'd get some nice women too. There'd be plenty of cash for that where he was going. This town and this country could just fuck off.

Two terrible acts to free him from a fucking nightmare.

Dave reached under the seat to retrieve the vodka and took another swig. He'd have to remember to smash back some coffee and get some mint gum before he went to work later. Probably would need another shower.

His first target was enjoying breakfast at the Costa Coffee opposite where Dave had pulled in. The target was a copper; Dave knew that, and his companion was someone Dave had asked out once in his younger less fucked up days. At least she'd been nice to him when she'd brushed him aside, but that didn't matter now. His escape from his fucking nightmare was all that mattered.

They left their seats inside the Costa. The male copper tidying away their empty plates before making for the door. As the shop door opened, Dave started the engine, stamped on the accelerator and lurched into the road. There was the screech of tyres from behind. An angry horn. Dave could see in his mirror a driver gesticulating.

He pushed the button so his window slid completely down.

Foot to the floor, the engine screamed as the car hurtled towards the crossing outside the coffee shop. Dave saw the two figures about to cross. He thrust the end of the shotgun out of the window and pulled the trigger. The kick of the gun surprised him, and he dropped it on his lap as the car lurched to the left. Grabbing the steering with both hands he wrestled back control.

He heard a thud, anguished cries, the clash of metal. He felt the car rocked twice, his vision blurred as he hung onto the wheel. Another crash as Dave swung around a corner, hitting the edge of a blue car. Keeping the power on, Dave felt his vehicle slid sideways as the wheels spun. Then the car straightened and he sped off down the street.

Dave's focus turned to getting to the drop-off point as he tried to steady his breathing and slow his hammering heart. Remembering what had been written in the instructions. Following the directions, he'd stored in what was left of his confused brain. Slowly his vision cleared as he regained control.

Was that a police siren? Or an ambulance?

Dave drove so not to draw attention until ten minutes later he turned into a courtyard surrounded by cheap garages anyone could rent. He found the one he wanted, the door already open and drove inside. Climbing out of the car, Dave shut the garage door and walked away clutching the shopping bag containing the things he would need later.

Only one more terrible act.

54

Z ack knew something was wrong as soon as they were
outside. He'd kept the dark car in his periphery while
holding the door open for Nadine as she fumbled
in her handbag for her keys. The sound of the over-revving
engine attracted his attention as soon as they stepped towards
the road. Nadine was ahead of him, oblivious as she was still
looking for her keys.

Zack didn't look around to see what was coming. He already
knew.

Rushing forward he grabbed the back of Nadine's blouse.
"Run Nadine, run." Shoving her with so much force Nadine
could only manage a few more steps before sprawling onto
the pavement on the other side of the road. Zack dived to his
right as he sensed the car. There was a loud bang, and he felt
pain searing down his left side.

Another voice cried out.

"Nadine." Zack hit the tarmac and instinctively attempted
to roll back up to his feet. Pain ripped through his left side.
He collapsed to the ground, vision blurring as he sucked in
as much oxygen as he could. There was more screeching of
tyres and crunching of metal on metal. More screaming.

Then he passed out.

55

There was the outline of faces above him as he opened his eyes. Zack thought he'd only been out for a few seconds, but he couldn't be sure.

"You okay, buddy?" One of the blurred faces spoke.

"My God, did you see that?" A woman's voice.

"Has someone called an ambulance?"

"We need the police; it was a terrorist."

"Does anyone know first aid?"

Zack's blinked to clear his vision, eyes focusing in on a spotty young man knelt over him. "Are people hurt?"

"A few pal, but nothing serious," the man said. "Made a mess of the Costa window though. You busted anything?"

Zack tried to get up again, but the pain was too intense. "Might have."

"Lie still, you might have smashed ribs or something."

"You a doctor?" Zack asked.

"Art student."

A familiar figure came into Zack's view.

"My God, are you alright?" Nadine had blood running down the side of her face. For once, her immaculate appearance had been thrown into disarray.

"No. I'm fucking pissed off that some mother has just shot at us." Zack closed his eyes for a second as he pressed his hand against his ribs. He'd broken and bruised them before. There was dampness on his fingers, and when he looked at them, he saw the blood. "Buckshot. Nothing vital." He nodded towards his partner. "Any get you?"

"No, because you pushed me so hard. But the son of a bitch has trashed my best work shoes." She held up a black stiletto that looked to Zack like all her other shoes. At least it was enough to make him smile. Laughing was out of the question.

"Anyone else hurt?" Zack said.

"Another woman was clipped as it drove away," Nadine said. "But just cuts and bruises I think. Some cuts from flying glass from the other side of the street, but no one took a direct hit."

"Anyone see him?"

"Ye man I got his plate," one of the men gathered around said.

Some good news at least, Zack thought. "You think it was our man?"

"No." Nadine shook her head as she tried to use her hands to comb some order back into her hair. "He wouldn't have been so stupid. When you pushed me to the ground I looked around and saw the end of the sawn-off waving from the driver's window. He was driving and trying to aim. A fucking amateur."

Zack nodded at the thought, resting his head back on the pavement. "Another one of his minions."

"Guess we're getting close." A lady in an orange summer dress offered Nadine some wipes which she held against the cut on the side of her face.

"And he's getting bolder." Zack realised that despite what was in the press, whoever was behind this obviously knew they were still investigating. Did they know that Zack and

Nadine didn't think it was the ex-teacher? This had to be a targeted attack.

The sound of sirens erupted among the shocked chatter of the people grouped around them. Nadine knelt beside him and squeezed his hand.

"Thanks for saving me, Zack. You're my hero."

"Fuck off."

56

The doorbell interrupted Miley's tears. She'd tried in vain to phone Uncle Jake after getting back from hospital. The memory of her dad nearly being killed only a year ago, was still intense. Despite his broad smile and insistence, he was fine as he lay in his hospital bed, Miley couldn't shake the images of those days when her dad was in intensive care. The moment she'd heard he'd been shot Miley had nearly collapsed on the ground. It had taken a few minutes for Nadine to get it through to her that he was okay and the wounds were superficial.

Her dad had told her there was no need for him to be in hospital, and he was only staying overnight on doctor's orders. Nothing was broken, just bruising and some puncture wounds from the shot. Words that did nothing to calm her fears of losing another parent. He'd tried to make out it some was psycho who was probably targeting the Costa, joking about the quality of the coffee. But she was a copper's daughter, and Miley knew a lie when she heard one.

When she'd asked if it was to do with the investigation, Zack had told her he didn't know. She'd questioned Nadine too on the ride home. But Nadine only offered for Miley to stay with her family for the night, or at least to come around for dinner.

She wished Uncle Jake would answer. He could've got some people together to find out who'd done this to her dad, or at least he was someone she could talk to that would understand.

It wasn't just the time her dad was badly hurt that made her so upset. It was the stark reminder of how much she missed her mum. If there was one person who could wrap her arms around Miley's shoulders and assure her that things were going to be alright, it had been her mum. Even up until the very end, until the only thing her mum could do was squeeze her hand weakly in the cold hospital room, there had been a reassurance that life was going to be okay.

Now there were only the faded memories of her smile and the collage of images she scrolled through on her computer. Her mum's pictures were in all the rooms of the house. Her dad never wanted to forget, and sometimes Miley caught him looking at the pictures with tears in his eyes.

Taking a deep breath, Miley headed towards the front door. She considered ignoring the caller who was likely to be some nosy neighbour on the pretence of offering a helping hand, which wasn't something Miley needed. What she wasn't expecting was a woman in a smart blouse and skirt flashing a charming smile while sporting a rosette showing who she supported in the coming vote.

"I'm sorry I'm not interested," Miley said as nicely as she could while pushing the door closed.

"I was hoping to speak to your father," the woman said. "Is he in?"

"No, I'm afraid not. But he wouldn't be interested either."

"Oh. Will he back soon, do you know?" Miley was surprised to see a look of genuine disappointment on her face. The woman glanced down at her rosette as if realising something.

"It's not about the election."

"No, he's in hospital, he's had an accident." Miley was hoping this would be enough to dissuade the woman.

"Oh my God, is he hurt?"

Miley hesitated, leaving the door open just a little. "He'll be fine. He was attacked. He'll be okay." Her voice broke. Tears came again, and before she could close the door the woman swept in, wrapping her arms around Miley.

"It's okay, Miley. It's okay. Come on, let's sit down."

Something about the woman's manner reassured Miley that she cared, rather than just wanting to pay lip service as the neighbours would, and Miley allowed herself to be led back into the kitchen where they both sat down.

"You know my dad?" Miley started to gather herself.

"He's been investigating my case. I snuck off from the campaign, pretending to hand out more leaflets. But really," the woman hesitated, as if not sure what to say next, "I wanted to see your dad."

"You're that woman, aren't you, the one that was attacked? The politician's daughter. God, are you okay? It sounded awful." Miley realised she'd said more than she should. "Sorry, Dad talks a bit about work. I don't tell my friends, I promise. You're Chloe, aren't you?"

Chloe smiled and slipped into a chair opposite. "Yes, and it's fine that you know."

"Was it awful? I would have been scared stiff." Miley almost forgot about her own worries. "And being stalked too. Sorry, I shouldn't know that. Shit, I'm such a blabbermouth."

"Hey don't worry." Chloe reached out and took Miley's hand. It felt good. "I shouldn't be here either, talking to him off duty. I just needed to see him. Has he really been hurt?"

Miley nodded. "Someone shot at him out of a car. Just bits of it caught him; he should be out tomorrow."

"Shot at?" Miley saw the colour drain from Chloe's face.

"Yea, some crazy with a shotgun. It's not the first time Dad's been attacked. He was stabbed back in London when we lived there. It's why we came to Oakwell. For the quiet life."

"He seems like a tough cookie." Chloe smiled. "I bet you are too."

"He is. I just wish he'd stay away from the bad guys now and again." Miley liked Chloe, she suspected her dad did too from the times he'd mentioned her, and now the woman was sitting in her house Miley could understand why.

"Well, he'll probably have to now," Chloe said. "Look I'm sorry for having barged in. I better get back on the leafleting before my mother starts badgering me. Are you here alone? Will you be okay? I'll give you my number, and you can call me if you need a chat."

"Thanks, that would be nice." Miley thought it would be nice. "I'm supposed to go out to a party tonight, but I'm not sure if I should now."

"Hey girl, sometimes letting hair down is the best thing, and I'm sure your dad would still want you to enjoy yourself."

"I'm not sure it's right, though, being he's in hospital." Miley decided not to tell her that going to the party was the last thing her dad wanted.

"And he's going to be out tomorrow right," Chloe said. "He's going to be okay."

"Ye I guess."

"Then what's the point moping around while your dad is being waited on hand and foot by the best nurses in Oakwell? Can't a girl have some fun too?"

Miley smiled. She knew how her dad hated being in hospital. Nurses or not. "I guess there's no point staying in moping."

"That's the spirit. Here's my number." Chloe scribbled it on a piece of paper from her handbag. "I'll message you when I've finished today. If you decide against the party, I can always come over with some ice cream and a girly film. Always works for me."

As Chloe left, she gave Miley another hug and though just meeting the young woman Miley knew she'd made a friend.

57

As the line of white powder disappeared in front of him, so too did the doubts he'd been having. When the effect of the coke wore off Liam's confidence vanished, and he mostly felt like a loser. It was then he thought about how pale and loathsome his body was compared to others, or how pathetic it was he'd never been with a woman until Alex had paid for one. When he wasn't high, Liam knew he wasn't worthy of being in the same room as someone as beautiful as Chloe, never mind sleeping with her.

Then he snorted the wonderful white powder Alex gave so freely, and the world became a much different place. Then Liam became the master of his own destiny. The one in control. Unstoppable.

While Chloe had showered that morning, Liam had watched one of the videos of her showering in her own home and had been tempted to storm into the bathroom and take her there and then. Alex had warned him about that feeling though, that he would have to control his urges and wait for the right moment.

That moment was going to be tomorrow.

Chloe had spoken to him after getting back in from the campaign trail for her wretched father. She'd complained about the heat and how her feet hurt, but never once asked how he was or how his day had been. For someone who was supposed to be sorry for the pain she'd caused him she didn't seem to give a fuck about his life. Alex had said that girls like her would always be self-centred. Far too concerned with her own life to give a fuck about anybody else's.

To think that he'd pulled her away from certain death. Kept her secrets from the rest of the world as she had asked, and yet she still didn't give a shit about him. The website of her pictures was no longer online, and though she'd thanked him, there seemed little gratitude for all he was doing. Liam was sure she avoided looking at his body. He made sure he covered himself up around her, so he didn't have to see the disgust on her face.

Liam listened to her go to her room. Imagined her getting undressed, perhaps slipping on one of those lovely silk numbers he'd seen her wearing. Then the light had gone out. Was she on her phone? Maybe messaging some of her friends and telling them about the disgusting man that she was sharing a house with.

Would she be so free with her news when he'd been on top of her, inside her, after ripping the clothes off her body and making her feel the pain he'd felt over the last twelve years? A surge of energy coursed through his body fuelled by the coke. Why hadn't he found out about this wonderful white powder years ago? They'd talked about drugs when they were younger. Alex had been dead against them back then, but now Liam could understand why he'd changed his mind. When Liam snorted coke, he could think about doing things he would never have dreamed of before. Even going outside didn't hold any fears when Liam was riding high on the power of the white powder.

He thought about it again. Not waiting, going in there to take advantage of the bitch. He could tie her up, whip her maybe. Liam tried to shake the thought as his trousers bulged. Instead, he delved deep into his archive of images he had of her. It was even more stimulating knowing that soon they would no longer be fantasies.

But he had to be patient.

Tomorrow they would go over to the house where Alex was staying. Liam's old friend had taken over the house the ex-headmaster of their school has owned because Alex said it turned out the previous owners didn't need it anymore.

Liam had told Chloe the ex-headmaster might know something but hadn't been seen for a while. Said they should go and check it out.

Chloe had agreed.

All the plans were falling into place.

"Are you sure you won't stay, Miles?" Alice tried to hang on to Miley's arm. "I know Josh has the hots for you. If you let him, he'd be all over you."

Which was exactly why Miley wasn't going to be dragged back into the party. "I've got to get back, I've promised my dad."

"Oh, come on, how's he going to know in hospital?"

"He's a detective; they know everything." Miley climbed into the back of the taxi with her friend still holding her arm.

"If you don't get with Josh then someone else will."

She knew Alice was right, but Josh seemed to care more about where he could get his hands than about getting to know Miley. Plus his getting her to try some pills because apparently everybody was getting wasted on them these days, was not Miley's idea of a good time. Not only did Miley know it was time to leave, but she realised this was not the sort of crowd she wanted to belong too.

"Then let them. Just be careful, Alice. It's pretty crazy in there, and watch your drink."

"Hey, I like it crazy, because I'm a crazy bitch." Alice spun round on her heels, allowing her short flowery skirt to flutter up. "Your funeral, Miles. I might just go with him myself." She turned her back on the taxi, heading toward the house.

Miley shook her head as she watched Alice stumble through the front door, worried her friend would not be able to look after herself.

"God, I bet this is how my dad thinks all the time," she murmured to herself.

"I'm sorry, Miss?" the taxi driver said.

"Talking to myself." Miley swung her legs inside the car.

"Back home?"

"Yes please." It was the same driver who had brought her to the party earlier. Luckily, he'd only been around the corner when she called.

As the car pulled away, she allowed her head to rest against the back of the seat. Closing her eyes Miley felt the world begin to spin, realising she'd drunk more than intended. The most annoying thing was her dad had been right. While not invited, the lads from the local college had simply waltzed in as if they owned the place, not that there was too much opposition considering they'd brought more booze. Once inside they'd taken over, and the fact that some of them made a bee-line for Miley had pissed off her new friends, who'd wanted to be in the limelight.

The attention from the boys in her year earlier during the night had made Miley feel great for a while, and she'd known how fantastic she looked in the sparkling blue dress.

While Miley was happy to dance she'd quickly dismissed any suggestions from the eager, adolescent boys to become more intimate. Only she found that others in her group of friends were not so shy. But as good as she felt about herself, Miley wasn't ready for going any further, even when the gorgeous Josh was encouraging her. When his hands were not roaming, he'd been trying to direct her hands inside his jeans. Apparently, all the girls did it, and it was no big thing. Miley had laughed at that comment, but Josh hadn't seen the joke.

Miley had no doubt her new friends would've been happy to do what he wanted. Sex seemed to be another part of being popular. It shocked her how free and easy Alice and Sara were with the boys, egging her on to do the same. The boys seemed to be expecting a whole lot more than a tongue down a throat or a hand up a skirt. Suddenly being known as a frump and a geek didn't seem to be a dreadful thing in Miley's eyes.

It was different from when she acted up on the camera. Willing to reveal more, talk dirty and dance like some slut. They were just anonymous faces or text chats anywhere in the world. Tonight, she'd realised just how real it could all get and was she any better than her friends for walking away? Hadn't her online antics paid for the dress she looked so stunning in?

Her dad had wanted her to keep away from these boys because he knew what they were like. What he hadn't known was what she was like when her bedroom door was closed. The guilt swamped her when she thought of her dad and she was tempted to text him to see how he was, ashamed at having defied him. Not just about the party but about everything she'd been doing.

Miley couldn't even kid herself anymore that she'd been doing it for the money, having been coining it in from the computer work. While not quite as much money as from the disciples that worshipped her body, it was a whole lot more than the average teen earned. The truth was she'd been doing it because it had felt good to be wanted and being able to tease the pathetic men on the other side of the webcam gave her sense of control. The power she'd wheeled over them felt amazing.

But at the party it'd been all too real and suddenly Miley hadn't felt in control anymore.

Could she tell her dad? Could she confess all she'd been doing and go back to being geeky Miley with friends that might fawn over her, but at least had some respect for her as a person. She even thought about Hacker Boi. He'd always been kind to her online, helped her learn some hardcore computer programming, and recently she'd been brushing him off because he just wasn't cool enough. She'd see if he was online when she got back, make it up with him.

Miley opened her eyes as the car stopped. The driver was getting out. As she undid her seatbelt, she looked round not recognising the street.

"Hey, you've gone wrong mister," Miley said as he opened the car door. "This isn't my house."

There was an intense smell. Alcohol at first and then something different, something stronger. The driver thrust an arm into the back of the taxi. Miley felt a rough cloth cover her mouth and panicked. She grabbed at his arm trying to push it away. A bitter taste filled her open mouth. A sweet smell crept up her nose. She threw a fist towards the man's face, but he wouldn't let go. Miley pulled a leg upwards and attempted to kick out but though her foot connected with something the man's hold remained.

She reached up to the cloth trying to push it away as the panic set. Nothing Miley did seemed to make a difference.

Everything went hazy.

59

Dave tried to grip the familiar steering wheel of his taxi as tight as possible to stop his hands shaking. His vision was blurring again, and it was all he could do to stay on top of the driving. He'd already pulled over once to throw up. He felt like doing it again.

The afternoon had been a nightmare when he'd seen the copper hadn't been killed. Having expected a visit, or a phone call from people he never wanted to see again. Dave was surprised when instead there'd been a message reminding him of his obligations as if he'd completed the first job. He'd been tempted to text back to check if the deal was still on then thought better of it.

The girl was lying on the back seat; her limp body stretched out. She looked so young, so innocent. He could barely keep his nerve, tempted to ditch the taxi and just run. The girl would wake up and be fine, and he wouldn't have every stinking copper in the land hunting him down.

Every time Dave saw headlights in his mirror, he was convinced it was the police. Certain there'd be a siren to pull him over. They'd pounce on him like animals, beating him before he was dumped in some squalid cell where they'd take turns spitting on him. He'd seen the TV programmes of how the coppers reacted when you went after one of their family. Dave could hardly blame them. He'd do the same.

At one point, a moan from the back seat caused him to nearly veer off the road as he looked around in panic. He should have had another slug of drink after he'd knocked her out. He'd drunk so much today Dave was convinced his driving was already erratic enough to attract unwanted attention.

The taxi radio was off. Dave wouldn't be taking any more calls from the office. That was a former life. Once he'd delivered the girl, he'd drive straight to Dover to catch the ferry. With the money in his bank, he'd replace this car and become a different person heading through Europe.

Dave had already singled out Thailand as the place to escape to. It looked fucking terrific on the web, and the women were incredibly cheap. The sound of a Thai bride catering to his every whim, while he hid out on one of the islands, sounded good. He could always ditch her if he fancied a change.

Finding his way to the driveway of a large converted farmhouse on the outskirts of town, Dave drove the taxi down the gravel entrance. The tyres crunched as they passed down the two hundred metres of the tree-lined drive until he emerged into a courtyard. Outside lights illuminated his arrival.

"Doing very well for himself whoever he is," Dave muttered. Not surprising considering the man could afford to wipe out Dave's debts in a flash. He wondered how much the girl was worth to him. As a copper's daughter, there must be a tidy penny for ransom, or some job worth a lot of cash. Unless the man had a hard-on for her. Dave couldn't blame him for that.

Maybe he could get himself a little more cash for his troubles.

As Dave brought the taxi to a standstill the large wooden door of the farmhouse opened to reveal a slim figure silhouetted against the light. Opening the taxi door, Dave climbed out. The man stepped across the gravel almost silently.

"Bring her inside," he said.

Dave reached into the back of the cab and slid the girl along the seat until he could hoist her onto his shoulders. "Up the stairs and the first room on the right," the man continued in a pleasant voice. "Lie her on the bed."

Dave grunted, shifting the girl's weight as he entered the house. An elegant staircase took him up to the landing, and a light in the bedroom was on, revealing a pristine room dominated by a double bed covered in a plethora of soft toys. Maybe the man was a pervert after all. But it was none of Dave's business. The weirdo could do what he wanted with her as long as Dave got his cash and was left alone.

"All good?" The man was at the bottom of the stairs waiting for him.

Dave nodded. "It went well."

"Unlike earlier."

"He must have dived out of the way, the lucky bastard. I'd been right on him." Dave didn't want to mention that his eyes had been closed. The man was smaller than Dave had imagined, average height average build, a nondescript face.

"Very disappointing." The man's face showed no emotion, but Dave couldn't help noticing his deep blue eyes never blinked and didn't waver from boring directly into Dave's soul.

"We still got a deal, right?" Dave's earlier ambitions of asking for more evaporated.

"I have something I need disposed of in the cellar," the man said. "Help me with that and we can consider our business concluded."

"What is it?"

"Just the bodies of the people who owned this house." The man's boyish grin was a sickening sight. "I fear they will begin to smell a little soon. Don't worry; they should be no bother."

Dave felt his stomach drop. "I don't know about this. Christ, bodies." He was sure he was going to vomit.

"You're in touching distance from a new life, Dave. Don't waste it now when you're so close. I'm sure you can find a place to dump them on your way from here. Then, when you've got rid of the car, you'll be long gone before the police even suspect you."

Dave didn't see a choice. He was already deep enough in the shit to spend the rest of his life behind bars. The sooner he got himself out of here and away from this psycho the better. He nodded his assent.

"Good." The man led the way through the expansive kitchen until they came to a door that opened to rough stone steps leading down into what Dave assumed was a cellar. The man indicated for Dave to go first. As Dave's foot hit the first of the steps, he felt a sharp pain and spun round, reaching for his neck.

"What the fuck." Dave saw the man was holding a syringe.

"Failure was not an option."

60

It was some time before the intense pain in Miley's head diminished to a dull enough throb she could bear. Even then tiny movements made her wince. She had to be content lying where she was until it all passed.

Miley remembered the taxi driver reaching over and forcing the cloth over her mouth. She'd tried to push him off, but he'd been far too strong. Why had he done it to her? The driver was nice enough when he'd taken her to the party, and she knew her dad had used the same firm when their car had been out of action.

It was obvious she was no longer in the car and appeared to be lying on something soft. Trying to figure things out like her dad would was what she needed to do. Whenever Mum had been stressed about something, Dad used to always be cool and collected. Probing at the problem until they found its weakness and the answer.

Miley knew she needed to be calm; think like her dad.

She was probably on a bed, and she could tell she was still wearing her dress, though wiggling her toes revealed no shoes. There was warmth on her bare skin, and the light behind her eyes meant this was probably a room with windows allowing the sun to shine through.

It was a good sign. Still dressed and not in some cold, dank cellar. Miley gently tried to move her arms away from her body making sure she wasn't bound. They moved freely.

Another good sign.

Opening her eyes, Miley squinted at the initial glare of sunlight through a large window to her left. Blinking she looked around. The bed was the size of her double bed at home, topped with a crimson cover and home to a large family of soft toys. Velvet full-length curtains bordered the tall window and rested against yellow walls before reaching down to a cream carpet. The bedroom was bigger than her own, even larger than her dad's. There was a wooden dresser in one corner with a mirror Miley would have loved to have in her room at home.

She pushed herself up, moving her limbs to make sure there was no pain and letting out a long breath as the last of the fogginess left her. A picture on the dressing table attracted her attention. At first, she thought it was a picture of her next to a boy she didn't recognise. Then Miley realised it was someone who looked like her when she was a few years younger.

Swinging her legs around, her bare feet landed on the soft pile of the carpet. With no sign of her shoes, Miley stepped over to the dresser and examined the picture. It could have been her, and whoever it was looked happy with her arm around a boy of around twelve or so. Miley saw another picture behind it. Just the girl this time in a purple dance leotard holding up a medal. There was a name badge, and Miley could just make out the writing.

Angel.

A shiver ran down her spine. Why were there pictures of a girl in the room who had the same nickname Hacker Boi had given her online? Was it the boy in the picture? Miley had assumed she'd been talking to an older teen or young man. He used to go on about following her dreams and seeing the marvels of the world. She'd suspected he'd never seen any of the things he spoke about and was just trying to impress her. She was sure that was after she'd sent him a picture of her. Boys generally changed the way they spoke to Miley once she'd sent a picture.

Out of the window, Miley could see an overgrown garden and beyond it trees with fading green leaves unmoved in the still air. There were no other houses in view. Nobody in any gardens to signal too. Miley tried to open the window anyway, but it was locked.

Looking around the rest of the bedroom there was no sign of her handbag or phone. Her breath getting short again, panic rose as she thought of the horrible things that might happen to her.

"Stay calm, girl. They'll be looking for you." She wondered when her dad would get back from the hospital. Knowing him it would be as soon as he could, and he'd be expecting her to be home. Her dad would leave no stone unturned to find her and if he called Uncle Jake she could almost feel sorry for whoever had taken her. Almost. A few years back they'd watched the film *Taken* and when she asked her dad if he'd go to as much effort to get her back, he'd joked about putting a pool table in her room. It didn't seem so funny now.

But she knew he hadn't meant it.

Miley walked over to the door. She listened. There was the sound of music, rock music, coming from below. Taking a deep breath, she took hold of the brass handle on the door and pulled.

The door opened.

61

"Miley, get down here right now." Zack waited at the bottom the stairs while the house still reverberated from the front door slamming. He was seething after a message from Nadine who'd seen pictures on Facebook of Miley at a party. She'd also found out the same party had been broken up by the night patrol after complaints from neighbours.

Furious, Zack had called Miley, only for it to go to voicemail. He'd discharged himself from hospital, not wanting to wait for some busy doctor to find the time to get around to him. The nurses had tutted and moaned about being too short-staffed to deal with headstrong coppers, but he'd ignored them and booked a taxi home.

Zack realised venting his anger on voicemail wasn't his smartest move and not surprising Miley had failed to pick up after that. Nadine had tried to persuade him to stay in the hospital while she went to see Miley, but this was something he had to deal with. A party getting out of hand was exactly what he'd warned his daughter about, and Zack had thought he could trust Miley to do as she was told.

"I'm warning you Miley, come down here now, or you'll only make it worse." He hoped she had a terrible hangover which would make his shouting even more painful.

No reply.

"Miley, I know you were at the party. If you think you were mature enough to go then, you need to be mature enough to face the consequences."

Zack listened at the bottom of the stairs. There was nothing. Had she got so drunk she was still out of it?

Climbing the stairs, Zack winced as bolts of pain punched his side where the gun pellets had struck. Her door was ajar with light shining through indicating the curtains were open.

"Miley, are you in there?" He glanced at the bathroom door, also open. With still no reply Zack pushed her bedroom door inward, revealing an empty room. Her bed looked as well made as it ever did.

Surely, she couldn't have gone out already.

"Miley, are you in?" He paused on the landing, listening again.

Had he frightened her so much with the voicemail she couldn't face him? Zack entered her room, trying to decide if she'd slept in her bed. There was no sign of her favourite handbag or her phone, so perhaps she'd gone to a friend's house after the party and stayed round because she wouldn't have expected him back last night. It was a pretty grim to think he might have scared his daughter to that degree.

Deflated Zack sat on her bed, rubbing his hand over her Hello Kitty pillow. It had always been her mum's favourite, which was why Zack knew Miley hadn't changed to more grown-up bed covers. Sometimes he forgot how brave she'd been when her mum had been sick, and they'd both watched Mary fade away. Zack had used work to distract himself while his daughter had got on with the practicalities of life. Sometimes Zack wondered if his daughter handled everything better than he did. Just like her mum.

His phone pinged, and Zack grabbed it out of his pocket expecting a message from Miley. It was Nadine, messaging him to say she'd spoken with a few of girls at the party and Miley had seemingly left before things started getting out of hand. She hadn't been there when the police had turned up.

"You're a sensible girl, Miley. I should've trusted you. But where did you go? Where are you now?"

He typed out a message to his daughter.

Let's talk about this honey. I don't want you to be scared to come and face me. I will always love you.

62

Expecting someone to be on the other side ready to grab her, Miley tensed as she pulled the door open. The landing outside her room was empty. The music grew louder.

Nothing made any sense. She was being held a prisoner in an unlocked room. Why was she even taken? It didn't seem to be the kind of house where a taxi driver would live. Listening to the music Miley wondered if it was one of the college boys. Perhaps it was their house, and they'd snatched her for a prank. She dreaded to think what they might have made her do while she was out of it so that they could post it on YouTube.

The carpet was soft on her feet as Miley moved out onto the landing. It had a luxurious feel that matched the rest of the house with its bright cream and yellow walls. Light flooded through a large window by the stairs while the other doors were all closed. She contemplated exploring other rooms for a way of escape, or maybe even a weapon she could use, but on peering over the bannister, she saw the front door in the large hallway below.

Keeping alert for movement, Miley ran to the stairs. Halfway down she saw the spacious hallway with its dark wooden floor. While there were other doors, Miley focused on the front one, leaping down the last few stairs until she reached it and pulled the cold metal handle as freedom beckoned.

It was locked.

There was an empty keyhole. After looking around in vain for a conveniently hanging key, Miley rattled the heavy door in frustration. With no way out she turned, leaning against the door as she considered her options.

He would be in one of the rooms. Her captor. Miley had seen enough horror films to know that any manner of horrendous things could be in store for her in this house. If it had been the college boys she would've heard them by now; laughing and joking as they sank some beers. Maybe he was playing rock music to drown out her screams as he went to work on her with his tools. Miley shuddered, vowing never to watch another horror movie again if she got out of this alive. Maybe she could face him down though, convince him to let her go. The bad guys seemed to like to talk a lot in the movies.

Miley padded across the dark floor towards the room the music was coming from. There was another opening to her left where Miley could see a kitchen on the other side. She wondered if there would be an exit into the back garden, but even if there was she knew it would be locked.

She had to face her captor.

Miley stepped to the outside the door where the music was coming from, readying herself to face whatever terror waited beyond. She imagined he would be there, sharpening a knife, as he shaped his plans for her. At least she hadn't woken up in some strange contraption like those *Saw* movies, where she might have had to cut off her arm to get away.

She glanced at the front door and wondered if she should try it again.

"Come on Miley; you can do this," she muttered to herself. After all, there was always one who managed to get away in the films. She pushed the door inward, convinced she was about to meet her doom.

Instead of a room of horrors, there was a long table covered in large screens, each showing either a myriad of colourful numbers or what looked like high definition camera footage of various locations. Some of the screens were attached to the walls down one side of the room. Though the main screen, twice the size of the others, was resting on the long wooden table. There were computers too, Miley could see. Slimline units on the table, all controlled from a central console sporting a wireless mouse and keyboard. Sitting by the keyboard a man slouched in a computer chair, his bare feet and legs resting the table next to a what looked like a large smoothie.

The man swivelled in the chair. A pleasant face looked at Miley, as she took in his *Game of Thrones* styled T-shirt and black shorts. She was confused by his appearance as he reached over to his green smoothie, slurping loudly as hi sucked through a thick straw. This was not the monster she'd been imagining. Maybe it was the college boys after all.

"You slept for a long time, my angel. But it's good to meet you finally." He stood up and held out his hand. "I'm Hacker Boi."

63

H is phone vibrating on the glass coffee table startled Zack awake. He snatched it up. "Miley?"

"No Zack, sorry. It's Chloe."

"Chloe?" Zack, still confused from the rude awakening, didn't register the voice or name.

"Yes. That is Detective Inspector Carter? Zack Carter."

"Yes, it is. Chloe. Sorry, I was asleep. Not really with it."

"Oh God, I woke you?"

"Ye, rough night."

"I'm so sorry I'll call back." There was a hesitation. "It's not important."

"No, no it's okay." Zack stretched his head back to ease the pain down his left side. He'd fallen asleep on the sofa. The last thing he could remember was sitting waiting for Miley to text him back.

Miley.

"Shit, what time is it?"

"Just gone three, sorry Zack I didn't think you'd be asleep. I wanted to check you got back okay from the hospital."

"Three." Zack glanced at the window. The sun was already on the opposite side of the house, making the room he was in stifling. His grey T-shirt clung to his skin, and there was sweat beneath the copious bandages which covered the areas of his arm and side scraped by the shotgun pellets. The air felt close, as though there was a storm coming.

"Yes."

"Christ those meds must have knocked me for six."

"Are you okay? I heard about the shooting."

"Fuck, where is she." Still holding the phone Zack jumped up and looked round to see if there were any sign of Miley.

"What?"

"Miley, my daughter, she went to a party last night, and she's still not back. I got back this morning, and she wasn't. I took some meds while waiting." The pain in his side had grown while he'd been stomping around the house looking for Miley, but he hadn't thought a few pills would knock him out like that. Maybe he should've listened to the doctors.

Zack hurried up the stairs, hoping to see Miley back in her room. Maybe she hadn't wanted to disturb him when she got in.

It was still empty.

"You've not heard from her?"

"Nothing. Shit." Zack sat on the edge of Miley's bed fearing the worst. Where was she?

"You tried her friends?"

"Not yet, I thought I'd wait a while. I didn't mean to fall asleep. I don't even know their numbers." Zack tried to regain his composure. "Sorry, Chloe you called me."

"It doesn't matter. I was just. Well, I just wanted to know you were okay. I'm sorry, I know it's stupid. I wanted to be able to do something and hear a friendly voice. But you've other things to worry about now."

"It's not stupid, Chloe. Look I'll need to make some calls, then I'll call you, okay?"

"Don't worry about me, just find your daughter. If there's anything I can do to help let me know."

"Tell me where a teenager who thinks she might be in trouble would hide out from her angry father?"

"That's easy for me, it would be the shopping or with friends. Preferably both at the same time."

"Then maybe she'll be back. She probably thinks I'm still pissed at her. But she would have messaged."

"Why would she think you were pissed?"

"Because she went to the party when I'd told her not to. I sort of ranted on the phone when I found out. I can kind of rant quite a bit when I'm mad." The guilt of how he had reacted returned. The last thing he had wanted was to drive his daughter away.

"She wasn't supposed to go to the party?"

"No, I didn't like the sound of it, and yes I know I wouldn't because I'm a cop."

"Shit, I didn't know." Zack heard the guilt in Chloe's voice. "I stopped by yesterday when doing my leafleting, you know for the campaign. Your daughter was in, she was upset about you having been hurt, and didn't know whether to go to the party or not. Sorry, Zack, I told her to go. I didn't realise. She didn't say she wasn't supposed to."

"I guess she planned to go all along." Zack found it hard to believe she'd always intended to defy him. He'd trusted her.

"She was really upset about you getting hurt, Zack. She told me about when you'd been hurt badly before. Part of the reason why you'd moved."

"For the quiet life." Zack jumped back to his feet, leaving Miley's room. He needed to walk, to think about where she could be.

"Did she say anything about going anywhere else? About who she would be with?"

"Sorry, Zack no."

"If you think of anything, let me know."

"I will, and let me know when she's home safe?"

"Will do."

Zack hung up before scrolling through his contacts when another call came through. It was Nadine.

"You heard anything yet Zack."

"No."

"Listen I've spoken to a girl called Alice who was at the party."

"She was one of her new friends." Zack stepped into the bathroom. He needed a shower and to think, but he didn't know if he should peel the bandages off.

"Alice told me Miley left the party and got into a taxi. Recognised it as one of Snowy's."

"I know the firm." Zack had used them a few times. "Small operation of half a dozen or so cars."

"Zack, one of their cars, went off the grid last night and they still can't get hold of the driver. The last they heard was he was going to pick a girl up from a party."

64

"I want to go home." Miley was sitting on one of the dining room chairs, a large strawberry smoothie untouched on the table in front of her. The man had introduced himself as having a real name of Alex, and after checking Miley had no ill effects from being drugged had gone to make her the smoothie. Something else to add to her confusion. He wasn't acting at all as she expected. But there was an edge to him, something behind those piercing blue eyes that told Miley she was in mortal danger.

"You told me you couldn't wait to get away from home." Alex slipped back into his chair before sweeping his finger across a touchpad in front of him. He brought onto the main screen an excerpt from a chat session. It was between Miley and the Hacker Boi. She remembered talking to him about wanting to travel the world. He'd spoken about how she could work from anywhere once she had the skills. Even saying at one point that he was working on a tropical island.

"I want to go home," Miley repeated.

"What you want is a better life."

"No, I want to go home. That was trash talk. You know that."

"You mean you don't want to visit all those wonderful places?" Alex leant back in his chair, putting his hands behind his head.

"Yes, I did, but not now. Not like this." He'd been so easy to talk to online, almost like a confessor where she could speak of her frustrations as he sent her pictures of the places he was working while she was stuck in little Oakwell.

"There will soon be little left of worth for you in this town, and this is not a place that will look after you. I will take care of you, Miley. I'll take you to the places you've dreamt of, and you'll be witness to visions of the earth few ever see. It's what you said you wanted. It's why I came for you."

"I want my dad." Suddenly he wasn't the pleasant young man anymore. If he'd done this because of their chats online, then he was a psycho. She wondered if he'd been one of the ones who paid to watch her as well and just used another name. That sent another shiver down her spine.

"After I've taken so much trouble to get you here. You told me your dad didn't care about what you wanted, that's why he wouldn't let you go to the party. I even arranged it so that it was easy for you to go there against your father's wishes. That's not very grateful, my angel."

"Please let me go." Tears came unbidden to Miley. There was something chilling about his casual manner. He seemed as friendly now as he'd been during their many chats, but Miley knew the danger she was in, and she was terrified.

"Angel thought she could look after herself. Told me she'd be okay, that she could take on the world. When those bastards took her, I wasn't strong enough to save her. She was like you, Miley. A delicate flower, full of steel. Soft of heart and so determined. I failed to save her from the darkness of this world. I will save you."

"I don't need saving."

"Oh, but you do, Miley." The man reached forward, swished his pad bringing photos from the party onto the screen. How the hell did he get hold of them? "So many boys ogling you, Miley. And look at these." There were images of when she had been performing on her webcam. "Baring yourself for all manner of old men to drool over. You're on the road to ruin if I don't help you. I was trying to guide to do more productive things with your time. I was teaching you how to control your own future, and all the time you were resorting to acting like a common slut."

"I was just trying to make a bit of extra money." Miley heard the disgust in his voice as he pointed at one of the pictures where she was topless. She blushed and looked away. Why had she been so stupid? "I'm not going to be doing that anymore."

"You see, I am already making a difference." Alex flicked the picture away. "You'll have a good life, my angel. You'll have the life you deserve. No one will ever hurt you and we can go to the most glorious places in the world." The images on the screen changed to bring up some of the places she remembered Alex had said he worked. At the time, she'd thought he was having her on, bigging up his life. Now she saw it was true. He stopped on a picture of island beach, golden sand bordered by a calm blue sea. There was a villa with fantastic looking hammocks swinging at the front. "I was there when I spoke to you once. We can be anywhere in the world.

"Please let me go home." Miley felt the tears flow down her cheeks.

"Your home is with me now."

65

"Th here's still no sign of his daughter." Chloe read Zack's message on her phone. "Maybe we should call DS Morris, see if she can help."

"Let's just go there, as we said." Liam had already grabbed his car keys. "If you've got to be back with your father, then we need to get moving."

Chloe knew Liam was right, and if they didn't act on Liam's discovery now, there probably wouldn't be a chance for another couple of days.

"You don't think it's too late at night?"

"I think you'll be busy tomorrow."

It was true. They'd been unable to do anything so far as she'd been out canvassing with her parents all day in the final push, and there was the post campaigning party tonight. A thank you to the troops who'd worked so hard. Despite what her mother had told her yesterday the latest opinion polls had shown her father slipping a few points, which meant the hero factor of his daughter had been called into play. Chloe had to admit it did seem to work, with no one rudely turning her away from their door.

"Okay, I guess there's nothing to lose."

After throwing on some leggings and a comfy T-shirt, Chloe pulled on her new sneakers and headed for Liam's car. She carried her replacement phone, to which she'd only given a handful of people the number. The upside of losing everything was there had been no more messages from her stalker. It made her wonder if it was Mr Hudson after all and this was just a wild goose chase.

"If the lights are all off, should we leave them?"

"We might as well have a closer look," Liam said. "It may be because they're on the cruise, or it may be something else."

"Like what? Oh." Chloe realised she was being dumb. Liam seemed to be relishing the situation and there was almost a twisted desire to make a gruesome discovery he could report to the police. Chloe found it hard to believe it their old headmaster had anything to do with it, but Liam was insisting that he couldn't have afforded the house they were living in on a teacher's salary.

He didn't stop going on about the things that had been happening in the town as they drove out of the town towards the house. Betting that it was another ex-teacher who'd been working with Mr Hudson and the headmaster. Maybe they'd all been selling pictures of the girls for years, while they'd been running the school. Liam talked about the pictures a lot. Chloe kept quiet, worried about what they might find and thinking she should be calling DS Morris. If only Zack had been able to talk to her, she would've felt a lot safer.

Chloe admonished herself for thinking so selfishly when Zack had his own troubles to deal with. She should be helping him find his daughter instead of playing Nancy Drew. After all, she'd told Miley that she ought to go to the party against Zack's wishes. Even though Chloe hadn't known, it still made her feel terrible.

"Here it is," Liam said as they drove onto a gravel drive.

"Look, the lights are on."

There were two cars parked in the courtyard in front of a large house, which sported a row of garages coming off to the left that looked as though they used to be stables in a former life. It was the type of property her mother talked about buying when Chloe's father was a top politician, and Chloe understood what Liam meant about an ex-headmaster not being able to afford it. "Looks like they have visitors. Shall we leave them to it?"

"Might as well ask a few questions, now we're here." Liam parked next to the other cars. Chloe saw one was a taxi and as she stepped onto the gravel noticed there was no driver sitting waiting, which seemed odd.

Liam strode over to the large door and pressed the doorbell. Chloe stood beside him, still looking around as she felt a shiver go down her spine despite the muggy evening. It had the feel of a place you stopped at when your car broke down, and you had trudged through the rain to find help. The sort of place once you entered you never left.

Her mother thought the couple were on a cruise, and her mother was rarely wrong. So why was someone here, why were there lights on and why was there the sound of someone turning a key on the other side of the door?

As the door swung open, a man appeared in knee length shorts and a grey T-shirt. It was then she looked at his face and took a step back as the breath left her.

"You."

"Hello again, Chloe." The man smiled. "Shame you didn't come to the party. I had a wonderful time with Jenny."

Chloe felt her stomach clench with a terror she'd never known before. His smile sent chills into her soul. Why was he here?

"Well don't stand on the drive. Liam bring your guest inside. I've just opened a lovely bottle of wine for you both in the kitchen."

There was a tight grip on Chloe's arm as she was propelled into the hallway with such force she nearly stumbled to the floor. Attempting to regain her composure she heard the front door close behind her.

"It'll be nice to celebrate our reunion," the man said. "Especially when there are not so many of us left these days."

Chloe was steered across the hallway into the large open kitchen. There was a table in the middle with four seats and a bottle of wine with two glasses in the centre. Chloe desperately tried to recall the man's name, even remembering the familiarity she'd felt that last time they'd met.

The man pulled out one of the wooden chairs. Liam pushed Chloe into it, her legs weak as she swallowed the bile down in her throat. As Liam took his seat beside her the man poured red wine into the two glasses.

"Sorry I don't drink alcohol." The man went to a large double fridge and retrieved a tall glass filled with a green liquid. He sat opposite Chloe. "I only drank water that night." He went on as though he thought that was why she had a confused look on her face.

"To old friends." The man lifted his glass. Liam followed suit before they both stared at Chloe to do the same.

"Who are you?" she said.

"See I told you she didn't recognise me, Liam. It's easy to disappear when you want to. Maybe it's because you didn't pay attention to the likes of Liam and me at school that you don't recognise me, Chloe. One of Liam's best friends."

"Alex." He was so different from the skinny, spotty boy she remembered from school. Chloe noticed his eyes first, brown in the nightclub and now blue. His hair was lighter too, and his broad smile showed perfect white teeth. He was different, but now Chloe could see the resemblance.

"Bingo. You see, it is a reunion." Alex took a large slurp of his smoothie. "Drink up Chloe; I know it will be to your taste. And I insist."

The jovial tone turned more sinister as he watched her and Chloe decided a drink was a good idea. She gulped down her wine, glad of its warm embrace.

"Did you kill Jenny?"

Alex smiled. "Your friend isn't with us any longer. A fun girl but she did complain a lot. A real screamer." He sucked on his smoothie. "Her body is in the cellar if you want to see. I'm afraid she might be a little rank." He shifted in his seat, blue eyes boring into her. "The question is, are you going to be a good girl tonight, Chloe? Or are you going to join your little friend in the cellar?"

66

Chloe screamed, her hair tearing as Liam used it to force her up the staircase. "Liam, you don't have to do this." The wine was sloshing about inside her, making her feel queasy. Alex had searched her, stripping Chloe of her phone and keys before letting Liam drag her from the kitchen.

"I want to do this." Liam's face came near her, hot breath on her cheek and eyes bloodshot from snorting coke in the kitchen.

They made their way to the top of the stairs, and Liam shoved her towards one of the bedrooms, pushing the door open with his foot before propelling her towards the bed. Chloe grabbed the edge of the bed to steady herself.

As she turned, Liam slammed the door. There was a wild, primaeval look in his eyes.

"Remember this, Chloe?" Liam walked towards a large dresser near the queen-sized bed where a laptop was replaying the exact moment she'd tricked Liam into exposing himself. It was edited to emphasise his naked overhanging belly and be as humiliating as possible.

"Liam, I'm so sorry about what I did. I know it was wrong."

"We can make a film tonight, Chloe. And this time you can be the star." Liam nodded to a camera beside the laptop pointing towards the bed. "Alex has provided some toys to enhance the fun."

There was a large holdall on the floor next to the dresser; Liam stepped over to it and emptied the contents onto the floor. Chloe saw all manner of devices better suited to some sick bondage film.

"You made those pictures, didn't you?" Chloe recoiled at the thought of some pictures she'd seen on the site dedicated to her. "You made the site. You made the images."

"Been making them for years. Every time I saw myself in the mirror I made a new one. Never thought I'd get the chance to make real ones." Liam reached to the floor and picked up a long wooden paddle and swished it through the air. "Be good to hear you scream for real." He grinned lasciviously, spit dribbling down his chin. "Or maybe I should use a ball gag."

"You don't want to do this, Liam." Chloe edged back on the bed, horrified at the evident madness in Liam. "You're better than this. I was a bitch. I know I was. Don't lower yourself to that level, Liam."

If she could speak to her younger self again, the one laughing on the endlessly looping video, she would scream at her to stop being so fucking stupid. To see Liam, who'd been so gentle and mild only wanting to be loved by someone like her, reduced to this slobbering animal broke Chloe's heart as much as it filled her with terror.

She'd enjoyed their time together when they'd been studying, despite what she'd told her friends at the time. To them, she'd described Liam as a fat disgusting pig who only wanted to slobber over her and get a look down her top. The truth was that it had been good to work with someone and not have to hide the fact she found most of the school work easy. Being able to use her brain without being labelled a geek freak.

She'd never felt good about what they'd done. Had only laughed at the video with the others because it was all part of being a member of their clique. Now she was faced with the horrific consequences.

The video showed Liam's young, eager face as she'd teased him with visions of her body, not realising his world was about to be shattered.

Liam saw her watching. "I bet even the game was fixed?"

Chloe nodded.

"I guess Alex thought of everything." Liam picked out a pack of playing cards among the implements on the floor.

As Chloe watched him, paddle in one hand and cards in the other, she knew he wanted her to feel terrible pain for everything she'd done, and how could she blame him? Wouldn't she want to do the same? Didn't she want the same?

But if this was going to happen it was going to happen on her terms. When she walked out of the last photo shoot she'd done in London, Chloe had been ashamed at how low she'd stooped and vowed never to be exploited like that again. But now she knew she'd grown up exploiting others as much as she'd been used up and spat out by the modelling industry. It was time for her to stop being the victim and take control.

Chloe stepped over and took the cards from Liam. "Okay then. Let's play for real."

67

L iam pulled the dresser chair across the room, sitting opposite Chloe who shuffled the cards.

"Are you ready?" she asked.

Liam felt like a boy again, like the one in the video. Rage replaced with an eager anticipation of what was to come. He swayed on the seat for a moment, dizzy, confused, excited. Almost disappointed she wasn't scared anymore.

"You first." Chloe cut the pack, handing half over to Liam who picked his first card off the top. A king of spades.

"Ouch. Your king beats my seven" Chloe kicked off her shoes, looking Liam in the eyes.

She drew another card. Waving a two of diamonds.

He had to beat that.

He had a five.

Chloe stood before him pushing her black leggings down, revealing, inch by perfect inch, sleek tanned legs. He could barely tear his eyes away from them as Chloe kicked off the leggings, sat and took another card.

"Finally." She waved an ace of hearts towards him.

After drawing a losing card, Liam took off his trainers.

"And again."

Liam's breath caught in his throat as she looked at him in such an alluring way, he felt totally out of control. Under her spell again. Liam failed to beat her queen and proceeded to drag off his socks. He wriggled his bare toes. His senses heightened, he could smell the sweet jasmine of her scent and thought he could hear Chloe's hair moving against her top. He wanted to know what her bare skin felt like to touch. He wanted to know what it felt like to be inside her.

"Not so good." She looked disappointed at her card. Liam fumbled peeling his own off the deck.

"A ten." He'd beaten her and realised her top was about to come off. Chloe lifted the edge of her T-shirt slowly, pulling it up with deliberate movements. For a moment, she had flashed her bra before lowering the grey top as though she wasn't going to do it. Then a coy smile, before the top came off completely.

"Nobody else here this time, Liam," she said. "No way to cheat the game now." She held up a jack of spades.

Liam stood to remove his shorts after losing the round. He was conscious of how hard he was, pressing against the inside of his boxers. Having dreamed so often of seeing Chloe strip off her clothes and witnessing her exquisite body clad in only her bra and panties had his body trembled with excitement. The sweat started to drip down his face, forcing him to wipe his eyes to keep his vision clear. It was too hot; it was hard to breathe.

"That's not good." Chloe held up a three of clubs.

His hand was shaking as he drew his card, beating her easily.

"I liked you, Liam. I enjoyed working with you." Chloe reached round her back. "There was no pretending when we were studying together. The laughs were real. The time I spent with you was one of the few times I felt I could be myself and not have to pretend." Keeping one hand pressed the bra against her breasts, Chloe slipped the bra over her shoulders until she was only holding it. "I shouldn't have done what I did, and I'll make it up to you."

Chloe cast the bra aside and sat with her hands on her lap. Liam's eyes were drawn to the perfection of her breasts, hardly believing he was so close to them and knowing he was going to touch them. His whole body was shaking

"King of diamonds." Chloe held up another card.

Liam was finding it difficult to breathe. He could hear his heart beating, wondered if he should have another line of coke. Would it help him calm down? He dropped his card at first. It was only a six.

An intense wave of shame passed over him at the thought of removing his T-shirt because he was convinced Chloe would recoil with revulsion and his dream would be shattered. But seeing her in her panties in front of him made him realise whatever happened he was going to have her. He peeled the T-shirt from his body, feeling a wave of nausea pass over him.

Chloe had taken another card from the pack and was holding it away from him. "Everything on this last card."

Liam nodded.

He picked from the top, heart sinking as he realised it was a three.

"Still beats me." Chloe turned her card to reveal a two of spades. "Guess it's your lucky day." She climbed to her feet, stepping in between his open legs. "Can a gentleman help a lady out of her underwear?"

Liam moved his shaking hands to either side of her hips. His stomach lurched. He took hold of the soft material. His vision swam, as if in some surreal dream where the most pleasurable things were just out of his grasp.

Nausea almost knocked him to the ground.

Jumping from the chair, Liam pushed Chloe back onto the bed to free his path to the en-suite. He slammed the door behind him and only just made it to the toilet.

68

The incident room was full of officers and civilians with grim faces and determined attitudes. Zack sat among the tables strewn with crushed Styrofoam coffee cups and the remainder of a plate of pastries brought in to provide a much-needed boost to sugar levels. He may not have been stationed at Oakwell very long, but he was one of them. He was a copper.

"We no longer consider Mr Gary Hudson the sole perpetrator in the hostel fire." Nadine was taking the briefing. Zack had to stay out of the way. Technically he was off the case as his daughter was involved, but no-one seemed inclined to evict him from the room. "Other occurrences in the town have led us to the conclusion there was no way he was acting alone, and it is possible he was being directed by someone else."

"One or more people?" someone asked from the front row.

"We don't know at this point," Nadine continued. "Could be both. Arthur and the ex-priest were killed by someone who knew how to handle a knife. Gary Hudson does not fit the bill. Various people have been trolled and blackmailed via untraceable means. Gary Hudson does not fit the bill for that either."

"Two days ago, Zack and I were targeted on the street, and

that night Zack's daughter Miley Carter vanished after getting into a taxi after a party."

Behind Nadine blown up images of Arthur and the priest were replaced with Miley's picture and a map showing where the party had been. "The last known sighting."

Zack swallowed a lump seeing her face projected onto the wall and felt the tension rise in the room.

"Is there a connection?" The same person in the front row spoke up.

"A lot of people that have been targeted all went to the same school at the same time, including Gary Hudson; you'll find information on that in your briefing packs." A few of them slid some of the files out of the grey folders that had been on the chairs. "However, we don't know the connection between them all. Our priority is to find Miley Carter. In your packs, there are instructions for each team."

"Bit light on people, aren't we?" a ginger-haired constable spoke up, and the others murmured with agreement.

DCI Sterling stepped up next to Nadine.

"Officers from Nottinghamshire and Derbyshire will be joining us as soon as possible to assist with the search effort. Dive teams will be heading to the canal. However, we do also have to maintain our civic duty, to make sure the voting goes smoothly today. Unfortunately, some resources will be required to assist."

There were general groans.

"I know, I know. You've got your packs. Your team leaders will brief you further. Now get out there and find her."

Zack was pleased to see the resolute looks on faces as the other members of the Oakwell police made their huddles to examine the briefing packs. He'd worked with Nadine to get search areas mapped and covered, so the use of the resources was as efficient as possible.

"You should get home and rest." The DCI had made his way over to Zack.

"I need to do something, Sir. I need to be involved." Zack scratched at the stubble on his jaw. The pain in his side was throbbing, but he was trying to stay off the medication to remain sharp.

"You know the protocol, Zack. I must take you off the case now you're personally involved. You're not even supposed to be in the incident room."

"I know, Sir. I appreciate that."

"Take some sleeping pills and get some rest while we do the work. I know you were out there all night and you won't do Miley any good if you're exhausted. When you've had some rest, come back in and go over everything you and Nadine have with a detective coming in from Derby. DI Scott Thatcher is a hell of a good cop. He won't let you down, Zack."

"I know, Sir. You're right."

"And it just became an order, Detective Inspector. Get some sleep, and I'll make sure you're kept in the loop. Do you understand?" The stern look told Zack it wasn't going to do him any good arguing.

"Yes, Sir." The DCI was doing him a favour, and it wasn't something he was willing to push. Zack also knew that agreeing with his boss didn't mean he would do as he was told. He could see his future. Another inquest into his subordination, another tale of sympathy and understanding of the good intentions of his actions as he was he disciplined. But he didn't give a fuck about what the future held so long as he got Miley back safe.

"Good," The DCI continued. "Now here's Nadine. I've to see the Returning Officer about the arrangements for tonight's count. This goddamn election is sucking up resources we need. Detective Sergeant Morris, please make sure this man gets some rest or don't allow him back into the station."

"I'll do that, Sir." Nadine gave Zack a stern but compassionate look. "We'll personally escort him home." Beside her, Adam was standing with his laptop on the crook of his arm looking as though he had something important to say.

"Excellent Nadine." The DCI beamed at her before making his departure.

"I don't need a babysitter." Zack took his phone off the desk and padded his pockets for his car keys.

Nadine held up her hand. "Zack, this is perfect timing. We were about to ask to go to your house."

"Why?"

"Because Adam's been on Arthur's computer." Nadine leaned forward. "Zack, we think Willow Moon was Miley."

69

"Liam, are you okay?" Chloe knocked on the bathroom door. The morning sun was streaming through the crack in the curtains. "I'm going to come in there if you don't answer."

"I'm okay." It was the first she'd heard from him since being told to leave him alone after he'd thrown up. Having waited outside for a while, offering to help him, Chloe gave up after a torrent of abuse and being told to fuck off.

Chloe had tried to get out of the room but the windows and doors were locked, and there was nothing to contact the outside world with. Instead, she'd buried herself under the duvet, lying there unable to sleep while the thoughts of what happened to Jenny somersaultedthrough her mind.

There was a knock on the bedroom door, and Chloe heard the key turning in the lock.

"Hello. He wants you downstairs."

Chloe recognised the voice and ran to the door. "Miley. My God, he has you too?" Chloe pulled the girl inside the room and closed the door.

"I'm fine. He hasn't hurt me. But I'll have to get back downstairs."

"What's he doing with you?" Chloe asked, checking her over despite what Miley has said.

"He hasn't touched me. He wants to take me away when whatever he is doing is over. I'm like someone he knew when he was younger. Some girl called Angel. I think something horrible happened to her."

There was a noise from the bathroom that startled Miley.

"It's okay." Chloe rested a hand on the young girl's arm. "Someone I know from school, Liam. I think he spent the night throwing up in there."

The door opened to reveal a dishevelled figure, his hair matted and stuck to his face. With little obvious attempt to clean himself up or wipe away the sign of the night's distress.

"You look like shit, Liam." Chloe shook her head. "How have you got yourself into this?"

Liam slumped onto a chair, barely acknowledging Miley's presence.

"Because Alex can do things I've only ever dreamt of, has access to software that's incredible, and I'd never been with a woman until he showed up again. He showed me how I could have the world, and Alex knew how much I hated you." Liam looked at the floor.

"He'd promised me stuff too." The quiet voice of Miley. "But I just want to be with my dad. He's planning to do a terrible thing today."

"Do you know what?" Chloe put her arm around Miley's shoulder.

"Something at the town hall when the most important people will be there."

"Shit the election," Chloe said. "Do you know what he's doing?"

"I've rigged the security," Liam said, still looking at the floor. "He can turn it on and off whenever he likes. He can turn off all the fire systems too. Like the hostel."

"You mean he's going to burn it down, with everyone in it."

Liam just shrugged. "I just rigged the security."

"Then we've got to stop him." Chloe stared at Liam, but he failed to acknowledge her.

"If we don't go downstairs now, he'll come and get us," Miley said. "He's doing breakfast."

"You're right. Go downstairs and tell him we're coming. Is there a phone, another way out?" Chloe steered Miley towards the door.

"Not that I've seen." Miley stepped onto the landing. He has a load of computer gear I might be able to use to get a message out if I get the chance."

"Liam, get yourself ready, and we'll go downstairs."

Liam climbed from the chair and retrieved his shorts from the floor.

"What should I say?" Miley asked.

"Just tell him we're coming. And if he asks we were both in bed together and I looked upset."

"Okay." Miley nodded and scampered off down the stairs. Chloe thought she was one hell of a brave girl.

"What we going to do?" Back in the room, Liam had a panicky look on his face.

"Act as though you fucked my brains out all night and made me suffer."

Liam looked at her and then nodded. "I can do that. I need some coke."

"No, you don't, Liam." Chloe went over and lifted his chin so she could look him in the eye. "All your life people have been using you, so end it here. We go downstairs and pretend like it happened the way you intended, and when we get a chance, we overpower him and get the fuck out of here."

"Okay." Liam sounded uncertain, and Chloe knew she didn't feel as confident as she was trying to make out she was, but they had to try and take control somehow. After all, there were three of them and only one Alex.

"Just remember," Chloe grabbed a flannel from the bathroom and began to wipe Liam's face to make him look more respectable. "You fucked me in every way possible and taught me a lesson. You were one bad mother fucker."

Chloe almost smiled at the startled look on his face.

70

M iley's back ached from the tension as she watched Liam and Chloe enter the kitchen. She'd been worried Alex would question why she'd taken so long getting back, but instead, he'd smiled at her and pulled out a chair for her to sit on, before pouring some orange juice.

"Ah, here at last." Alex grinned as Liam and Chloe entered the room. "Good morning. I hope you've slept well after your night's activities."

"I know I did." Miley saw Liam was trying to put a smug look on his face. Chloe was looking down; her hair was more messed up than earlier and Liam was pulling her by the arm.

"And how was it for you, Chloe? Do you think you've repaid the humiliation you put Liam through?" Alex was busying himself with plates on the side of the kitchen, while Liam sat at the table with what Miley thought was a ridiculous fake smile plastered on his face.

"You are both sick bastards," Chloe spat.

"Please take a seat." Alex began putting the plates on the table, indicating for Chloe to sit. She sat opposite Liam and next to Miley.

Liam bragged about how fantastic Chloe had been, how adventurous she was, though how poorly she had handled the whip. Miley concentrated on watching the butter slowly melt on the warm croissants in front of her. Normally she loved croissants, and it was rare they would have them at home, but she didn't feel like eating this one. Miley didn't dare look at the other two as Liam spoke about his night. She knew he was lying.

Alex pushed the bowl of jam into the centre of the table, before pouring out strong coffee into the four mugs. He was wearing a black polo neck sweater with dark trousers, which Miley thought made him look like some professional hitman when combined with his slicked back hair and a clean-shaven face. It seemed to transform him from the smoothie drinking T-shirt and shorts dude of the previous day.

As Alex took his seat, he placed a gun down on the table with a dull thud. "Now eat up everyone while they are still warm."

Miley froze, fixated on the gun, wanting to look at Chloe but unable draw her eyes away from the weapon. She'd seen guns before, even fired a handgun at a range with her dad, but there could be no doubting the implication of its place on the table.

Only Alex ate, delicately buttering each piece of croissant before applying a dab of jam. "Liam, you should be a man enjoying your breakfast. Especially after the night I imagine you had?"

Liam nodded and poked at his plate.

"Then why the reticence?"

"What's the gun for Alex?" Liam asked.

"Normally they are used for killing people, and today you will use it as your initiation into a better life."

Miley looked up and saw Liam go pale. She could barely breathe. Was it going to be her? Was she going to die?

"What do you mean?"

"She can't come with us Liam; we talked about that." Alex bit off a chunk of croissant and chewed it slowly before continuing. "Chloe has no place in our new life and you've had your fun now, so it's time to finish it."

"You can't mean to kill her." Liam visibly shrank in his chair.

The momentary relief at it not being her about to be shot was replaced with the horror of realising Liam was being asked to kill Chloe. Almost choking, Miley looked across at Chloe whose eyes were wide with terror.

"I'm not one for small talk. We have a lot to do today so kill the bitch, and we can get on." Alex picked up the gun and offered it to Liam. "You want the life I have offered you?"

Liam nodded.

"Then there will be plenty of other whores who will gladly fuck you for the wealth you'll have. So, don't be a fucking retard and shoot the bitch." He slammed the gun down in front of Liam, making the plates jump on the table.

Miley watched Liam stretch his shaking hand towards the gun. He had almost grasped it when he let his hand fall back to the table.

"I can't."

"Pity." Alex picked up the gun. "I guess I'll have to do it."

He pulled the trigger.

Miley screamed.

71

"What the hell was she thinking?" Zack sat on Miley's bed with his head in his hands. The shock at what the three of them had read on her computer still sinking in. He felt sorry, angry and ashamed at the thought of her actions over the last few months. Most of all he felt he'd let his precious daughter down. To think his little girl had been living a secret life in their own home and he'd trusted her so much, never thinking to check what she was doing online. After all, she knew a hell of a lot more about the online world than he did, and she knew the dangers.

"Looks like she was mainly paid in Amazon vouchers and to a PayPal account." Adam clicked through the emails of Miley's alternative accounts. He said he'd have missed them if it hadn't been for a folder she'd left open, showing mirror accounts for almost all her social media interactions. It seemed Miley hadn't gone to great lengths to cover her tracks. Either she didn't think her dad was savvy enough to access anything or she didn't care.

"I'm sorry, Zack," Nadine murmured.

"Stupid thing is I'm as mad at myself as anybody. Jesus." Zack shook his head.

"Do you think she knew it was him? Arthur," Nadine said.

"Can't see any names used anywhere." Adam was rapidly

scanning through emails. "If she did, she wasn't saying."

"All the times he helped us out at the station and all the time he was looking at my daughter." Zack was furious, Arthur had been an excellent work colleague, a friend. They'd even shared a few beers together and moaned about the state of the country. Arthur might have paid for his perversion in the end, but it was little consolation. "Where are you, babe? Who are you with? There's got to be something on there to tell us. It has to be someone she's been in touch with."

Adam shook his head. "I'll keep going, but her most common contact on this account seems to be Silver Wolf. There are others, but not as frequent. I'll get some of the techs in head office to try and trace them."

Zack nodded, there seemed no end to this nightmare.

"Do you think Arthur was killed because of this?" Nadine said. "Or his connection to the case?"

"Could be either, but I'd say because of Miley." Zack stood and walked over to her makeup dresser, trying to fight off the despair. He could smell her coconut perfume lingering in the room. Miley's smell. "Can't say I'm bothered about him now, except if he could provide any clues to where Miley is."

Nadine rested her hand on his shoulder. "We'll find her."

It felt as if everything was happening in slow motion. Zack knew all the effort everyone was putting in to help find his daughter, but they seemed no closer, and more and more resources were getting called away to make sure the polling around the town went smoothly after the incident at the hostel.

Nadine's phone rang and when she answered, it was evident she was talking to the DCI as she told him where they were and what they were doing. Concern spread across her face as

Zack watched. His stomach clenched as she hung up.

"Chloe's mother has rung the Boss because they can't get hold of her. She was supposed to be at a meeting an hour ago."

"I've got her new number," Zack said. "I'll try."

There was an element of relief it was not the news that he feared, as Zack pushed the call button and put it on speaker. It went straight to answerphone. Another two attempts received the same message.

"Have you got Liam's number?" Zack asked.

"No, they'll have it back at the station," Nadine said. "I'll get it."

"Don't worry; I'll go around." He needed to do something and had a feeling it was connected.

"Zack, I'm not sure." Nadine started.

"Guys, this is interesting," Adam interrupted. "She first started talking to someone new about six months ago in a separate chat system I've not seen before. Someone called Hacker Boi. It looks like it's encrypted, so unless you have a key sent from the person you're talking to you can't get it working.

"This guy was helping her out with her computer work, some real hardcore programming." Adam scrolled through some of the messages. "Kinda nice guy, boosting her confidence of how good she was and how she will be able to go far. Helping her do some freelance jobs not many could handle. He keeps calling her an angel. Some messages are a bit creepy though, telling her how special she is and how she should be looked after in this cruel world."

"What did he call her?" Nadine was by Adam, looking at the screen.

"He refers to her as Angel, or his angel sometimes."

"Angel," Nadine said. "Shit. It can't be."

"What is it?" Zack was already at the door when he turned around to see Nadine had paled.

"A case when I was probationary. Just on the fringe, but I'm sure it was about a girl called Angel. I don't understand. Zack, I need to go and see the case files. They'll be at the station."

"Okay." Zack trusted his partner not to question her further. "You do that. Adam see what else you can uncover. I'm going to see if I can find Chloe because I can't believe she won't still be caught up in this. Ring me as soon as you have anything."

Despair was a thing of the past now. Zack was going to find his daughter.

72

It was the screaming Chloe heard first. Looking across the table she saw Miley's contorted face, her mouth wide as every muscle strained to push out a scream. But it sounded dull, as though it was from another, more distant room. There was something else. A high-pitched ringing that threatened to drown out all other noise. Chloe realised it was in her ears.

Her face was wet and Chloe wanted to reach up and wipe it away, only she feared what it was. Faint smoke hovered in the air over the table, almost vanishing as she watched it spiral up towards the wooden beams of the ceiling. There was a sharp metallic smell and the taste of copper in her mouth.

Was she still alive?

As if the world was in slow motion she turned toward Liam as his body crumpled, slumping sideways at first, before slipping to the floor like a drunk man passing out at a party. If it weren't for the fact half his face was missing she might have thought he'd simply fainted.

She was alive. Alex hadn't shot her.

The gun. What about the gun?

Relief gave way to panic that the weapon would be turned on her. Chloe forced herself to focus on the end of the table. On Alex, whose hand was still holding the black gun resting on the wooden surface. As the ringing in her ears faded, Chloe began to make out his voice above Miley's frantic screams.

"Miley my angel, Miley, calm down. No one is going to hurt you." Alex reached out, touching Miley who pulled away, but her screams dropped to rasping breaths. "Liam was going to join us; only he wasn't worthy. He couldn't do what needed to be done."

"You killed him." Miley forced out each word between gulps of air.

"Yes, Miley. He lied to us. He was weak. He never did to Chloe what he said he would. I have ways of knowing these things."

It looked as though Miley was about to burst out into screams again as Alex stood and moved to her side, lifting her from the chair with such ease she might have been a rag doll.

"Come on my sweet, let me get something to calm you down."

Miley was shaking as he wrapped his arms around the girl before carrying her from the kitchen the shock having drained all the fight from her. Chloe found herself short of breath as she tried to get control of her shaking body.

He'd killed Liam.

There was crimson spattered across the pale table top. Deep red spots on the back of her hands. Other colours too, and tiny lumps that could only mean one thing. She wanted to wipe her face again sure that bits of gristle were sliding down her cheek. But the idea of touching it, seeing it, was more terrible than knowing what it was.

He'd killed Liam.

Chloe thought she was saving him by what she'd done, stopping him from raping her and being a criminal for the rest of his life. As much as it had been her fault he'd turned into a crazed young man; it was now her fault he was dead. Blood dripped from her onto the table as Chloe fought the urge to cry out in anguish, battling for mastery of her own body. She knew she had to calm down.

Liam's lifeless body settled on the floor near her chair. A pool of blood spread out from where the remains of his head rested on the cold tiles.

"Would you have preferred to be in his place?" Alex walked back into the kitchen, standing near the body.

Chloe shook her head. "You didn't have to kill him."

"Because he was a victim? But he was happy enough to take his revenge, wasn't he? Liam was pleased to know your friends had come to unfortunate ends. He's helped me loosen the dark secrets of this town, helped bring on the inferno they will see tonight. That made him as guilty as anybody else. If he'd chosen the right path, he'd still be alive. You talked him out of it last night, didn't you?"

Chloe stared at him and said nothing.

"You're a smart one, Chloe Evans. Then again you were always smarter than you seemed. Maybe I'll have some use for you yet. Depending on the path you choose?"

Chloe looked him in the eye. Something hardened inside of her. "If you're going kill me then just do it, you fucking prick."

"You are full of surprises." Alex stepped around the body and Chloe's heart sank when he retrieved the gun from the table. She could've grabbed it while he was out of the room. She cursed herself for being so stupid.

"You're going to kill me anyway," she said. "I know who you are so you can't let me go."

"When this is over, everyone will know who I am Chloe,

and your knowledge will be no threat to me. Now this place is a mess, and I hate mess. We need to clean it up."

73

There was no one at Liam's house and no car parked outside. The curtains were still drawn. Zack tried the front door, banging on it for a few minutes before moving around the small front garden and through the back gate to the rear of the house. A patio style backdoor was also locked. He peered inside at the kitchen. There were a few odds and ends on the side, but nothing to indicate anyone was inside. Zack tried ringing Chloe again.

Voicemail.

In frustration, he called Adam. "There's no one here. You found anything else?"

"Zero," Adam said. "I'm going to unhook the hard drive so I can send it to the lab. They'll find anything I can't. I'm getting them to try and trace where the Hacker Boi messages were from. My guess, it will be like Chloe's stalker, and we won't find a thing."

"The same person?" Zack queried.

"Could be."

"How long for the techs to get results?"

"This kind of thing could take days."

"I haven't got time for that," Zack said.

"I know. I'm doing the best I can."

"Sorry, you've been great." Zack rested his head on the back door, feeling the energy drain from him. "Can you see if you can get hold of Chloe's parents or campaign team? See if she's turned up yet."

"Probably where she is," Adam agreed.

"Well, let's find out for certain." Something told Zack she wouldn't have shown up there either. "Then can you get them to run a plate check on Chloe's car to see where she was heading? It's not here."

"On it."

"In fact, let me ring them," Zack decided. He was outside the house of someone he was sure was involved in all of this. Outside a house that could well contain the evidence he needed to find his daughter. It was time to bend the rules. "I need you to get over to Liam's to help me on the computers."

"I thought you said no one's there?"

"There isn't; I'm going in any way."

"If you do that, anything I find-" Zack could hear the concern in Adam's voice.

"I know the rules." Zack had seen there was a shed in the backyard and hopefully there would be something he could use to break in. "This is not about corrupting evidence Adam; it's about finding my daughter. I'll say you were never here. I'll take the flak." Zack knew even the lenient DCI would not be able to back him on this call. If the shit hit the fan, then the arse covering would be colossal. He knew the score; he'd been there before.

And he didn't care.

"Don't worry, Detective Inspector Carter, I'm a big boy now and I'll be right over."

Zack thanked him before ringing off. He called into the station to get them to run a check on Chloe's car and see if he could get an expedited warrant to trace her phone. He knew they already had a trace for Miley's phone, but these things seemed to take so long. Pocketing his phone he stepped across the yard.

Zack opened the shed door, unleashing a wave of flies. The smell was dreadful in the stifling heat, making Zack wonder if there might be something dead in there. Wrinkling his nose, he poked around the sparse shelves until he found a rusty length of metal. Swiping away the cobwebs he headed for the back door.

It took three efforts on the patio frame to force the door off its runners. It tumbled to the floor with a clatter Zack hoped wouldn't bring round any nosey neighbours.

"Hello, is anyone home?" Zack made his way through the downstairs' rooms, keeping his eyes peeled for anything that might indicate where Chloe and Liam were. As he stepped into the hallway, his phone rang.

"Found them?" It was Nadine.

"No sign," Zack replied. "I'm in their house right now."

"Really?"

"Don't ask. You got anything?"

"Zack, I know who the Hacker Boi is."

C hloe had already thrown up once while attempting to clean the kitchen, gagging every time she looked at the remains of Liam's face. In contrast, Alex was an ocean of calm instructing her as though it was a regular cleaning job. He'd fetched some thick black plastic, which he cut with kitchen scissors to make a larger covering. Chloe wasn't sure if mutilated bodies like this were supposed to smell as the air was filled with the stench of disinfectant as Alex prepared two large buckets of steaming water.

"Work on cleaning the floor and the walls, Chloe. I'll see to his body."

He placed some of the plastic on the floor, before rolling Liam's large body onto it. Chloe turned away and heaved as pieces of brain flopped onto the tiles.

She plunged her hands into the hot water before sloshing it over the floor, and smothered the red and grey bits in soapy bubbles while Alex partially wrapped the body in the thick plastic. He used grey masking tape to keep it together as best he could while Chloe moved onto cleaning the walls.

All the time, her mind was racing as she tried to think what his plans might be for her, and how she might affect them. Despite what he'd said, Chloe couldn't imagine he was going to let her go, and what of Miley? It sounded like he was going to take her away after tonight. Chloe had to seize any chance she could get to stop him.

It was difficult to remember much of Alex when they were at school. While he was part of Liam's group, he was just a nerdy nobody for the most part. She recalled him gaining a certain infamy for a brief time when his parents were murdered. Even Chloe's mother had been aware of him then because the killings had followed on from another murder. A girl not much younger than Chloe had been savagely cut down. Chloe's mother had gone on for weeks about how she needed to stay safe.

There wasn't much about Alex after that. Chloe didn't even know when he left school. He just wasn't there one day. She wondered what it was like to lose your parents like that. Was that why he was doing what he was now?

Alex bent down to re-adjust Liam's body on the plastic when he looked around as though he sensed Chloe looking at him. She hadn't realised she'd stopped cleaning, lost in her thoughts.

Alex grinned at her.

The urge for action taking hold, Chloe grabbed one of the buckets of hot water that was now half full and hurled it towards him. She hadn't been a victim in her own home, and she wasn't going to be a victim now.

Alex stumbled back, and Chloe followed up the water by barrelling into him, knocking him to the ground. She considered going for the gun in his pocket but instead opted for the large scissors on the table. Alex leapt nimbly to his feet as Chloe threw herself at him again, stabbing the scissors towards his face. For a moment, she thought she'd pierced his skin before a hard blow caught her on the side of the head.

Dazed, she felt another hit to the other side of her head, and for a moment everything went blank.

The scissors clattered to the floor in front of her, as she sank to her knees.

"You still have a lot of spirit, Chloe. I like that. I'm not going to kill you if that's what you're worried about. Not unless you force me to. You see, letting you live knowing your parents have suffered because of what you did is much neater. Letting you live while the lives of all your friends have been destroyed is your punishment."

Pain tore through her scalp as he yanked her up by the hair, pushing his face up against hers.

"I can imagine how your life will be when this is over, Chloe. Maybe you'll wish I'd killed you. And you never know, I might call on you again if you're bad. Perhaps prick those pretty eyes out of your head." The scissors were in his hands now, sharp blades hovering just in front of her. "I think I'll leave you to think about that for a while with your old friend here. One hand released her and reached into his pocket, producing a set of handcuffs. "I bought these especially for you and Liam to have fun with. They might as well not go to waste."

As she realised what he was doing Chloe used the last of her strength to try to push him away, kicking out with her legs at his stomach. She felt the ripping of her hair again, as Alex took a firm hold. Then her head smashed against the kitchen table.

hloe had already thrown up once while attempting to clean the kitchen, gagging every time she looked at the remains of Liam's face. In contrast, Alex was an ocean of calm instructing her as though it was a regular cleaning job. He'd fetched some thick black plastic, which he cut with kitchen scissors to make a larger covering. Chloe wasn't sure if mutilated bodies like this were supposed to smell as the air was filled with the stench of disinfectant as Alex prepared two large buckets of steaming water.

"Work on cleaning the floor and the walls, Chloe. I'll see to his body."

He placed some of the plastic on the floor, before rolling Liam's large body onto it. Chloe turned away and heaved as pieces of brain flopped onto the tiles.

She plunged her hands into the hot water before sloshing it over the floor, and smothered the red and grey bits in soapy bubbles while Alex partially wrapped the body in the thick plastic. He used grey masking tape to keep it together as best he could while Chloe moved onto cleaning the walls.

All the time, her mind was racing as she tried to think what his plans might be for her, and how she might affect them. Despite what he'd said, Chloe couldn't imagine he was going to let her go, and what of Miley? It sounded like he was going to take her away after tonight. Chloe had to seize any chance she could get to stop him.

It was difficult to remember much of Alex when they were at school. While he was part of Liam's group, he was just a nerdy nobody for the most part. She recalled him gaining a certain infamy for a brief time when his parents were murdered. Even Chloe's mother had been aware of him then because the killings had followed on from another murder. A girl not much younger than Chloe had been savagely cut down. Chloe's mother had gone on for weeks about how she needed to stay safe.

There wasn't much about Alex after that. Chloe didn't even know when he left school. He just wasn't there one day. She wondered what it was like to lose your parents like that. Was that why he was doing what he was now?

Alex bent down to re-adjust Liam's body on the plastic when he looked around as though he sensed Chloe looking at him. She hadn't realised she'd stopped cleaning, lost in her thoughts.

Alex grinned at her.

The urge for action taking hold, Chloe grabbed one of the buckets of hot water that was now half full and hurled it towards him. She hadn't been a victim in her own home, and she wasn't going to be a victim now.

Alex stumbled back, and Chloe followed up the water by barrelling into him, knocking him to the ground. She considered going for the gun in his pocket but instead opted for the large scissors on the table. Alex leapt nimbly to his feet as Chloe threw herself at him again, stabbing the scissors towards his face. For a moment, she thought she'd pierced his skin before a hard blow caught her on the side of the head. Dazed, she felt another hit to the other side of her head, and for a moment everything went blank.

The scissors clattered to the floor in front of her, as she sank to her knees.

"You still have a lot of spirit, Chloe. I like that. I'm not going to kill you if that's what you're worried about. Not unless you force me to. You see, letting you live knowing your parents have suffered because of what you did is much neater. Letting you live while the lives of all your friends have been destroyed is your punishment."

Pain tore through her scalp as he yanked her up by the hair, pushing his face up against hers.

"I can imagine how your life will be when this is over, Chloe.

Maybe you'll wish I'd killed you. And you never know, I might call on you again if you're bad. Perhaps prick those pretty eyes out of your head." The scissors were in his hands now, sharp blades hovering just in front of her. "I think I'll leave you to think about that for a while with your old friend here. One hand released her and reached into his pocket, producing a set of handcuffs. "I bought these especially for you and Liam to have fun with. They might as well not go to waste."

As she realised what he was doing Chloe used the last of her strength to try to push him away, kicking out with her legs at his stomach. She felt the ripping of her hair again, as Alex took a firm hold. Then her head smashed against the kitchen table.

75

As Nadine spoke Zack saw Adam pull up round the back. "One second Nadine, Adam is here." Opening the back gate, he let the intern in.

"The house is clear and there's an office upstairs, " Zack said and Adam simply nodded, rushing past him.

"Go on." Zack spoke back into the phone as he followed Adam up the stairs.

"Seventeen years ago, a twelve-year-old girl called Angel went missing," Nadine said. "She lived in a run-down part of town, though her street hadn't been known for trouble. It's gone now, demolished and redeveloped, and that's because of what came later. I was a probationary at the time when I was drafted in to help. I spoke to the mother at length and a close friend of Angel, a boy, called Alex Ryan. They'd been neighbours, but Angel's father had lost everything in a financial scandal that had hit the company he worked for. He killed himself. Angel and her mother had then hit hard times, having to move to the shitty Yeoman estate.

Alex was a good lad, helped us where he could, desperate to find his friend and showing some of the secret places they used to go. It was clear he thought of her as more than just a friend. A week later she was found barely alive, having been beaten and tortured. She was a real mess and died of her injuries a few days later. I've sent a picture of Angel to your phone. It's a scan but good enough."

Bringing up the image of Angel on his phone Zack gasped. "Shit."

"The spitting image of your daughter."

"I would say so." Looking at the picture of this sweet girl from long ago made him even more desperate to find Miley. He needed to know she was safe and yet the more he heard, the less certain it seemed. "But I don't get the connection."

"At the time, we couldn't trace who was involved, but what we did uncover was the neighbourhood was waist deep in sordid activities, some of which Angel was part of. Three women, all addicted to either drugs or drink, were performing through webcams or even taking part in videos that were being shot in one of the houses on the street that had been converted into a mini studio. Angel's mum, an ex-actress, was one of them.

"Only it looked like the men involved Angel as well. When her mum was out of it on the drugs, Angel was often the star attraction. Apparently, it paid for her acting and dancing lessons, as she aspired to be a Hollywood star. It'd been considered a to be one of the quieter parts of the estate, but that was because they were very good at concealing what was going on. Apparently, the drugs and booze to keep them all going was delivered by the local ice cream man."

"Jesus, no wonder I never trust them," Zack said.

"Well, they bulldozed the entire cul-de-sac in the end. Three years after Angel's murder most of it was gutted in an arson attack. Nearly all the houses had been doused in petrol and set alight. Angel's mother was pulled out of her house. At first, it was thought she'd died of smoke inhalation until the autopsy revealed a cocktail of painkillers and booze in her system."

"Suicide."

"And arson. Any of this starting to become familiar?"

"It is." Was this why Miley had been taken. Because she reminded someone of a girl from the past. "Did they ever find who was responsible for Angel's death?"

"There were a lot of suspects after what was uncovered on the street, but nothing could ever connect them to her death. They all seemed to love her, and not just because she was making them money, which was somehow the creepiest of things. They would all say how she loved to act and that there was no pornography, just arty films. They tried to justify a twelve-year-old girl dancing naked on video as some sort of art. Bloody pedos. Three of them died in the fire. They'd done their time and returned to the street. It's like whoever was behind it was patient enough to wait.

"Anyway, I'm getting ahead of myself. Before that there was an attack on Alex's house a few weeks after Angel's death. He got away, but his parents were murdered. It was then Alex told us about the three men he and Angel had discovered in an abandoned house in the woods at the end of the street Angel lived on. It seemed the men had been using it as some sort of drugs base.

"Alex and Angel had decided they were going to steal the drugs, expecting the men not to be there. Angel's mum was a junkie and Angel suspected the drugs were being supplied by these men. She wanted to get rid of them. It also appeared she had a keen sense of adventure and not too much regard for danger. They'd been caught by the men and though they'd managed to escape when Alex set fire to the house, it was because of this Alex reckoned Angel was killed. He blamed himself for everything because he hadn't told us sooner. We worked out who the men were in the end. A crew from Guilford who had been run out of the town by Romanians and had been looking for a new place to set up. The street was quick to give them up when they realised they could have killed their precious Angel. But it looked like they had skipped town.

"Ten years ago, a detective from Leeds came down because there'd been a triple murder in the dales which looked drug related. The bodies were found in a holiday let they'd seemingly taken over during the winter. There wasn't much left after the fire but enough DNA for them to trace it to two of the guys there was a warrant out for. They'd done time before.

"There were no clues to who'd killed them. The charred bullets at the scene couldn't be traced."

"Alex," Zack murmured. He looked at Adam who seemed to be doing a lot of frowning and complaining as he typed at Liam's keyboard.

"While never in the frame for anything at the time that's why I wanted to do some digging," Nadine said. "To find out what had happened to him."

"You find anything?"

"The night of the arson attack on the Yeoman estate he vanished off the face of the earth. With his only other living relative not wanting to take him in after his parents had been killed, he'd kicked about a few foster homes, until he seemed to settle into one until he was sixteen. After that night, no one ever heard from him again, and he hasn't turned up on any database anywhere. But there is something else you should know."

"Go on."

"Six months after he left the last foster home it burnt down. Everyone escaped apart the foster father who'd been strangled by his own belt."

"Did they get anyone?" Zack already knew the answer.

"No. But this is the real kicker, Zack. Alex was in the same year as Chloe and Liam at the high school, and from what I can understand Alex was Liam's best friend."

76

Miley's stomach squeezed tight as Alex stroked her hair while she lay on a large red sofa in the lounge. She must have fainted; she remembered him picking her up then waking up on the sofa. Or had she been drugged?

When Miley closed her eyes, she saw Liam's head bursting apart like a melon, as if it was a movie in her mind playing over and over. Alex sat on the edge of the coffee table, a glass of milk beside him as though she was still a child. She wished she still a kid now and could be wrapped in her daddy's arms and told everything was going to be okay.

"It wasn't a nice moment, but the world is full of things we would rather not happen. You know that Miley, don't you? You know about the horrible things that happen. It will be over soon. After tonight you won't have to worry about your past anymore, and your future will be filled with wonder."

"What wonders?" Miley steadied her breathing as he continued to stroke her hair. When she looked at his face she was confused by the adoration he seemed to show for her, it was like some of the boys in the computer class when she'd first swept her hair back and stopped hiding away. Not the lustful desire of those on the webcams, but a look of worship. Alex looked on her almost as a kind, decent man, yet only a short time ago he'd shot Liam right in front of her.

"Let's start with somewhere you have always wanted to go. I've been, and it's kind of cool." Alex produced an envelope from his pocket and handed it to Miley. She opened the flap, revealing tickets for flights from London to Florida early the next morning. One of the tickets was made out in the name of Susan Angel.

"That's not me."

"That's not a problem, Miley. You will be in the morning."

"But my passport, my clothes."

"We'll buy anything we want when we get there. As for a passport, something else that isn't a problem. No need to worry anymore, I'll take care of your every need. It'll be a holiday of a lifetime and the start of a great adventure." His hands cupped underneath her chin as he looked into her eyes. "I've changed my plans for you Miley, so we can do what you always dreamed of. You just being here makes me look at the world a different way. There were things I was going to do, other vengeances for what they did. If we're together there'll be no need anymore."

The fact he looked at her as her father would terrified Miley. His hands were smooth and it was hard to imagine them being the hands of a killer. Deep blue eyes looked at her with love, not hate, and a boyish twinkle hinted of mischief, not murder. Yet she knew the truth of what he was capable of.

"I want my dad."

"I will look after you now, my angel." He drew her to him, further wrapping his arms around her. "Now rest some more and eat something. I've things to prepare for tonight. When I'm back from the town they'll be so busy they'll not notice us slip away. It's what you asked for, Miley, and I will make your life special."

Miley went to speak again, but he hushed her lips with his finger before standing. She watched him disappear out of the room. If he expected her to go with him quietly, he was sorely mistaken. She was a copper's daughter, Detective Zack Carter's daughter.

Miley listened to the sound of movement as her captor went about his business upstairs. She could hear nothing of Chloe and wondered if she was okay. There was the sound of a shower. Or at least water running.

Miley darted to the door of the lounge and peered around the empty hall, seeing the door to the dining room was open. Miley went to the kitchen door. There was a strong smell of bleach, and on the ground, she saw's Liam's body.

Then she saw another figure lying close by.

Chloe.

She was still. Dead.

Stifling a cry, Miley hurried to the dining room and threw herself into the leather computer chair, pulling her knees up to her chest and hugging them. It was a few minutes before she could gather herself to look more closely at the screens. The rig was a set up beyond anything Miley had seen before, controlled by an elongated pad in front of her which she could run her finger over to scroll and control the pointer across the screens. The keyboard next to it was flat and thin, ready to roll up and be packed away at a moment's notice.

Most of the screens were showing various video images of Oakwell, as well as some that looked as though the camera was inside people's houses. There was the continuing flickering of charts and numbers on another which Miley assumed was some sort of monitor on the stock markets. The main screen had an editor open, and Miley recognised the programming language that she used in her machine learning projects.

"Having a little wander, are we?"

Miley jumped at Alex's voice. She turned, and he was right beside her. She could still hear the water running upstairs, but his hair didn't look wet. "Found anything interesting."

"Chloe's dead, isn't she?" Miley said.

"I hope not. I've still got use for her."

He stepped further into the room.

"You understand this." He pointed at the central screen.

"It's learning isn't it, your program. You are teaching it something."

Alex smiled. "How to weed out the corrupt and unworthy from the human race." His face seemed to show no anger and yet his calm words instilled made Miley tremble. "I can let you watch a while. But perhaps I need to be able to stop you from wandering." He stepped over to her and placed his hands in his pocket.

77

When Chloe opened her eyes, she felt like crying. Not from the pain in the side of her face where she had hit the floor but the sight of the semi-covered body of her once childhood friend lying beside her. She could see the side of his head that hadn't been blown away by the bullet. He looked so at peace from that angle. Chloe wondered if he'd known any peace since the night she tricked him.

Having tried squeezing her own hand out of the cuffs, Chloe spat on them like she'd seen in films. A lubricant to allow her hand to slip through so she could escape and have a happy ending. Another joke of Hollywood. She was stuck fast.

Her head throbbing, Chloe lay on the floor beside Liam feeling desperate for him, despite the fact his actions had brought her here. His prize for not going through with his revenge on her in the end? Lying on a kitchen floor with half his brain stuck to a black plastic sheet.

Searching the kitchen again Chloe tried to find some inspiration for an escape. Staying on the floor attached to a dead body was not an option. Miley was in the house somewhere, and tonight Chloe knew that her parents would be the target of Alex's wrath. Would Zack be there too? They needed a Hollywood hero and he'd be perfect, even though he would be more interested in whisking his daughter to safety rather than worry about some slut who'd spent her life using other people to get her own way.

Though a fat lot of good that had done her.

No, if she wanted a way out of this mess Chloe had to come up with it herself. There was the thought of trying to seduce Alex, promising him all manner of sexual delights if he'd let them go, but Chloe thought that was more likely to get her killed. And he seemed more interested in Miley.

She sat up, feeling the weight on her wrist where the handcuff was restrained by Liam's arm, and stretched to see the kitchen tops. There was a bottle of washing up liquid beside the sink. Maybe that would be the lubrication she needed. Positioning herself the best she could, Chloe reached for it but it was too far away.

"Work with me on this Liam." Chloe managed to spin round and rise to her feet getting both hands on Liam's arm before pulling. At first her feet slipped, but soon could get enough purchase to drag the big man across the floor inch by inch, using the black plastic as a makeshift sledge. After a final yank, Chloe stretched out to grab the bottle of green washing up liquid.

She squirted it on her wrist and arm until it was green and slippery, before trying to squeeze her hand through again. Trying every conceivable position there was so much liquid it was pooling on the floor, but it was all in vain.

Chloe collapsed onto her haunches, taking a moment to feel sorry for herself.

"No fucking way Chloe, he's not going to get the better of you." She jumped up and began kicking out at Liam's body with her bare feet. It might only have been causing pain to herself, but for a few minutes it felt good. After all, he'd brought her here. She might have felt guilty about the past, but the idiot had brought her to this fucking place.

When her anger was spent, Chloe paused to catch her breath and await further inspiration. There was a set of knives nestled in a large wooden block on the other side of the sink. She'd seen them before but knew they'd be no good against the handcuffs. It was something from the movies that gave her an idea.

"Not that desperate," Chloe said out loud, glancing down at her wrist. Then she looked at Liam's arm.

It needed another exhausting pull on Liam's body to get Chloe in reach of the knife block. Most of them were too small, but there was one she thought would do the job with enough weight behind it. Taking the knife in her free hand she squatted beside Liam, already feeling sick.

"Just like chopping a leg of lamb," Chloe said, to convince herself.

Laying her arm carefully down onto the floor, Chloe hefted the knife.

78

"Christ Zack, anything we find in there now will be inadmissible." DCI Sterling held his head in his hands, and Zack knew his boss was close to losing it.

"I know Sir, Liam isn't our man, but I think he can lead us to who's behind this." Zack had risked going back to the incident room, a place he was supposed to stay clear of. The DI from the neighbouring force was already there reviewing the evidence with Nadine, who was at least still on the case. Rashid had pulled Zack and Adam away from the other DI as soon as they'd entered the room.

"Did you find anything?" The DCI looked at Adam who shook his head.

"He's locked his stuff down good," Adam said. I think it's rigged so after several failed attempts the drives will be wiped. I've got the drives here with the right people; we should be able to extract some data."

"Can we get computer forensics team on it?" Zack asked unperturbed.

The DCI threw his hands up in the air. "And this is why detectives personally involved in the case aren't be allowed to investigate. I said I'd keep you in the loop Zack and I meant it. This is going too far. He could sue us to hell and back for

288

this."

"And wouldn't you do the same if it was your daughter?" Zack stared down his boss. He liked Rashid, but he wasn't going to back down. The job wasn't worth it. "Liam's got the motive and the skills to be involved in this. We find Liam, we find Alex and we find Miley and Chloe."

"Except Chloe's mother has rung to say Chloe has messaged that she's gone away for a few days with Liam. Something about not being able to take the pressure of being in the spotlight."

"When was this Sir?" Zack couldn't quite believe it.

"Just a few minutes ago."

"Can we trace the location of the call? Can you authorise that Sir?"

"Give me a good reason why."

"Because this was the same trick pulled with her friend Jenny." Zack knew this was no coincidence. "And she still hasn't been seen.

"I'll get her mother to call her back, to give you reassurance, but her mother seemed convinced and didn't want any fuss. She was just angry Chloe had gone off on such a key day for her father."

"No fuss. He's got them Sir. I can't just sit by while my daughter is missing."

The DCI's voice softened as he placed a hand on Zack's shoulder. "I would be doing exactly what you are Zack, you know I would. But in my position, you'd be thinking the same. We'll find your daughter, but we need to bring to justice whoever is behind this. To do that we must play by the rules, I have to play by the rules to make sure the case we bring doesn't get thrown out of court."

Zack's shoulders slumped. He knew Rashid was right.

"For what it's worth, I think you're right."

"Tonight's going to be the end game," Nadine said as she walked over to them in the corner. The other DI was behind her. Zack thought he was wise to keep his distance, but he looked pissed at Zack's appearance and Zack knew his boss would probably catch some heat for this.

"Alex has been moving his pieces while we've all been running around like dummies," Nadine continued. "He's been planning this for a long time. Hell, we didn't even know anything was wrong until a week ago."

"That sort of calculated behaviour fits his profile." The DCI nodded in agreement. "That was some excellent work, Detective."

"You think Alex fits the bill?" Nadine asked.

"Like a glove, if you will forgive the cliché. I only wish we had a better description to go public with and hand to the uniforms tonight."

"The count is still going ahead?" Zack was surprised.

"We'll increase our presence, but yes, it is. While I concur with all your findings, there is just not enough of a credible threat to the count itself. A lot of supposition. Good supposition I'll grant you, but we need hard evidence. I've spoken with the Returning Officer and division, and they insist on the count going ahead. We'll increase our presence as a precaution and keep the response teams on high readiness. We've got a team of bomb dogs coming in to clear the building. There are still some who don't want to look beyond our dead homeless ex-teacher. We've got to put as much down to normal security precautions as possible."

"Can't they see this man is fucking serious?" Zack muttered, letting anger get the better of him.

The DCI didn't try to cover his irritation. "I would like to inform you, Detective Inspector, that it wouldn't be a good idea to go to the hall tonight, but I suppose this is another piece of advice that you won't follow."

"I'm due some holiday if you want me to take it now." Zack was ready to walk away.

"Why do I suspect during this vacation you may suddenly find yourself interested in politics?"

"Everyone needs a hobby."

"Listen, Zack, I can't keep you away from the hall tonight, so I won't even try. Detective Sergeant Morris."

"Sir." Nadine brought herself to attention.

"Stay with him tonight and stop him from generally messing up the investigation. Wherever he might end up."

"Be pleased to, Sir." Nadine put an arm around her partner's shoulders. "He'll be a good boy."

"Adam." The DCI turned his attention to the intern.

"Sir."

"You have my permission to expedite the forensics on any computer you need, if relevant to the case. I'll get you a car to Peterborough and warn them of you coming. It's already blown as admissible evidence, so let's just get what we can from it."

"On it." Adam turned on his heels and jogged out of the incident room.

"Nadine, you are the only one who can remember Alex on our team, so work with the photo guys to come up with something.

"If you see him, stay calm and make contact. If you see anything or hear anything, then let me know immediately.

You both got that?"

Nadine and Zack both nodded as the DCI patted them on the back. "And Zack, you can't be in here now. I'll need to brief your replacement." The DCI turned towards the new DI.

"Best we get suited up then, cowboy." Nadine put on the worst Southern Yankee drawl Zack had ever heard.

"I've got to find her, Nadine."

"I know. We'll stop this, Zack. We'll get them all back."

79

Chloe splashed water on her face, trying to wash the last of her vomit down the silver metal plug of the sink. She didn't care that the noise might bring Alex as her whole body still wretched from the sickening sounds of the kitchen knife hacking through gristle and bone. The cuffs were still on her wrist. Just not attached to the other hand which was now lying next to the rest of Liam's body.

While she felt awful for desecrating his body, she was relieved to be free.

There was a loud tap on the window.

Chloe jumped.

Another.

She glanced at the window, expecting to see Alex, only to see large drops of rain bouncing off the outside of the window.

"Get a hold of yourself, Chloe Evans." She took in some deep breaths to calm herself and considered her next action. Miley was somewhere in the house, and she needed to get her so they could both escape.

Stepping around the dismembered body of her former school colleague Chloe made her way into the hallway. Through the large windows she could see dark clouds had gathered overhead. It was almost strange to look out of the tall windows and not see the blue sky anymore. The closest door was opposite Chloe, so she stepped across the tiles keeping alert for any other movement before listening outside the door.

With the sound of the rain hammering down, Chloe couldn't hear noise in the room and decided to take a chance. Taking hold of the handle, she pushed the door inward, ready to spring back and make a run for the front door if she saw Alex. A chair in the room moved.

It was Miley.

Chloe glanced around, but couldn't see anyone else.

"Are you alone?" She whispered.

Miley nodded. "Yes. You look awful."

"It's not been a great day." Chloe entered the room. "We need to get out of here."

"Can you get me out of these?" Miley swung the chair around, revealing her hands restrained by cable ties.

"Give me a minute." Hurrying back through the hallway Chloe retrieved one of the other knives from the kitchen. She returned to Miley and set to work on the cable ties. The plastic was tough but it was not nearly as gruesome as when she had freed herself.

"Thanks. He caught me trying to snoop." Miley rubbed her wrists where there were angry red marks from the ties.

"Come on, we need to find a way out." Chloe went to take hold of her arm. "Did you find any phones?"

Miley shook her head and spun the chair back around towards control pad. "Everything is hooked up in here. I need to find a way to get a message out. He's going to destroy the town hall."

"Can you get on?" Chloe was working out their options as Miley brought the large screens to life with a browser.

"There's so much blocking software on here to stop him being tracked, I can't get out through the usual routes." Chloe saw Miley's attempt to get onto sites such as Facebook or Instagram met with failure.

"Then we can't tell anyone?"

"He's got his own messaging software. Custom stuff that feeds into these other sites. It's got a password lock to send the message. Probably using some encryption and routing to avoid being traced. It's similar to what Uncle Jake uses to talk to us."

"I've no idea what you are saying," Chloe said.

"Some people like to keep secrets."

"I get it." Chloe glanced at the door expecting Alex to burst through any moment. "Can you use it?"

"I can't break the encryption, but a little misdirection might be helpful." Miley's fingers tapped at the keys. "He'll be looking for a hack, but probably not for something piggybacking his own code."

"Shouldn't we just try and get out?" Chloe couldn't understand the screens Miley was working on. If it wasn't Word or PowerPoint, then Chloe was usually out of her depth on the computers at work. Something sprung up that looked like a crude chat window, at least there she could see snippets of conversations she could read. Others were incompressible jumbles of letters, numbers and symbols that seemed to mean something to Miley.

"We need to get word back somehow." Miley glanced over to Chloe.

Chloe realised they were a long way from other houses if they were just to run out into the road, and the chances were Alex would catch up with them before they could find any help. "No. Keep going. You're right it's our best shot."

"Do you know the address here?" Miley returned her focus to the keyboard.

Remembering it from when she came with Liam, Chloe reeled it off. It had only been the previous evening, but that seemed a long time ago now.

"Great, if I've got this right it just might work."

"What is it?" Chloe leant her shoulder.

"Just something any decent script jockey should be able to put together. I might get a message to Uncle Jake." Miley paused for a moment looking up at the screens. "If he's listening."

"Your Uncle Jake?"

"Ye, Dad's brother. Don't see him much because he's abroad all the time, doing stuff he says I don't want to know about. We've got special chat software to talk to him, so it can't be traced."

Chloe raised her eyebrows. The Carter family was something else.

The main screen showed the CCTV of the town hall, though it was blurring with the rain pouring down the lens of the camera. They could see people rushing in and out of the building, but none of the faces could be recognised. "Right, let's see if I can log in."

"You know his password?"

"No and I don't need to. I just need to make it look as though I've been trying. But I need him to log in to get my message out."

Chloe watched Miley bring up a password box. She hit a series of letters to log in.

The first attempt failed.

"How do you know all this?" Chloe saw her second attempt had failed.

"Had plenty of time to think about it while I've been sat staring at his screens."

Chloe thought she heard something upstairs.

"He could be coming." Chloe moved over to the dining room door and closed it. Still holding the knife, she strained to hear anything above the noise of the rain.

"I think he's on the stairs. Look like you are still tied up."

Miley nodded and pushing away from the desk she moved her hands behind her before twisting the chair, so they were out of sight of anyone entering the room.

Chloe knew she'd have one chance as he entered the room.

The door swung open.

She launched herself at Alex.

80

Zack had told Nadine that he needed to get back home, get a few hours' sleep and freshen up while she was working the case with the replacement DI. It wasn't a total lie, he needed down time, something which Nadine had been nagging him about, but he really wanted time to think. Having spent the night chasing loose ends he knew that wasn't the way the problem was going to be solved. Being afraid and thinking dumb thoughts wasn't going to help his baby girl.

To get her back, Zack was going to have to do what he did best and that was finding solutions among the data. He also wanted to talk to Jake. Talk through what he needed to do. Zack sent him everything he had on the case as soon as he got home. He just had to hope his brother wasn't in the middle of nowhere.

Shedding his clothes and turning the shower to cold, Zack let the rivulets of freezing water wash away the sweat caking his body. The shock of the freezing water forced Zack to suck up the air, feeling a surge of adrenaline. The cold water helped clear the grime from his body and wasteful thoughts from his head.

Towelling himself down, Zack pulled on some dark pants and a black T-shirt. From the bottom of his wardrobe, he dug out army-style boots. Not the most comfortable in this weather but he felt he needed something heavy duty.

By the time he was dressed, the coffee had brewed in the kitchen and Zack poured a mugful, strong and black. He slid himself into the chair at the kitchen table and flipped open his laptop to bring up the file on Angel that Nadine had sent him.

His phone beeped. Nadine telling him what time she'd be at the town hall, and that the explosive sniffer dogs weren't going to get there. Some foul up in the communications.

Alex was good, really good.

There was an email with only one word.

Online.

Zack felt a rush as he typed in a key combination that brought up a chat window his brother Jake had installed for them after he'd left the military and embarked on a new career where being off the grid was a great advantage. Zack had sent everything he had to his brother in the hope his long tendrils into the murky worlds Jake moved in might through up something. On entering the password another box opened.

JAKE: You found her?

ZACK: Not yet. Trying to figure it out.

JAKE: I got the files. Your conclusion?

There was no messing from Jake. Brevity and efficiency were traits he prided himself on. There was a problem and it needed fixing. That's all that mattered right now.

ZACK: The fire officer suspected the oven and taps had been turned on to release the gas before Gary Hudson had ignited it. But there was nothing about how he'd done it without being fried. It leads me to conclude a remote detonation of some sort.

JAKE: Agreed, Technology again.

ZACK: Yes, but there's nothing to tie it with Alex.

JAKE: Apart from we know he likes fire and was into his tech.

ZACK: Exactly.

JAKE: And Alex is?

ZACK: A loner. He stays behind the scenes mainly, behind the screens even. But something lures him out. He likes to get up close and personal.

JAKE: Military training?

ZACK: : He's had years to perfect himself as a killing machine. If we looked hard enough we'd find traces of him. Cold cases maybe, or wrongful convictions he's engineered.

But what he does best is manipulate people. Get them to do what he wants by foul means or fair. And that means his reach is long.

JAKE: He wants to rip the heart of the town because they ripped the heart of his life.

ZACK: Which means the election at the town hall.

JAKE: And how will he do it?

ZACK: Same as the hostel. Remote device which will lead to a fire. But he'll be there for this one. He'll want to feel the flames.

Zack brought up google maps and zoomed into the streets around the town hall.

ZACK: Plenty of buildings he could hide in.

JAKE: I could get a team to come over. It'll be tight but there are some people who owe me favours.

ZACK: If it's not you on the team bro, I don't trust them.

JAKE: If I could get there I would.

ZACK: I know that.

JAKE: Make sure you are carrying, Zack.

ZACK: Not wise for a copper in England.

JAKE: Do you really care about that?

ZACK: No.

JAKE: Then do it.

ZACK: OK.

JAKE: You got this brother. Find him and you'll get Miley back. I've got our techs on it. If they find anything we'll let you know.

ZACK: Thanks Jake.

JAKE: Go get her.

Zack slapped down the lid of the laptop and rose from his chair before walking through the door joining the kitchen to the garage. The car was pulled right up to the back of the garage, instead of its usual place on the drive. Squeezing past, Zack went to a large wardrobe covered in flaking paint resting against the back wall. It had been left by the previous owners, probably because it was too big to move and too ugly to want.

Pulling open the stiff wooden doors Zack took out the assortment of old jackets and bags of wires, until he revealed a chunky metal toolbox at the bottom. Placing it on the workbench beside the wardrobe he chose the smallest key from his bunch before using it to remove the padlock and prise open the top of the toolbox.

On the top tray, there were the usual tools and assortment of screws and nails anybody would've expected to find, but Zack ignored them, lifting the tray out to reveal what he was looking for. Two Glock 9mm pistols taped together, four magazines and half a dozen boxes of ammunition. Beneath them, a sturdy Bowie knife. Souvenirs Jake had brought from Iraq before they'd started to clamp down on what the returning squaddies had in their kit boxes. Zack had been mad about it when Jake had turned up at his house asking him to store them, but he was glad of them now.

Zack lifted out the pistols, a box of ammunition and the knife from the bottom of the cold metal box. Removing the tape, he returned one of the pistols before the toolbox was locked and placed back in the wardrobe.

Back on the workbench, Zack stripped the gun down, checking the mechanism and applying oil where it was needed before putting it back together.

After pushing open the garage door, Zack climbed into the car. Outside the rain had begun and already Zack could feel the air cooling.

There was going to be a massive storm tonight.

"I'm coming to get you, Miley."

81

Outside the door Alex had sensed something was amiss. The rain obscured any sounds, but he was convinced he'd heard voices. Glancing at the kitchen door it was still closed. Perhaps he should check on Chloe, but it was impossible for her to escape.

Pushing the door open he saw Miley in the chair. His eye was attracted to the login box displayed on the main screen showing attempts had been made to try and access some of his software.

A knife flashed towards his face. Raising his arm, Alex stepped forward, deflecting Chloe's wrist with his forearm. The blade sliced his skin before passing down his side. Fractions later, his right elbow connected with the side of her temple. Not at full force, Alex knew he didn't need that, but enough to stun the frantic woman.

Finally, he swept Chloe's standing leg, sending her crashing onto her backside. The knife clattered to the floor and Alex stepped forward flicking it away with his foot and sending it spinning across the carpet to Miley's chair.

For a moment, Alex thought Miley was going to make a lunge for the knife. He'd already seen her hands come around, showing she wasn't tied. Alex remained still and stared at her intently, waiting for her to make her move. Miley looked up at him, Alex could see the tension in her body, the indecision. She slumped back down.

Chloe came again, kicking up from the floor, targeting his groin. Alex twisted to his side, again letting her attack pass him by, before sinking to his knees and delivering a cruel blow to her throat with the side of his hand.

"You're a tigress, Chloe. No wonder you bested Gary so easily. But stay down and don't try my patience any longer."

He didn't expect a reply. Chloe was gasping for breath, holding her reddening throat. Alex saw the cuffs on her wrist, blood smeared around one of them and knew there was only one way she could've done that. She really was something.

Taking hold of her hair Alex dragged Chloe to her feet. "I've got work to do tonight. A meeting with your parents. Would you like to say any last words to them?"

Chloe tried to twist away, but he could see the cloudiness in her eyes from the blows she'd received.

Alex looked up at Miley. "You can come with me. As you both seem to be getting on so well, you can take care of each other."

Alex turned, leaving the room and forcing Chloe to scramble to her feet to follow him by grabbing her top. Her breathing was laboured and she probably wouldn't be able to speak for a while after the damage he'd inflicted.

When he reached the kitchen, Alex saw Liam's body across to the other side of the room, with his wrist severed. Chloe really was a resourceful girl. They reached the cellar door, which Alex opened by sliding back the big metal bolts. The smell, when the door opened, was horrific. While he'd wrapped the bodies of the houses' owners in thick plastic, no doubt the other corpses were a little worse for wear.

"Get in. You never know you might find a friend."

Alex didn't give Chloe much choice. Thrusting her through the door. Her cry came out as a hoarse croak as she tumbled along the narrow passage that led to the top of stone stairs. "You too." He indicated to Miley who'd followed them meekly from the dining room.

"I don't want to go in there." She started backing away.

"I know you don't my angel, but you can't be trusted yet and I need to go out for a while. So be a good girl and do as you are told." He added a degree of menace in his voice as he stepped towards her. She looked about to run so Alex grabbed her arm and pushed her after Chloe. He didn't want to be so rough, but she was proving troublesome. Perhaps he was going to have to tame her. Teach her properly how to act.

A few hours in the cellar would certainly help.

"I'll be back when it's over ladies. Think about your priorities. It could make the difference between living and dying."

Without waiting for a reply, Alex slammed the door shut and slid the bolts back across. He glanced at the clock in the kitchen.

It was nearly time now.

He needed to contact a few more people to confirm his escape route and safe house after it was over. There was also the house to prepare, wiping away the evidence he didn't want found. After tonight they'd know who he was, but he'd already have vanished. Until he wanted to be known again, he would once more be a ghost in their machines.

Before leaving the kitchen, Alex moved over to the gas pipes being fed into the house, confirming the device was armed.

82

There could be no denying it any more. Peter had wrestled with the knowledge of what one of his devices might have done for the last few days. But the silly woman in the awful brown hat had confirmed his suspicion. One of the devices had been used on the hostel.

And that was not what he'd agreed to.

The realisation hit in the chest as though someone had punched him. His struggled to regain his breath and was forced to grab a nearby table.

"Are you okay Peter, dear?" It was Mary Evans who enquired.

"Yes. Sorry, I think some of the wine just went down the wrong way."

"Well, you deserve to celebrate with the amount of money you've raised for us this week. Mrs Brown said. "It's amazing I just can't imagine how you've done it?"

Peter tightened his grip on the table. No, they had no idea how he'd escaped the financial trap the man had laid. They had no idea of the cost in innocent lives. Peter might not have been a fan of the wave of immigrants flooding Oakwell but he would never have sanctioned such a barbarous act. Where else was the man going to use the devices? What were his other targets.

"I'm so glad it looks like Thomas will be representing us in Parliament. He's an excellent man." It was a woman new to their little gathering who spoke. An elderly woman sporting a lot of jewellery who was supposed to descend from aristocracy if one looked back far enough in her family tree. At least that's what she told everyone.

"Too bad you didn't see that until a few days ago." Mrs Evans remarked. "Still it's always good to welcome the latecomers."

The silver haired woman gave Mrs Evans a frosty stare.

Peter wanted to get away from the group. The whole swell around Mr Evans had increased in the last few days because it was so clear he was going to be the winner. It made Peter sick. Okay, maybe he had the advantage of backing the winner from the beginning but that was because the Evan's family had always been strong supporters of the charity. Even if they may well be doing so because it looked good in the press.

So much of this world seemed corrupt.

He'd tried to find out if the other device had been used at Chloe Evan's house. Her mother seemed to think the man had started the explosion with a lighter. But she'd heard from Chloe that the homeless man had intended to go on and attack the school. So maybe one of the devices had been destroyed in the fire.

Which still left one.

Peter started to panic. If the stranger wanted to teach the town a lesson then there could be no better place to do it than here. There could be no better might to do it than tonight.

He looked round frantically as though expecting to see the device on a table or attached to the wall. That was stupid thinking. The devices were designed to be attached to gas pipes, to rupture the casing before igniting the gas. They wouldn't be up here; they would be in the building where the gas entered.

Without a word, he left the group and hurried across the floor towards one of the doors. When he'd first met the stranger, the man had been dressed as a caretaker suggesting he had full access to the town hall, and more importantly to any of the infrastructure he'd need to cause maximum damage.

Finding a set of stairs, he descended while trying to work out the best route to take. Peter knew he had to see if he was right. And if he was he had to warn people. Fuck what they would find out about him. He could not be a party to any more killing.

83

Z ack pulled up in a car park which gave him a good view of the town hall. The rain had eased a little, as darkness descended, but he could still sense the thick air was ready to unleash another deluge.

In the car, he had toyed with the idea of tucking the gun in the back of his trousers before scoping out some of the areas Alex was likely to be. In the end, he'd decided against it. Zack wasn't going to be using a gun where people gathered.

He messaged Nadine.

Going to check around the outside of the building.

Don't do anything stupid I'm on my way. The DCI is already pissed we're not together and DI Watson is calling you a loose cannon.

Fuck Watson let's just get this done.

Agreed. Be there soon.

After leaving his car, Zack spent a few minutes under the shelter of a tree in the park. He watched the people scurrying towards the main door and scanned the people to see if there was anything that would give Alex away. There was a strong police presence, and bags were being searched. The media were camped out in front in force, even though their vans had been ordered to park well back.

It was approaching ten o'clock and soon the polls would

close around the county, allowing the ballots to be brought and counted. The candidates would arrive, to wait for the result while enjoying a charity dinner organised for this special night.

Zack moved from under the tree, pulling his hood up as he skirted the road next to the town hall and looked towards the vantage points he had identified. Zack passed around the building, seeing nothing. He wished he had spotters at strategic positions looking for Alex.

It would've made sense for Zack to look around the inside of the hall. He was still suspicious about the bomb dogs being called off, but if that had been his work then it only confirmed Alex would be nearby.

"Anything?" Nadine said, as he approached her on the steps outside of the hall.

"Nothing. But he's around here somewhere." Zack was calm, focused. All the panic and emotion of the day had been pushed aside, allowing him to concentrate on what he needed to.

"They've all got the photofit image and control has extra people on the cameras. If he shows his face, we'll get him."

Zack nodded, eyes darting about the people in the crowd, looking for the nervous, the concerned. With the rain falling steadily most people were wearing jackets with their hoods up making it even harder.

"They swept inside too?"

"Yes, and they keep sweeping. We haven't found anything."

"Pity about the dogs," Zack said.

"Ye, some communication mess up." Nadine then looked at him. "Or do you think it was him?"

"Got to be." The phone in Zack's pocket started to ring. It was from a number he didn't recognise, from abroad.

"Hello."

"I've got something."

"Shit, this is an open line." Zack recognised his brother's voice. "Tell me."

"Nearly missed it. A message from Miley."

Zack could hear the excitement in his voice. The DCI was heading towards them from inside the doors. Nadine stepped forward to speak to him.

"Tell me," Zack said into his phone.

"A message came through saying the town hall is the target. And where she is Zack."

Zack's heart skipped a beat. "Where? How."

"Looks like she's got a message out by hacking onto chat software like ours. There's an address I'm sending you now."

"Thank you, Jake."

"No, thank your daughter. It's on, Zack."

Zack flicked off the call, switching to see the message which simply told them Alex was targeting the town hall and to tell her dad, Detective Inspector Zack Carter, the address they were at. It was her, and she was okay.

"Sir, you've got to clear the building." Zack stepped over to the DCI and Nadine. "We have a credible threat." He showed the message on his phone to the DCI.

"Miley."

"Looks like it." Zack nodded. "Sir-"

Rashid held up his hand for a moment as he whipped his radio out of the inside of his brown jacket pocket.

A shrill ringing filled the night.

"That's the fire alarm," Nadine said looking at the town hall in bewilderment.

"Get everybody out," the DCI screamed at the uniforms on

bag checking duty. He turned to Zack. "What's going on?"

"I have no idea. But boss, I'm going for her," Zack said. The alarm having been sounded, people were already leaving the building. There was nothing for him to do here.

"You should wait for back up," Rashid said. "I'll call an armed response to the address."

As he started passing that order down the radio, Zack snapped.

"It could be too late, and we'll need eyes on the ground to see what's going on."

"Zack, I understand but I can't authorise that. You must let the professionals handle it now. It's the best thing for Miley." His boss tried to keep a measured tone with him while listening in on the radio to the evacuation. The fire crews were on the way, but nobody inside could locate a fire.

"I'm a professional, Sir. It's what I do."

"Not anymore." The DCI shook his head. "Zack, you're in a different world now, you know that. Different rules." He placed an arm on Zack's shoulder.

Zack snatched his phone back as he did so.

"I'm going for my daughter. If it's against the rules, you'll have to arrest me."

Zack stepped back and spun round. The rain had increased as the tempo of people leaving the town hall grew. They only started hurrying once they got into the rain.

"Zack, stop." The DCI turned to Nadine.

"I know, Sir. Go with him and stop him doing anything stupid."

"Exactly," Rashid said.

Nadine jogged up to Zack's shoulder.

"He's right you know," she said.

"I've got to go."

"I know that too." Nadine pulled her fluorescent jacket tighter around her shoulders. "And it looks like I'm babysitting again."

There was a burst of lightning in the sky. Thunder cracked overhead, and the heavens opened once more.

The town hall exploded.

84

The fire alarm took Alex by surprise. There'd been no calls on the police band that one of the press liaison officers had been sharing on loudspeakers to the other journalists.

For Alex, it was the perfect place to hide.

It was easy to look like an aspiring journalist, eager to get to the front to get their own story, that no one looked too closely at his faked credentials or noted the paper he said he was from. Alex had been able to watch all the dignitaries climb the steps into the hall. Each one turning to smile and wave at the media. Chloe's father had the biggest smile. His victory was almost assured, if the polls were to be believed.

The moment the people started pouring out of the hall, Alex slipped his hand into his jacket pocket and pressed the large call button on the old-style phone. He counted down the ten seconds from the moment the gas pipe would have been punctured until the incendiary was released. Gas fuelled flames burst from any weak points in the old structure before dissipating in the cool night air. Even from this distance, he could hear the screams as skin seared in the heat blast.

The flash of lightning and crash of thunder had been unexpected but added a welcome dramatic touch. Alex knew the cameras would be rolling and probably streaming this live. Now they would know who he was and soon they would realise why he'd done this.

More lightning illuminated the scene, and Alex gave a satisfied grin at the number of casualties being dragged from the main hall. Flames and smoke burst from the main windows while the screaming became a backdrop to sirens. It would be another busy night for Oakwell's finest.

They would rebuild again. Alex knew that for certain. While there were many traits mankind had he found deplorable, Alex couldn't deny the power of the human spirit to fight back in the face of adversity. When he'd burnt down the Yeoman estate, little had Alex realised that he was clearing the way for much nicer homes, ridding the neighbourhood of undesirables so decent hardworking families had been able to move in.

The rain battered the scene, and Alex could already see it was helping dampen the fire. It didn't bother him, beyond the punishment to the town that had let Angel down, he wanted to send a message to the rest of the world. He wanted them to know that you couldn't treat people like shit and get away with it. He wanted them to remember Angel.

The fire crews rushed into the area in front of the town hall. Ambulances roared through the street, sirens piercing the night. Wafts of smoke would occasionally pass over the media tribe, some of whom had surged past the cordon to get better pictures.

He would've liked to have stayed and enjoyed the carnage a little more, but surrounded by chaos and confusion he knew it was time to slip away. It would take time for them to react and lock down the surrounding area. By the time that happened Alex wanted to be well on his way.

85

Everything happened at once.

Zack felt the wave of heat pass over him, lightning streaked across the sky, rain battered broken bodies flung from the front steps of the town hall. Darkness engulfed the scene after the flash until the flames sprouted from the town hall.

"Shit. Nadine, you hurt?" Zack shouted. Nadine was picking herself off the floor beside him.

"I'm good. Did everyone get out?"

"I don't know." Zack looked over at the mayhem surrounding the town hall, seeing the bodies on the floor. "My car will be good. I've got to go, he'll be on the way."

He saw Nadine look to where the DCI had been. Rashid was staggering to his feet, blood dripping down the side of his face and he looked at the two detectives.

"Go and get her."

Nothing more was said as Zack and Nadine slipped through the crowd until they reached his car. Screams and panicked cries sounded all round them, the air thick with acrid smoke and hot ash billowing from the building. Some people were still running from the front of the town hall, while others were hurrying between the houses to see what had happened. Many stared in bewilderment at the unfolding scene.

The rain was almost painful, like stinging slaps to the face as Zack reached his car and slid into the driver's seat. Despite his coat, he was soaked through.

"Can you find this place?" Zack tossed his phone to Nadine who wiped the screen and looked at the message as she slammed her door shut.

Nadine nodded. "I know it. Head south towards Melton, it will get you on the right path."

Zack fired up the engine before screeching into the road, honking his horn to get people out of the way and driving down a side road after he was forced to mount the pavement to let a fire truck through. After narrowly avoiding a couple and their dog, who were too busy watching the flames, Zack found his way on the main road out of town.

"Shit, this is bad," Nadine said. Zack could see she was gripping her seat tightly. Her face was white with shock.

"One hell of a psycho. I just hope he was nearby. Might give us a chance to get the girls out."

Nadine nodded. "You think it was early."

"Got to be. He knew the alarm had been raised and the people were coming out. Something didn't go to plan. Maybe someone spotted the device and hit the alarm. Whatever happened, it's not our problem now. We have to focus on getting to the house before he gets back."

"We'll get there." Nadine's voice had little conviction. "But we need back up."

Their progress was agonisingly slow as they passed through the outskirts of Oakwell. The torrential rain forced Zack to be careful. Eventually, they broke out of the town and made better progress along the country roads. Zack was playing the odds now. He knew Alex might have moved Miley nearby so he could escape quickly. Or he might have managed it all remotely from the house, watching it live on the news channels.

"We're nearly there." Nadine was almost too late with the instructions as she peered through the rain swamped windscreen. "There's a long driveway through the trees to the house." Zack braked sharply, and the car juddered to a halt before he backed up until they were at the entrance of the drive. He pulled into the mouth of the drive, blocking it. From where they were he couldn't see the house.

"A damn good place," Zack muttered. "I need to take a look."

"It's the old headmaster's house," Nadine said.

"What?"

"Oakwell High School. The old headmaster who was there when Gary Hudson and Chloe were there."

"You thinking it was him?" Zack wiped the front of the windscreen which was steaming up now they had stopped.

"He's got to be at least sixty."

"Did he live alone?"

Nadine shook her head. "I think his wife was a teacher too."

"I'm going for a look."

"The backup is on its way, Zack." Nadine held up her phone to show the message. "Boss reckons ten minutes."

"I know." Zack undid his seatbelt, before turning to look at Nadine. "I'm going to get closer to see if there is anybody there. I'll message back what I find so you can pass it on. If he's not here, then I might have a chance to get them."

"I'll come with you."

"No. Wait for the backup."

"You need to wait for the backup."

"I have my own." Zack reached across Nadine and, opening

the glove box, he pulled out the gun, knife and two spare magazines.

"Shit, Zack, where did you get those?"

"Sometimes a few souvenirs found their way back from active tours."

"You can't have that. If people found out."

"I'd be in big trouble. Right now, I'm glad I have it, and I want you to stay in the car. The more intelligence we get for the response unit, the quicker we can get them out of there. I know what I'm doing. Trust me. I've been in a shooting war before."

Nadine nodded as Zack switched his phone to vibrate and checked the setting to give him a mini torch beam. There was a flashlight somewhere in the boot, but he didn't want to waste time hunting for it. "Message me as soon as they're near, and I'll relay back what I see." Opening the door, Zack climbed out into the rain.

Nadine reached across and put her hand on his arm.

"Be careful."

86

Zack lifted his jacket hood to keep the rain out of his eyes. There was a gravel track winding through the small copse of trees, and he was thankful the rain masked any sound of his approach. Lightning and a crack of thunder startled him halfway along the track, but the flash of bright light gave him the chance to picture route towards the house.

Zack could visualise Alex at one of the windows waiting to see if there was a figure making its way towards the house, or waiting to see if a streak of lightning would show him an approaching intruder.

Stepping on the side of the track, Zack edged his way down the rest of the drive as quickly as the awkward movement allowed him. The occasional thick clumps of grass threatened to trip him but he knew he had to stay hidden, stay careful. Miley's life depended on it.

The closer he moved to the house, the faster his heart was beating, forcing him to use techniques he hadn't practised for years to calm himself. With each step, his body remembered his training and Zack stayed close to the shadows of the trees allowing his eyes to adjust to the darkness. A good pair of night vision goggles would've been handy. Pity Jake hadn't thought to bring some of them back with him.

The house loomed out of the darkness. He squatted for a minute to examine the scene. There were no lights, no sign of glowing devices that might give him a clue to people being inside. Zack considered the best way to approach. The drive was all gravel right up to the house and there were probably security lights. Thunder growled across the sky as the rain beat down even harder. Zack shivered, his jacket and T-shirt were soaked through. But he had to shrug that off and focus on the task at hand.

There was a long stone building with a low roof off to the left of the house. It looked like a set of old stables, but the doors showed it had been converted into garages. Zack counted enough for four large cars. For a moment, he contemplated risking using his phone to get a google earth view of the house.

"Too late now sunshine," he whispered to himself before darting from the edge of the drive to the cover of the low buildings after another flash. He pulled out his phone, knowing he was sheltered from view, and messaged Nadine.

All dark. Can't see anybody. Two cars in drive. One a taxi.

The missing one?

Can't see plate.

Where are you?

Near the garages. Taking closer look.

Don't go any further.

Be in touch.

He needed to get closer. Miley was in there, he knew it, he could feel it, and he didn't trust anyone else to get her out. Especially not a response team, no doubt full of rookies who'd never seen any action. He knew their training, he knew they would be good at their job. But they weren't as good as he was.

Zack ran down the side of the garages towards the two cars and, at the last moment, darted between them so he was only a few metres from the front door.

Taking a deep breath, he sprinted across the gravel until he was right next to the large wooden door. There was still no reaction from the house. He strained to hear anything above the rain.

Nothing.

He reached for his phone again.

Going in.

Without waiting for the reply, Zack replaced the phone in his hand with his gun.

He pressed down on the black metal handle of the door. While it was bound to be locked, it would be stupid not to try.

He pushed the door.

It was locked.

Pulling the Bowie knife from his boot, Zack went to work with the tough steel blade.

In a few moments, he was in.

87

Darkness and the rain were agents Alex used to cloak himself. The elements were not to be feared but embraced. Something his instructors had drilled into him at various training camps around the world. He'd gone to them a soft, white, western boy and been close to leaving on so many occasions, unable to take the taunting or the punishments. Then he would picture Angel. Remember the pain she must have gone through in the end. He'd recall his parents' dead bodies after the bastards had cut their throats and how the town had cast him off to foster carers. Memories had fuelled him through the gruelling training routines, and this, in turn, had transformed him into the lean muscled individual he was now.

He retrieved a black jacket from the car, pulling the hood up, not as protection from the rain, but as cloaking that combined with the rest of the black clothing he wore. Where his face would have been exposed it was covered by night vision goggles; he adjusted them to give him the best view of the forest.

In one training camp, in the jungles of Columbia, they'd spoken of using all your other senses to compensate for darkness. Then he could become one with his surroundings. But Alex didn't have time to spend years mastering those arts, and why bother when he could make up for it with technology. His goggles also sported infrared capability. US military grade kit you couldn't buy in the shops.

Alex made his way through the trees with only a few bumps and scrapes. His car was round the other side of the woods from the main driveway, towards which he was now skirting.

"Hello, who are you?" It was the heat signature of the engine that showed up first before he realised there was a person sitting inside the car. He suspected hero boy Zack would've gone after his daughter and it was probably the woman detective. Alex had no quarrel with her as she'd shown him compassion when Angel had gone missing, the only copper to take what he said seriously. At the same time, Alex couldn't leave anybody to sneak up on him when he least needed it. She would need to be taken out of the game.

Nadine was in the passenger seat on the side of the woods he was in. It meant he didn't have to try and edge around the car to get close. Alex removed the goggles and waited a moment for his eyes to adjust. Crouched behind one of the thicker tree trunks he could see she had her phone on by the faint glow it was giving off.

Alex took in some sharp, rapid breaths to oxygenate his blood while flexing his fists to feel the wet leather squeezing in his hands. He rose and stepped out from behind the trunk.

With his plan thought up on the spot, as many plans were, there was always a chance things could go wrong as all the angles couldn't be covered. What Alex hadn't considered was lightning spearing across the sky the moment he moved away from the trunk. Nadine looked up, and he saw the look on her face as she spotted him.

He broke into a sprint.

Alex's right fist exploded through the glass of the passenger window, clearing a path for his left arm to pass through to where Nadine's head should have been. Only she'd reacted by throwing herself backwards out of his reach.

His left fist hit nothing.

Yanking at the handle, Alex pulled the door open to stretch towards her, as she manoeuvred herself into the driver's seat. A high-pitched noise filled the inside of the car with a painful screeching. A rape alarm. The sudden sound assaulting his ears made him pause long enough for Nadine to thrust her heeled foot towards his head. Alex swayed aside. It struck his shoulder.

"Alex stop," she cried out, reaching back with her hand to let herself out of the car. He grabbed her leg to pull her back, but the rape alarm also functioned as pepper spray. Alex twisted away, avoiding a full blast in the face but still felt a stinging sensation engulf his eyes, and as he tried to clear it he was forced to let go of Nadine.

The car door opened. The sound of Nadine scrambling away. Alex pushed himself into the driver's seat, not wanting her to get a head start while his vision cleared. He tumbled out of the driver's door onto the wet gravel. Rain swept across his face, offering some relief as he rolled onto his heels, realising he was vulnerable to attack.

Alex leapt to his feet, his eyes clearing enough to see Nadine running into the trees. She might have gotten away with it too, had it not been for the glow of her phone she was fumbling with as she ran.

Alex reached behind his back to release his gun from the belt holster under his jacket. He would get two shots before she was out of range.

88

As Zack entered the house, he heard the distinct shriek of a rape alarm. Nadine? He hoped the backup would help his partner but if it was Alex attacking her, then maybe the house was clear. Miley had to be his priority now, however guilty he felt.

Zack pointed the gun around all four corners of the entrance hall before covering the stairs. For a few moments, he stood in the centre of the hall. Alert. Listening, vulnerable.

The shots made him start and spin towards the front door even though he knew they were in the distance. Then there was the sound of muffled shouting. Girls voices.

Miley.

Zack pulled his phone from his jacket with his left hand and switched on the torch beam. There were two doors as well as the stairs. The beam of light followed the bannister up, ready to catch any movement. Not that he was expecting to see Alex now. The gunshots had told Zack where he was. They also told Zack he didn't have much time.

"Miley, Chloe. Can you hear me?" he shouted, before waiting to see if he could make out their location above the sound of the rain. He heard them again. It was coming from the door on the opposite side of the hall. Thunder crashed overhead as Zack raced across the tiled floor and smashed the door open with enough force to hit anybody trying to hide behind. While he didn't think Alex was here, Zack wasn't going to take any chances.

All four corners again. A rapid sweep followed by a slower one to ensure the room was clear. Something on the floor attracted his attention and Zack shone the torch onto the body of Liam. There wasn't much left of his face and a hand was missing. Zack swallowed at the thought of what the hell could have gone on in the house.

"Miley, Chloe?"

"We're in here." Zack's heart lifted with joy at the unmistakable sound of his daughter. "In the cellar."

Casting the torch in the direction of her voice he spotted another door with large bolts drawn across. He sprang over to the door before slamming the bolts back and pulling it open to reveal grateful faces.

"Are you okay?" He scanned Miley's body for injuries as she threw herself at him, wrapping her hands around his neck.

"I'm sorry dad," she whimpered. "I shouldn't have lied to you, I shouldn't have gone to the party."

"Slow down, honey. It's okay," Zack gave her a good squeeze feeling breathless with joy at having her in his arms again. "But I suppose it's not the right time for me to say I told you so."

"For getting us out of there, I think you've earned the right." Chloe emerged from the cellar. Her voice was hoarse and shining the light on her face Zack saw her throat was badly bruised. She looked around. "Where is he?"

"Close by," Zack disengaged from his daughter suddenly very aware of the gun he was holding. He slipped it back into the back of his trousers. "Backup is on the way, but I've heard shots. We've got to get out of here fast and careful. There's a backdoor." He flashed his phone to the door at the other end of the kitchen. "We'll try that."

"It'll be locked." Miley let go of his neck. "Everything is locked."

"Not everything to me." Zack produced his bowie knife again. "Come on."

A loud popping sound dominated the room.

Zack winced at first, as if it was a gunshot and then paused to listen as he heard the unmistakable sound of hissing from somewhere within the kitchen. There was a strong smell of burnt eggs which almost made him choke before he detected the gas. His mind flashed back to the recent fires.

"Shit, get back in the cellar." He grabbed the two women.

"What? No." Ignoring Miley's protest, Zack shoved her roughly back through the cellar door. Chloe had been behind her with no chance to get out of the way before Miley bundled into her.

"Get as far as you can."

To his relief, the girls reacted quickly and he saw them descending the stairs. Zack had only just reached the top of the stone stairs when the kitchen exploded.

89

Alex reattached the night vision goggles, adjusting them until all the sensors were focused. There was a human-sized heat signature on the ground where he was sure Nadine had fallen. He waited to see if she was going to move, sure that he'd hit her, but police sirens began nearby and Alex could tell they were getting louder. This place was going to get very busy very quickly.

Turning his attention to the house, Alex jogged a few yards down the drive so the dark outline was visible. He couldn't see anyone outside the house itself, and the goggles wouldn't show anybody inside those thick walls.

His time in Oakwell had come to an end. It was a pity there wasn't a chance to finish it off neatly. It was painful he wouldn't be able to take Miley with him as there was no time for sentiment now. He was convinced obsessing about her had already slowed his thinking and perhaps it was best to allow many years of planning to unfold without being distracted by memories of better times. If they were still in the cellar Alex knew the girls would survive the blast. They would find what he'd left there for the police.

Inside his jacket pocket was the final old phone. Rain bounced off the grey surface as Alex checked the signal strength and his finger hovered over the green call button.

"Goodbye, again, Angel. I'm sorry we couldn't be together again."

He dialled the pre-set number and Alex heard the connection. There was a click before he rang off, pocketing the phone again until he'd trash it in some random bin before the night was out. Even if the police found it, there'd be nothing which would help them trace him.

He glanced round to where Nadine's body lay. Still prone and no threat.

Alex moved back into the trees, silently counting in his head, and when the count reached ten he heard the explosion and sadness descended over his heart. The mission had gone well. The town would learn the lessons of what happens when you turn the other cheek and let evil fester in your midst. Maybe this time they wouldn't let the cancerous thinking, which had allowed Angel to be abused and murdered, grow back.

People like Chloe and Elliot's father shouldn't be allowed to hold the reins of power, taking dirty money for their campaigns and manipulating others for their own ends.

He'd sent a message and put himself on the map. The establishment knew what he was capable of.

This was just the beginning.

90

The force of the blast propelled Zack down the hard-stone stairs. He heard Miley squeal and tried to reach out to her but only floundered against the solid walls as he tumbled to the bottom where the two girls lay.

"Are you hurt?" He tried to push himself to his feet. Dazed by the hits to his head on the steps.,"Okay, I think." Miley said.

"Chloe?" Zack asked. He grimaced at the pain ripping through his ribs, as he struggled for breath. His body was screaming it'd taken too many knocks and needed to stop and he felt an ominous pain in his knee.

"Nothing bad," Chloe croaked. "What happened?"

"Gas explosion." Zack got himself into a sitting position, retrieving his phone. Its screen was cracked, but he managed to at least get the light to come on. "Stay here, I need to see if we can get out."

"Dad, I don't want to stay down here."

"It will be safest."

"There are bodies down here, Zack." Chloe was getting to her feet.

"What do you mean?" Zack shone his torch down at his feet and realised there were at least three bodies. Two were wrapped head to foot in black plastic, while the third just had some plastic thrown over it. "Shit. Get onto the bottom step, but don't come any further until I say."

Zack tried to climb to his feet but his knee threatened to give way forcing him to lean against the walls for support. Taking deep breaths, he pushed off with his good leg, gaining a few steps before having to use his bad knee again and this time it failed. Already he could feel the brutal heat from the flames and black, choking smoke that was belching out of the kitchen. There was no way through the house. He stabbed at his phone.

"Ah, shit," Zack said.

"What's wrong?" Miley said.

"Damn phone's smashed up. Can't get a call out."

"What will we do?" Zack could hear the panic in his daughter's voice. He was struggling to keep a grip on things himself. "Won't we burn down here?"

"Not if we stay back. There's nothing for it to burn on the stairs." Zack used his light to confirm the stairs and walls were stone. "The smoke could be a problem, though." Zack coughed again, as another plume of smoke was pushed down towards them by the sheer force of the heat. "What else is there down here? Does it go any further back?"

"There are a few rooms I think," Chloe said. " I tried to see when we were trapped here. But I didn't want to go far in the dark. I didn't know if there would be any other bodies."

"We've got light now, and we need to need to see if there is another way out. But I've got a problem."

"Your leg?" Chloe said.

Zack nodded. "I'm going to need help."

"We'll help you, Dad" Zack felt Miley's hands cling to his jacket.

"Can you stand?" Chloe said

He pushed himself up onto his feet, gingerly testing the bad leg. "Just."

"C'mon, we can help you," Chloe wrapped her arm around him. "Miley, can you get the other side?" Zack sensed his daughter to the right of him and couldn't help but give her a squeeze as he felt pride at how brave she was being.

"Come on. We'll do this together." Chloe coughed, her voice breaking.

Passing through the small room, they almost tripped over one of the large bodies. Zack shone the light on the swollen face.

"The taxi driver," Miley said. "He put something over my mouth and the next thing I knew I was here. I should never have gone to that party, Dad. I've been such an idiot. I've done such stupid things." She buried her face in his jacket, sobbing.

Zack stopped and held her for a minute. "It's okay, baby. Let's just make sure we survive this first." He'd already forgiven her. Zack just wanted them to get out alive, so they could start over.

Making their way through to another large room, Zack could see it contained tables and chairs, all worn, and badly stacked against one wall. Opposite was a single table and desk containing boxes of paper. Above the desk, hundreds of newspaper clippings and pictures clung to the wall. As he scanned them with his torch, Zack knew they weren't there by accident.

He then swung the light round to the other side of the wall.

"Oh, Jesus." Zack felt Chloe almost give way as his gaze fell upon the naked body lying on the mattress.

"Jenny?"

"Yes."

"She's dead." Jenny almost looked peaceful but Zack could tell from the angle of her neck.

"Let's keep on going," Chloe urged, coughing as more smoke made its way down to them. The next room was some sort of old musty store with racks upon racks of wine. Zack cast his phone around for another way out.

There wasn't any.

Zack slipped to the floor as exhaustion engulfed him. "Dead end."

91

Chloe felt cheated.

Each time there was a glimmer of hope something happened to dash it. Tears sprang to her eyes that she wiped furiously away before anyone noticed.

"Not quite trapped yet," Zack said. "Look up there."

From where Zack was sitting on the floor he was scanning the roof with the light from his phone.

"A trapdoor. I bet it goes into the garages. Let's hope it still opens."

Chloe couldn't see anything to get them up to the trapdoor. "The wine racks," Zack said as if he was reading her mind. If we can drag them over then we can stand on them."

He started to climb to his feet but collapsed.

"Hold the light for us," Chloe said. "Miley, can you help?"

The girl nodded and moved over, helping drag some of the crates across. Whenever the light flashed onto Miley's face she saw a grim resolution to find a way out of there.

"I hope they weren't expensive," Zack said, as wine bottles fell out of the racks and smashed on the floor. "And watch your feet." He shone the light down on Chloe's bare legs and feet. "You better stand back."

Stepping away from the crates, Chloe trod around the broken glass and stood on one the bottom crates.

She coughed. The smoke was starting to enter the room and her already sore throat was throbbing with intense pain.

"Zack shut the door and see if you can block any gaps." Zack shrugged out of his jacket and pushed the door closed, using his coat to block as much of the gap under the door as he could. With smoke still coming through Chloe saw him peel off his T-shirt and cover as much as he could until only a few wisps could squeeze through into the room.

"I can hear something," Miley said. "Sirens."

"Backup, I hope," Zack said. "Chloe, can you reach the trapdoor now?"

Chloe stepped onto the highest crate, being careful not to tip it over before pushing hard on the trap door. It seemed to give a little but she couldn't open it.

"Help me up there." Pushing himself up on one leg Zack hopped over to the crates and handed Chloe the light. Miley stepped over to help her dad scramble onto the crates until Chloe could move down. Grabbing another crate, Zack used it so he could lie on his back and push up with his arms. Chloe watched him give a mighty shove which saw no movement. As he adjusted his position to try again Chloe couldn't help noticing his lean build as muscles rippled in the light. Zack tensed and drove his body upwards. For a moment, the trap door seemed to open before it came to a stop.

"Fuck, there must be a car parked overhead or something."

With the sirens close above them in the courtyard Zack gave another massive heave, but it only moved as before. Then he stopped with a fit of coughing. Chloe saw the smoke was gathering at the ceiling. Looking back at the door it was coming around the edges even thicker now, and there was no way they were going to be able to stop it.

She heard another grunt from Zack and swung the phone back around to see he was trying again.

"Fuck it," Zack cried, before another spasm of coughing. He rolled off the top crate onto the ones below, clearly in a lot of pain.

"We need to get their attention," Chloe said. "I'll try and bang on the door." Chloe pulled a long chunk of wood from one of the collapsed crates and clambered back on the makeshift tower before hammering on the trap door with all the strength she could muster.

"Hey, Miles," Zack said after a brief pause. "Have you still got a monster scream in you?"

"I'll try, Daddy."

Despite having heard her scream in the kitchen earlier Chloe wasn't quite ready for the shriek which filled the room when Miley let loose. But after two ear-splitting screams, Miley was reduced to a sickly cough. Zack pulled her lower like Chloe had seen them do on the television to get below the smoke. What she would give for a handy window to climb out of like there'd been in her father's campaign office.

She battered on the door again, but her strength was fading and she slipped off the top crate, landing heavily next to Zack. The light was shining towards the ceiling illuminating the deadly smoke gathering above them.

Chloe thought she heard voices. Was there was a light? People beckoned to her. Called her to the light.

The smoke engulfed her.

And then nothing.

92

L ight drizzle descended from the sombre grey clouds that swept across the cemetery, as the dark teak coffin was lowered into to the grave. Zack stood watching in his worn black suit as the woman he'd partnered since moving to the town was laid to rest.

He'd been taken to the hospital along with Miley and Chloe after they were hauled out of the cellars by the fire crews. Miley's piercing scream had alerted them and the cars blocking the trapdoor had been manhandled out of the way.

So, concerned had Zack been to know Miley was safe, he hadn't given a moment for Nadine. But when DCI Sterling had stood in his hospital room, pressing his hands together the noise of the two gunshots came back to Zack. Two bullets had burst through her chest and killed Nadine instantly.

The colleagues surrounding him at the funeral were as much in shock at the recent events as grieving over a lost comrade. Over a dozen had died at the town hall, with scores injured in the explosion that had ripped the heart out of the town. These were the type of events they expected to hear about on the news, not in their sleepy, friendly town.

Zack felt a tightening of an arm around his waist as Miley, her face peering from out of the hood of a blue jacket, snuggled in closer.

"You good?" he said.

She didn't look at him. Just nodded. "I liked Nadine."

On his other side, he felt Chloe brush his injured side as she held a black umbrella over all three of them. She'd been there for his daughter over the past few days, as it had taken much longer for him to recover. Though he knew Miley had also been a great comfort to her. Chloe's parents had only just made it out of the town hall and were still in the hospital. Her father had spoken to the media from his hospital bed to pay tribute to two of the candidates, including Elliot's father, who'd lost their lives. There'd be another vote soon, and the town had no doubt who the winner would be.

With the vicar's final words, the crowd began to break up, most heading to the hotel for the wake. Across the grave, Zack saw Nadine's husband staring blankly at the sodden earth being piled on the top of the coffin. Rain dribbled down his unprotected head, mingling with tears, while he held the hands of his two children for whom there could be no consolation. For a moment, he caught Zack's eye and there was the nod of acknowledgement between those who knew what such a loss felt like. Zack could remember holding Miley's hand the same way and trying to explain to her why terrible things happened to such wonderful people.

He couldn't hold the gaze. Zack had heard the rape alarm and heard the shots. He'd known Nadine was in danger while he went for his daughter. No-one begrudged him and Zack didn't regret his decision, but neither would he forget the look on the two boys' faces as they saw their mummy lowered into the earth. He'd left his partner on her own and then not gone to help when he knew she was in trouble.

As they turned to walk down the uneven path between the

gravestones, Chloe slipped her arm around Zack's. He knew it was as much to steady him as herself. After the tumble down the stone stairs, his leg was taking its time to heal. At the iron gate leading to the main car park, Detective Chief Inspector Sterling was shaking hands, with extra words for the colleagues who were closest to Nadine.

"How are you all coping?" Zack had not seen the DCI since coming out of hospital. There'd been a debrief, but it had been conducted by the Independent Police Complaints Commission. The biggest manhunt for many years was now on and Zack was no longer part of it. His actions would be scrutinised for any wrong doing and he knew they'd find plenty of that.

"Getting there, Sir."

The DCI looked at Chloe. "I hear your father is on the mend."

"He and mother will be back home soon."

Rashid gave Miley a smile before turning his earnest gaze back to Zack, who looked at him expectantly.

"We haven't a clue, Zack. They've combed the area again and again, and there's nothing. We've got his description all over the country, all over Europe and there's not been a single plausible sighting. The guy's a ghost." The DCI bowed his head, as if in acknowledgement of the failure. It wasn't a surprise to Zack.

"Because he planned his escape as well as he planned everything else," Zack said. "He was able to be a ghost for years before all this. Alex knows how to stay off the grid."

"You're right." Rashid paused looking back at him. "I think they're going to want to interview you again. Everyone is involved now. You know I might not be able to protect you as well as I want to."

"I get it, boss." Zack nodded. He knew things were bound to come out in the internal investigation. They'd pour over the actions of all the officers involved and that would show up the times when Zack had acted outside the spirit of the rules. And no doubt in some report it would be written up that Zack was found with a gun.

"I think you should take your vacation time, Zack. Just get yourself away from here. Take your daughter to Disneyland." Rashid tried another weak smile at Miley.

Zack felt his daughter burrow deeper into his side.

"I don't want to go there anymore."

93

" It should be on its way to your email now, Zack. You know, the other account." Zack had taken Adam's call while sitting by the pool of the villa they'd rented for the week. Miley might not have wanted to go to Florida anymore, but they'd both wanted to get away and a plush villa on the Spanish coast was proving a big hit. It's huge private pool and easy access to the beach was courtesy of his brothers' generosity. Jake was sitting at the other end of the pool talking to Miley and Chloe.

It was good to see his daughter smiling after what she'd been through, and it seemed to help that Chloe was with them. They'd become like sisters, and while a little jealous of his own lack of attention, Zack was relieved to see there were no ill-effects.

He didn't know when they'd next be able to afford a holiday. There wasn't going to be a job for him to go back to. While the fact he'd had a gun with him was being kept quiet in most quarters, he'd been advised to resign without a fuss. Zack saw the sense in that.

"Thanks Adam, I appreciate it." Zack walked inside to the spacious lounge and flipped open his laptop. Logging into a new Gmail account he'd set up just for this.

"You think you can find anything?" Adam said.

"I don't know. I guess I just wanted to look at this stuff." Zack downloaded the file attached to the email. "I think the son of a bitch left it deliberately."

"I don't doubt it," Adam said. "The guy's a genius the way he's put things together. I've got friendly with one of the techs drafted in to enhance the forensics on all the computer gear, and he says they've seen nothing like it. Layers upon layer of disguise and some gigs were farmed out to other people, like Liam, to carry out. Just a pity we didn't get Alex's rig from the house. It was melted mush by the time we got to it."

"How friendly are you?" Zack asked. Adam was a good-looking guy, but Zack realised he'd added fast working charm into the equation.

"Friendly enough." Zack could hear the smile in Adam's voice.

"Keep asking questions?"

"You not done with this, are you?"

"Not even close."

"I'm your man. Look I'd better go, you're out of bounds for now."

"Thanks, Adam, and I think I could be out of bounds for a long time. Let me know if you get anything more."

"I will. I liked working with you. You're the kind of person who gets things done."

Zack extracted the files into a folder before examining them. They were scanned copies of everything which had been pinned to the wall, or on the desk in the cellars beneath the converted barn. Files which Alex had collated about each of his victims. Even those on people from the town not mentioned in the case. Zack knew this had been left on purpose because Alex wanted them to know who he'd targeted and why. He wanted them to know just how long his reach had been.

Zack jumped for a moment at Miley shrieking until he realised it was just Jake throwing her in the pool. This was quickly followed by Chloe making a splash and the sound of his older brother's loud laughter. A sound which filled Zack with love for all three of them. Jake had insisted he pay for the villa and had made sure he could get over for a few days. Zack was glad.

Flicking through the files he saw the familiar faces of those victims he knew about. There was Chloe's friend Jenny. Implicated by Alex as part of the gang in his school days that made other peoples' lives a misery. She'd been raped before her neck was broken and her body was abandoned in the cellar.

Chloe's crimes were listed together with photographs of when she was younger, including the time when the modelling world had made her take desperate measures. Arthur, the gentle man who it turned out had been part of a ring exploiting Angel with the old priest and headmaster many years ago. There were transcripts of online chats, not just with Miley, but with no end of other young girls. There was Peter, the charity man with a shady past who had built the devices which had started some of the fires. Peter's body had been pulled out of the wreckage of the town hall. In the end, he'd set off the fire alarm and tried to get people out of the building before succumbing to the smoke and flames.

There were so many conflicting emotions as Zack scanned through the records. Alex had been relentless in his horrific pursuit, and while some of them were clearly nasty individuals it was hard to believe any deserved his brand of justice. Yet when Zack considered the people who'd exploited the likes of Chloe and Miley, or even Chloe's own exploitation of others, it became hard to differentiate between the victims and perpetrators.

His gaze fell upon a familiar face, not one he had come across as part of this investigation but because it was the Member of Parliament who'd retired a few months before on health grounds. An unexpected retirement forcing the by-election. Reading on, a realisation dawned on Zack that sent shivers across his body. His mouth went dry as he completed reading the document. At the bottom of the file, as with every other, were the full contact details of the person in question.

Zack picked up his phone and punched in the number. It rang for a few moments before a male voice answered.

"Mr Cunningham?" Zack asked.

"Yes, who is this?"

"I'm Detective Inspector Zack Carter."

"How did you get this number?"

"From the files of the most wanted in the United Kingdom."

"Oh. I see."

"Mr Cunningham, you didn't resign because of ill health, did you?"

First to know

Building a relationship with my readers is one of the best things about writing. If you enjoyed this book and would like to find out about further books when they are about to be released then please sign up below. I'll only ever send you stuff about my books and never share with third parties. You'll also be the first to know about any new material.

http://www.sjdavison.com/sign-me-up/

I need you

If you enjoyed this book you can help me.

Reviews are so important for me to get attention for my books. Not only that it helps the ranking so many more readers can become aware of my books.

So if you liked Angel of Death I would be grateful if you could spare five minutes to write a review. It can be a short as you like.

Thank you very much.

About the Author

I'm based in the East Midlands, England. Having served for ten years in the Military I embarked on a career in Information Technology which included creating and running my own company for a number of years before it was sold.

With a passion for technology and the human psyche, I love to explore these themes in my work.

Still working at a leading tech company in the UK, I write in my spare time. When not writing I love the movies, watching anything and everything no matter how bad.

I make my online home at http://www.sjdavison.com/